The Sisterkin

SJ Howarth

Cover artwork: © Emily Southwell 2023

First edition 2023.

ISBN: 978-1- 7396258-2-5 (paperback)

ISBN: 978-1-7396258-3-2 (Kindle)

Note: this book features dying as a theme and some readers may be experiencing grief or thoughts of suicide. There is help and support available, which includes (UK):

Cruse Bereavement: www.cruse.org.uk

Hope Again (under 25s bereavement support): www.hopeagain.org.uk

Samaritans — free to phone on 116 123, 24/7 for support with suicide, bereavement or anything troubling you.

HOPELINE UK (under 35's support with thoughts of suicide, or concerns for someone else with thoughts of suicide): 0800 068 41 41

Printed by Kindle Direct Publishing 2023.

The Sisterkin

'Deeds, not Words'

Emmeline Pankhurst, Manchester, 1903

Part One: Backwash

Chapter 1 – Something of an Aftermath

Daisy felt herself lifted as strong arms pulled her from the cliff edge. She fought hard, desperate to get down the steps to the beach, but in one swift movement she was up over Pol's shoulder. Daisy jiggled awkwardly as Pol marched toward the cottage, pinned tighter as she tried to wriggle free. Pol carried her upstairs before setting her down gently on Morfydd's bed. Stepping back, she blocked the doorway, arms folded as she fixed Daisy with a hard stare.

"Don't even think about getting off that bed."

Daisy twitched with adrenaline, her heart still racing. As she tried to sit up, she reeled sideways. Forcing herself to take slow, deep breaths – anything to feel more in control – she moved to the edge of the bed. She had to look for her dad and wanted to check on Suni. If she was quick, she might be able to dart past Pol and down the stairs.

"I will stop you leaving, Daisy."

"This is nothing to do with you. I've got to look for my dad!"

Daisy launched herself from the bed and dashed at Pol, diving between her legs on her hands and knees. She almost made it – but Pol snapped her legs together and held her fast.

"What did I tell you, Daisy."

Scooping her up like a wayward kitten, she returned her to the bed. Daisy turned on her with a smouldering glare, ready to explode, then heard Morfydd and Arwen on the stairs. Reaching the bedroom, they stopped talking but not before Daisy caught the end of something Morfydd was saying, "...and I'm so sorry, you missed your chance."

Arwen's eyes were red and bleary. Squeezing by Pol she laid a hand on her arm and she seemed to shrink, relax into something softer. Morfydd weaved around the two of them into the small, increasingly overcrowded, bedroom.

"Thank you, Pol," she said. "I think Daisy understands now."

The words were intended for Pol, but it was Daisy she gave a grave look. As she joined her on the bed, Morfydd suddenly looked much older. Daisy pulled her knees to her chest and backed into the corner.

"Morfydd, please, please let me go to the beach, my dad –

Morfydd rounded on her. "You know as well as I do, Daisy, he's not on the beach –

"In the sea then," Daisy snapped frantically. "I can't lose him again."

"Daisy," said Morfydd, softer than before, "your dad is not on the beach, or in the sea. Arwen will talk to you. For now, I know it's hard, but try and get some rest. You've had a shock."

Daisy threw Arwen a questioning look, hoping she might say more. Arwen looked at her, but gave nothing away. The watery sadness in those green eyes, that permanent frown; the poor girl was desolate. Perhaps Gwen had been right, cautioning against Daisy not being ready for the Sisterkin. She felt that Pol and Morfydd had been a touch hard on her, given the circumstances.

"I'll talk with Daisy. Can you two deal with everything else, see to Suni, whilst I do?"

Neither resisted. Morfydd left the room without speaking, Pol giving Arwen a quick kiss on the head before clomping downstairs. Arwen sat beside Daisy, smoothing out her dress as she made herself comfortable. "Right pet, just us now," she said smiling, "perhaps you'd like to talk about what's happened?"

Pol looked down at the beach. The incoming tide was swollen, crude imitations of the moon rippling over the surface. Scanning the water there was no sign of either man. She knew there wouldn't be, but had checked nonetheless, for Daisy. The men had gone somewhere, which Pol considered no great loss to her or the world at large. Where they had gone, she was far less sure.

Hearing a noise, she turned to see Morfydd had joined Gwen, who had remained beside Suni, bringing a thick blanket which she wrapped around him. Gwen had kept track of his pulse as it fluttered fragile and unsteady, Suni still unconscious. "This one'll need an ambulance," she announced with an air of finality.

"What shall we tell them?" Morfydd asked. Her tone was unsure, as though deferring to Gwen.

"Do you have a ladder, Morfydd?"

Morfydd looked confused. "A small one? In the outhouse."

Gwen got up and waddled out of sight, returning a few minutes later with a ladder. She extended it and propped it against the guttering, repositioned it a couple of times, then kicked it over sharply.

"He fell, clearing out the guttering."

"In the dark?"

"He fell earlier. Went unconscious unexpectedly."

Morfydd nodded, glancing at the fallen ladder, then at Suni flat on the ground. It made sense enough. "I'll call them."

Fifteen minutes later, an approaching siren could be heard. Gwen had volunteered to wait by the roadside, show the paramedics the way. Walking them through the trees, she gave them a summary, in a tone that suggested there was no other explanation; planted the idea in their minds.

The paramedics were unable to revive Suni. One of them, an older woman with spiky purple hair spoke with Morfydd and Gwen, as the younger, blonde and painfully thin, listened impassively. Both gave similar accounts, being sure to mention the thud as his head hit the ground. They explained they had sat with him, not wanting to move him, as he'd complained of feeling dizzy. He had drunk some water and sat wrapped in a blanket. Then he had blacked out, not long after. There was no need to tell them anything of the bright light, or of Gabriel and his assailant. The only person who might remember, might say something different, was Suni — and right now that was an unlikely prospect.

"Is there someone we can contact?" the younger paramedic asked as they helped manoeuvre Suni carefully onto a stretcher.

"His best friend Daisy will have numbers. She's inside, do you need to see her?" Morfydd asked calmly. Just a regular accident with a ladder, nothing more.

"Nah. This one's going to the hospital near Aber. Please ask Daisy to tell his family, soon as."

Back at the roadside an owl hooted, a brisk wind whipping up from the sea as the paramedics lifted the stretcher into the back of the ambulance. Morfydd hovered, as the older paramedic leaned against the ambulance as if deep in thought, then slapped the side before climbing into the passenger seat. She waved briefly as they pulled away. Morfydd watched the ambulance disappear over the hill, the flashing lights weaving along the coast road, sweeping solemnly across the water.

That was that. Suni would be in the right place. Gabriel and the other man had gone into the light. More importantly, Morfydd thought, moving quickly through the chilly night back to the warmth of her cottage, for now at least, Daisy was exactly where she needed to be.

Chapter 2 – Betwixt and Between

Daisy pushed into the cold, lumpy pillows. Twisting around to rearrange them, nothing made them any warmer or softer. Arwen had been downstairs a while and when she returned, she was carrying a mug of steaming liquid. "For the shock," she said handing it to her.

Daisy felt shock, having replayed all of it whilst Arwen was downstairs. That man who had attacked her dad, the swirling bubble of light...her dad and the man pulled upward and outward, not downward, as though gravity had been caught napping. Then they were gone, just as the light blinked out.

Whilst she'd been trying to arrange her thoughts into some kind of order, Maya had chirped from the drawer of the chest and not long after Socrates had skulked into the room, jumping on to the bed and freezing at the sight of Daisy, before curling into a tight ball at the far end of the bed.

Daisy sniffed at the tawny liquid. It smelled like dry soil. Sipping it, it tasted like dry soil. She swallowed it down in as few gulps as possible. Whatever it was, it made her gums tingle and not long after she felt herself sink into the pillows. The duvet suddenly lighter than air; the mattress bottomless.

Arwen tilted her forward and rested her on her shoulder as she reached to adjust the pillows. Socrates opened an eye for a moment, before turning away. Tucking the duvet in around Daisy, Arwen settled next to her; close like a mother. As Daisy fell deeper into the softness, concern for her dad and Suni remained, but the tea had subdued her panic. It was like contemplating it all from further away.

The sharp peal of a siren had Daisy straining to look out of the window. From the bed, she could see only dark sky, the faintest hint of moonlight peeping in at the corner. With a hand on her shoulder, Arwen encouraged her back into the pillows.

"That'll be for Suni, he's still unconscious."

"Will he be alright?"

Arwen wasn't sure what to say. Suni would make a full recovery, but not without a few turns in the road, for Suni and for Daisy. "In time, yes. It could feel a little worse, before it gets better."

Daisy grimaced. That was Suni, always sucked into her drama. As Pol had carried her inside, she had seen him lying on the ground not moving, but wasn't sure how he had ended up there.

"And my dad?"

"Your dad is safe and well, Daisy –

"How do you know that?"

Arwen looked at her. "That bright light at the cliff...I've been through it – and look, I'm perfectly alright."

Daisy looked crestfallen and Arwen sensed no matter what she said, it wouldn't be enough. She felt for Daisy. She was lost, having already turned over many stones to find Gabriel.

"Daisy," Arwen started, hoping to move things on, "Morfydd has asked me to talk to you about what happened..."

Daisy shifted position as she slid under the duvet. It was like getting ready for a bedtime story, but she felt this one wasn't going to be quite so soothing. "Earlier, you looked upset...is everything –

As Arwen got up and closed the curtains, a stiff breeze pushed through the open window, carrying with it the sound and the smell of the sea.

Now wasn't the time to answer Daisy's question. "Do you think you're ready to hear what I have to say?" Arwen asked returning to the bed.

"Ready...as I'll ever be," Daisy replied, her words felt woolly now, her mouth numb.

Arwen laid her hands neatly in her lap, turning to Daisy as she spoke. "Some years ago, much of what happened today, was foreseen," she said, the shuddering waves mingling with the lilt of her accent, "and you are not here with us by accident, Daisy."

Arwen paused, trying to read Daisy. She had expected a flicker of fear, but had seen none so far. Daisy felt heavier and drowsier, barely able to reply.

"Uh-huh..."

"One of the gifts I bring to the Sisterkin, is being able to read what's coming. Through scrying and —

"Scrying?"

As Daisy tried to focus on Arwen the room tumbled further away, gradually consumed by the dark. Arwen, however, remained visible, seemingly illuminated by an inner radiance. Whatever had been in that tea, Daisy thought, was pushing her faster and faster toward a fuzzy slumber.

"Some call it peeping. It's a way of seeing what may come to pass. Like Tarot, or tea leaves. Some read flames. Personally, I prefer a bowl of spring water. A full moon is welcome, but not essential. I see images, visions if you will, within the water. Have you ever looked into a fire, seen shapes in the flames?"

Daisy nodded slowly, eyelids drooping as she turned onto her side, barely registering the pillows anymore.

"I'm like that with water. I saw you Daisy, here with us. We knew you were coming," she paused, smiling at something.

"You saw...the future?"

Arwen nodded. "I did, I do. You are important Daisy, to the Sisterkin. Not just because of who you are –

"Hmmm..."

"But because of *what* you are."

"What I am?"

"After the light on the cliff, you will feel different; changed. Suni too, and your dad."

Daisy nodded slowly. Trying to take in everything Arwen was saying was feeling harder and harder.

"There is much to come, Daisy," Arwen said with a quick sigh. "You can walk away, you're completely free to make your own choices. We hope that you want to spend time with us, rather than feel you have to?"

Daisy waved a hand encouraging her to carry on. Usually, the gesture would have been straightforward, but now her arm seemed ludicrously heavy, like it was off doing its own thing.

"I like it, so far..."

"And we like you, Daisy."

Arwen smiled warmly and slowly brought her fingertips to Daisy's temple, holding them there. "There's more for you to know, but right now, rest is what you need most."

"But I...I...you said something...about being changed?"

"Anyone who passes through the light, or is touched by it, will feel different. It's a beautiful different. Like magic, leaking through."

"Leaking through? What, from somewhere else?"

"Rest, Daisy."

Daisy felt warmth radiating from Arwen's fingertips, her skin soft. It reminded her of something, a feeling she couldn't bring to mind.

"Sleep now, Daisy."

As Arwen withdrew her hand and backed away from the bed, the warmth remained. She was now just a vague shape lingering on the threshold, before closing the door gently behind her. Tiny orbs of pink and green light danced across the air. Globes of sparkling energy that flared, then slowly faded. Daisy could no longer keep her eyes open and she gave in, floating into a realm far beyond the bedroom; far beyond the cottage walls.

~

Daisy slept for the best part of a day. Sitting up slowly, she did feel better; much calmer. Clambering out of bed, she padded downstairs yawning as she tied her hair back. Morfydd and Arwen were sat by the fire talking in low voices, but stopped when they heard her on the stairs.

"Daisy," said Morfydd cheerily turning in her chair, "How you feeling?"

"I feel alright, thanks. How's Suni? Any sign of my dad?"

Perching on the table between the chairs, the fire welcome after the chilly bedroom, she waited for them to tell her something – anything.

"There's no sign of him, no," replied Morfydd. "And no news on Suni, yet"

Daisy frowned and wrinkled her nose. "I'm gonna have to call his parents...I should have already, probably."

"The paramedics said he was going to the hospital near Aberystwyth."

"Do you feel up to calling them?" asked Arwen.

"I'm not looking forward to it, but I'll do it."

"We'll give you some space Daisy."

The two of them headed upstairs. The fact Daisy even had numbers for his parents, was down to Suni. The year before, after bingeing on too much late-night *X-Files*, he'd insisted they swap numbers — "in case we go missing in a weird way; get taken." Daisy thought it ridiculous and had laughed in his face. "Eeeww, what if I accidentally drunk-dial your dad?!" — "And what if he replies!" Suni had howled.

It seemed more practical to call Mr. Panchal, but when she tried, his number was out of service. She tried a few more times, each attempt making her more anxious. She dawdled, smoking a cigarette as her finger hovered over calling Mrs. Panchal. She would be upset, but she needed to know. Suni would want them there when he came round.

Mrs. Panchal had been upset. She was silent for so long Daisy wasn't sure if she was still there. It was awful ringing a woman to tell her that her son — her only child — was in hospital, whilst also being vague about the circumstances. Then she had started crying and Daisy hadn't known what to say. Her sister (of the shiny-Christmas-pound-coin) would drive them and they were leaving as soon as she arrived.

Daisy had held herself together on the phone, but afterwards she was overwhelmed. The weight of it all, the responsibility, was too much. Had it not been for her, neither Suni or her dad would have even been there. It was hard to shake and she was still chewing it over when Morfydd and Arwen returned.

"How was it?" asked Arwen.

Daisy jumped up. Patting her pockets, then looking around for her car keys, she realised they were probably at her dad's house. In trying to recall where she had left them, the previous morning seemed like a lifetime ago. "Terrible, I need to go. Go see Suni."

As she paced the lounge her panic returned. All she could think about was talking to her dad, the time he'd hugged her and she'd jumped, felt that weird static energy, wondering if it might somehow have passed from him, to her.

Maybe, there was something she could do to help Suni after all.

Chapter 3 – Digging for Cress

He could hear an insistent bleeping, like the sound of a reversing lorry. It took him a while to realise that what he was hearing, was the melody of his life. His heartbeat, remixed and remastered through a chirping monitor.

As he became more accustomed to the bleeping, or at least nudged toward accepting it, he found himself questioning how and why he could even hear it. What business had this machine, mimicking the cresting of his heart? Then it hit him: his breathing wasn't how it usually was, something he found momentarily petrifying. He could still breathe, but it felt more complicated than usual. And everything was black...

All he needed to do was open his eyes. When he did, he immediately wished he hadn't. What he had expected, he wasn't sure, but a room on an Intensive Care Unit, was not it. All the angles were sharp, the walls abandoned to listless magnolia paint, curtains held together by ancient stains; an all-pervading reek of disinfectant. He squeezed his eyes shut, convinced he wasn't properly awake and opened them again. Still, the hospital persisted.

A commotion of people in white smocks and blue plastic aprons whirled around the room, the artificial lighting bringing a searing milkiness to proceedings. Bodies wove in and out of one another around a bed, as if dancing to the chirp of the monitor, as they checked and adjusted various tubes and wires.

Suni stood in the corner of the room watching. Looking down at himself he was relieved to find he was wearing clothes. Beside him was an empty chair, presumably for visitors. He had no memory of getting here and wanted to see who was in the bed. As he strained to look, he felt panic – it could be Daisy, or one of his parents. Trying not to get in the way he edged nearer, until he saw it was...him in the bed!

He giggled nervously, immediately clamping his hand over his mouth, making a muffled yelp, not unlike the sound a dog might make if you stood on its paw by accident. He needn't have worried, no one heard him. No one could hear him say, or do, anything here.

He watched fascinated, as the nursing staff fussed over his body: a rigid, plastic mask obscured the lower part of his face and a fat plastic tube was wedged down his throat. Other equipment seemed to be fastened to, or stuck into, his arms; a plastic bag of clear liquid hung from a metal stand.

One of the gowned women broke away from the bed to talk with a man who had just entered the room. From the expensive navy-blue suit, the lustrous gold silk tie and greying hair – expensively styled and swept back from his garishly tanned face – Suni reasoned he must be a consultant. They whispered to each other, whispering Suni could hear perfectly, as one of the man's eyebrows arched like a caterpillar contemplating a new leaf. Suni heard them mention a fractured skull and swelling of the brain.

"Excuse me, I know you're busy," Suni began leaning toward the pair of them, "but can you please tell me what's happening?"

The woman and the consultant continued – excited talk about sharing spicy chicken wings and sticky fingers after their shift. Suni took a few steps nearer to tap the consultant on the shoulder. Try as he might, his hand wouldn't make contact, so instead he waved frantically between them.

"Hello. Hel-loooo!"

Neither even blinked. The consultant bent closer to the woman, decanting suggestions into her ear. She flushed and hurried back to the bed, glancing back with a bemused look.

Suni pushed his hand against the man's chest. The consultant didn't move, or show any signs of registering this, but instead jammed a fingernail between his front teeth as though digging for cress. Studying his nail briefly, he turned and left the room, Suni trotting after him.

"Hey, hey you...WHERE YOU GOING?!"

The man pushed through a door marked STAFF ONLY. Suni stared at the door, glancing up and down the corridor: endless rooms, a few empty trolleys abandoned at inconvenient angles and cheap plastic chairs along the corridor wall.

"Don't bother pal, he can't hear us."

The voice was gruff and Mancunian. Suni looked up and down the corridor, trying to find the owner of the voice.

"In here, buddy..."

Suni walked through an open door into a storeroom. It was a small, square room that smelled of cleaning products. There was a large, low sink, a parliament of mops in various stages of fatigue and shelving filled with boxes of gloves, tissues and other supplies. Sat on a small round stool beside the sink was a boy of around seven with blonde hair and plump red cheeks. He was wearing a medical gown dotted with faded logos and swinging his bare legs back and forth.

"I've been here fucking ages, man. No one can see us, or hear us."

Suni slouched against the door frame as he considered the boy. His hoarse voice belonged to a middle-aged smoker or daytime drunkard; the wrong voice for a small boy cheerfully swinging his legs in a hospital storeroom.

"My name's Suni. Hello."

"Good to meet you, man. You can call me...Loki."

"Hey Loki. Are we, dead?"

The small boy glanced up at Suni with a glint in his eye, with just enough of a hint of danger for Suni to pay attention.

"Nah. Not yet anyways."

"What are we then?"

"You're shining, did you know that?"

"No, I didn't realise," Suni answered confused.

"We're stuck," Loki said grinning. "Apparently, the guy that's meant to come for us, has gone AWOL. There's a bunch of women down the next corridor, were on a trip to an owl sanctuary in Llandudno. Bus came off the road and now they don't know whether they're coming or going. Fucking noisy lot an' all."

Without wanting to make a big gesture out of it, Suni folded his arms and reaching round pinched his left arm. Feeling nothing, he pinched harder. Turns out, pinching yourself doesn't necessarily do what you need it to, when you need it to.

"You aint dreaming, pinching yerself won't do owt."

Reluctantly, he unfolded his arms and they hung at his sides with nothing better to do. "I can't just wait here. There must be someone in charge, I'm going to –

"You're not getting this, are you," said Loki, before letting out an exaggerated sigh, "think of us as invisible. Like them *Missing 411* folk."

"I love that show," said Suni. "Blows my mind that so many people just vanish into thin air...and so often in the woods."

"Your mind a bit less blown now?"

Suni nodded slowly. If he was right – and he was by no means sure that he was – the facts were thus:

1. He wasn't dead.
2. He wasn't fully alive either.
3. He was standing in a hospital storeroom, with what looked like a child, but talked like an adult.
4. He wanted answers, or at least something loosely fitting an explanation.

"There's a fifth one..."

"Fifth what?"

"You were making a list in your head. There's a fifth point."

"There is?"

"Number 5. This could last a while."

Loki slid off the stool, barely reaching the height of Suni's waist. He offered Suni a tiny hand to shake but when he reached for it, their hands passed through one another.

"Kinda tickles, don't it."

Suni nodded as he turned his hand palm up and stared at it.

"Well pal, I'd love to stop and chat shit, but I've got people coming. Come and hold me hand, sit round the bed. Fall out with each other."

Suni realised that as far as he knew, no one had been to visit him. He wondered if anyone even knew he was here.

"Thanks Loki, for talking. It's helped a bit."

"Pleasure pal, you take it easy."

Suni watched him saunter down the corridor, his bare feet making no sound. As he was about to disappear around the corner, he paused and looked back at Suni. Flipping him his middle finger, he ran giggling out of sight.

"Yeah, you too," Suni said to an empty corridor.

Returning to the room where he remained motionless in the bed, the clamour had eased. There was talk amongst the gowns of the patient having been stabilised. They moved on quickly, discussing a vending machine that was taking money for ginger beer, but giving out nothing in return.

He flopped onto the chair and waited for them to leave. There was no door for them to close and once the room was empty, he listened to the frequent bleeping of the monitor, catching scraps of conversation drifting in from the corridor.

He crossed the room to the only window. It was behind patterned curtains that had given up in 1993. The mechanism was broken and although he wasn't able to open them, he peered through the gap, hoping to get see his surroundings, scope out a landmark. He jumped back, startled. It was night time, but the sky was crammed full of fireworks – furious bursts of colour that ruptured the firmament before dwindling away in rainbow showers; one whirling display after another. Each burst coming without any sound. He found himself thinking about his dad as he struggled to retrieve a memory; something about special people and fireworks.

Gabriel blinked away floaters as he realised (and not for the first time) that he was sprawled face-first on the ground. He thought he should be soaking wet, the sea perilously close only seconds before, but he was dry and smelled a perky fragrance of bruised leaves and crushed vegetation. His throat throbbed from Mr. Bliss trying to squeeze the life out of him with hands of granite.

Rolling onto his back he sat up. Deep forest surrounded him, darker and fuller than the woods near his cottage. Gone, was the snow and the cold. This forest was dense and humid; pubic. The light that had engulfed the cliff was nowhere to be seen.

Sagging in the heat, his velvet jacket wasn't helping and he shrugged out of it and hung it over his arm. Unbuttoning his shirt, he was relieved to find the eagle carving still around his neck. He rubbed it thoughtfully, listening to the different sounds coming from the trees. He heard rustling overhead, bird calls and bright coloured fluttering higher up. He was convinced he spied Howler monkeys too, scuttling through the trees. They sniggered; none braving a roar, yet.

A few feet away, Mr. Bliss was tangled up on the ground not moving. Gabriel shuffled across the carpet of leaves, startling a gigantic purple butterfly in the process and nudged him with his foot.

"You alive?"

At the second nudge – more of a kick which Gabriel enjoyed tremendously – a long, low groan could be heard as Mr. Bliss curled into himself. He groaned again as he hesitantly unfurled himself, like the world's most disappointing flower.

Repositioning himself and leaning back against the trunk of an immense tree, he folded his arms. Gabriel wondered whether he should mention the spider – larger than a handspan and meaner than a van of bailiffs – that watched Mr. Bliss from the rippled bark.

Gabriel clapped slowly. "Brilliant work, all but killing the both of us."

"I hate overdues," Mr. Bliss said sourly.

It was only now, not having to fight for his life, that Gabriel appreciated just how bland the man's face was: like cheap butter, prone to slippage at any moment. "Well, neither of us seem overdue right now."

Standing left Gabriel momentarily dizzy, so he decided that finding food and drink needed to happen as soon as possible. He stretched, cautiously at first, before easing out a loud yawn. He walked on the spot, testing his legs whilst Mr. Bliss stayed sat by the tree. He looked pale, grey and sad; the deathly equivalent of a rainy Tuesday in Stoke-on-Trent. Gabriel sighed and shook his head, walking over.

"Let me help you up?"

Mr. Bliss stared at his hand like he had never seen one before, then took it guardedly. The spider tensed, relaxing as the men moved away from the tree it was merrily claiming as its own.

"Are you hurt?" asked Gabriel.

Mr. Bliss smoothed down his clothes before scraping back his greasy hair with both hands. One of his trainers was missing, exposing a fluffy white sports sock.

"I've lost a shoe, but I'm not hurt."

He looked around, peering deep into the tight tree cover on all sides, then turned back to Gabriel asking, "Are we, dead?"

Gabriel threw his head back and laughed. Here they both were in some curious forest having passed through – through what he wasn't entirely sure – and now Death, was asking him if they were both dead. "Correct me if I'm wrong, but aren't you, Death?"

His reply was sharp. "I'm fully aware of the irony," he said with a weary moan. "I just wanted your thoughts on the matter. Forget it."

"I don't think we're dead," Gabriel said as he finished rolling a cigarette and lit up. "It doesn't feel the same as when I died before. I'm still Gabriel," he offered cheerfully as he exhaled. "Smoke?"

Mr. Bliss glared at the tin in Gabriel's hand. "No, those things can kill you."

Apart from a sore neck and the syrupy humidity, Gabriel felt wonderful. Light and airy as lime mousse. He wandered away, straining for a high branch. He jumped to grab at a ripe orange fruit, getting it on the third attempt.

"What on earth are you doing?"

"It's a mango," replied Gabriel sniffing it. "Ripe too," he added with a squeeze, slipping it into the pocket of the jacket over his arm. "I wonder where we are..."

Gabriel walked on, forcing his way through a compact barrier of bushes, the like of which he had not seen before. Heavy, bulbous black blooms bent for the ground and aquamarine ferns grew waist high. There were showy bundles of dusky figs to his left, clustered bananas above him. Higher up, secretive coconuts waited for their time to drop. Higher still, a filigree canopy in every shade of green, pierced by shafts of sunlight.

Moving carefully, he froze as another spider larger than his hand moved ponderously along a stout branch. The two of them were very close, with no kind of greeting; an utter absence of ground rules around personal space. As he stepped back and gave the spider a polite bow, there was a violent rustling in the undergrowth. Instantly, he pictured a snarling panther...a fat, poisonous frog...a concealed snake. All manner of creatures he wasn't sure existed here, but held responsible for the shifting shrubbery. What he couldn't see, was an elderly and somewhat portly, armoured edentate going about its loud workaday business.

Although the flora and fauna were closely woven, Gabriel managed to squeeze into a narrow passage. Although not neatly cut, it did look deliberate; the result of a tenacious ingenuity. Mr. Bliss was following, loping slightly with only one shoe, ducking at every sound. Catching up with Gabriel, he called out, "I don't like this, Gabriel."

"Try taking your other shoe off, level yourself out."

Winding deeper into the forest, Gabriel was fascinated by the turn of events. As a dying man, he welcomed any unexpected excursion, such as sauntering happily through a faintly perilous forest, all but leading Death by the hand. Any minute, he expected to wake up in his armchair, or find himself sprawled outside Morfydd's cottage on the kinder side of a cliff plunge, a crescent of worried faces peering down at him.

"Will you not go quite so far ahead!"

"For a man who's put so much effort into ending my life, you're in no position to make demands," Gabriel tossed over his shoulder. "Keep up. Or who knows, you might die!"

Wriggling between trailing vines, Gabriel was forced to take a slower pace, stepping over fallen trees and submerged roots. He wondered how Daisy was doing, couldn't recall where she had been when he was hovering in thin air over the sea, Mr.

Bliss grabbing at his generous velvet lapels, before the light had embraced them.

No glowing tunnel, no fantastical music.

Just instant arrival in the forest.

As the trees and shrubbery began to thin, it looked like there was a clearing up ahead. Gabriel heard the wondrous sound of gurgling water and licking his lips, decided he would be drinking it, regardless of where it came from, or what colour it was.

"Why have you stopped?" Mr. Bliss demanded. He was hot and flustered, wearing his standard look of angry fatigue.

Gabriel ignored his question. "Did you bring us here? I mean, did you mean for us to end up here, when you grabbed me?"

Mr. Bliss shook his head quickly, looking awkward.

"So, this," Gabriel said spreading his arms, "isn't your doing?"

"No. I have an idea where we might be."

"And would you care to expand on that?"

Mr. Bliss shook his head again. "Not particularly."

Gabriel chuckled. At least he was consistent. "Fair enough. You hang on to that air of mystery. It does seem important to you."

He followed the bushes and trees as they petered out, until he reached a round glade. After the forest cover, the sun felt hotter than it should. Sweat poured inside his clothes, as though he'd pulled his clothes out of the washing machine mid-cycle[1].

---

[1] Yes, washing machines will not usually allow you to open the door mid-cycle, but this is a work of fiction.

Beyond the clearing was a wooden building – single storied and balanced on fat wooden stilts raising it a metre or more from the ground. In the shadowy space beneath, moving water could be heard softly conspiring with stone. A short set of wooden steps at the left-hand end. It looked like a beach hut: a beach hut, sorely lacking a beach.

Whatever it was, it appeared to have been meticulously assembled from limbs of the forest. Used as they were found this gave the hut an air of being both alive and purloined. At the centre was a pair of closed doors made from sandy-coloured split young logs. Around the building was a neat, railed veranda, wattled without daub. The roof was thinner logs, lashed together with vines and sloping to meet the veranda. To the right of the doors, at the far end of the veranda, was a hammock strung between the corner pole supporting the roof and a plump trunk nearby.

Winding from the clearing to the steps, was a path of smooth, round, glassy blue stones set into the ground. Stepping along the stones, Gabriel found a small, tubular metal table by the steps. It looked out of place, carried here by the water no doubt, elbowing its way between plastic bottles, wet wipes and gluey condoms, before being repurposed.

"Let's see if there's anything to eat, I'm bloody starving!"

Mr. Bliss remained apprehensive, holding back. "How do you do it," he asked keeping his distance, "just take life as it comes?"

"There's no benefit in not doing, in resisting. I'm far happier flowing downstream. Get there in the end."

Mr. Bliss folded his arms stood on the spot. If they had arrived where he thought they might have, food would be the least of their worries...

"Hello? Anyone home?" Gabriel called out as he examined the table. A series of short planks had been lashed to the tubular frame with fraying, sea-rinsed rope. On the table was the following:

A small hand-painted sign which read:

Homemade lemonade – free to all

Five empty glasses and a glass bottle filled with a cloudy, pale-yellow liquid. Beneath a jagged lump of coarse pink rock, was a pamphlet flapping in a gentle breeze.

"I probably wouldn't drink the..." Mr. Bliss began, not bothering to finish as Gabriel uncapped the bottle, filled a glass and drained it down.

"Man, this is SO lemony! It's divine!"

Gabriel filled two glasses, emptying his once more before walking over to Mr. Bliss and handing him the other. He took the glass and sniffed at it. It did indeed, smell very much of fresh lemons. He took a cautious sip, feeling the bubbles on his tongue, the cool liquid soothing his dry throat. He took a second, deeper gulp. Gabriel, meanwhile, emptied a third glass before setting it down on the table. It was only then, he noticed that even after filling four glasses, the bottle was still full.

"Thank you, that was refreshing."

Gabriel cast the words in the direction of the hut, unsure whether anyone was around.

Holding the warm pink stone in place, he slid out the pamphlet. The white paper had been folded repeatedly (and precisely) to make it more manageable. A title was handwritten in bright green crayon:

Advice for the Newly Arrived

Gabriel opened it. There was no contents page and the inside cover was blank. The second page had more writing, in the same hand, this time in purple, with a cartoon drawing of a glass of very fizzy lemonade:

1. Go with it.
2. This will happen countless times – as it already has.
3. Enjoy the opportunity to rest and repair – and the everlasting lemonade.

Gabriel handed the pamphlet to Mr. Bliss who had gradually come closer. "Look, at this, painting for lemonade."

Mr. Bliss stared at it blankly. Gabriel fished out the mango and having hung his jacket over the railing, began tussling with the fruit, wishing it came with a zip for easy opening. Still fiddling with the mango – which staunchly refused to reveal its private parts even when he poked at it with a stubby pencil he had found in his pocket – Gabriel wandered along the veranda leaving Mr. Bliss at the table.

He smelt the wood stretching in the heat, and an earthy fragrance from broad-petalled indigo flowers that wound from under the veranda; peaty, with a citrus note. It was then, just as he was about to slide open the wooden doors and nosey inside, that he realised they were not alone.

"Oh, hello there…"

As Gabriel scaffolded his impromptu greeting with a friendly grin, he saw the hammock was occupied; filled, in fact. It looked like a woman lying on her side, facing away, buttocks soaking up the sunshine; knees curled to her chest. There was a loud yawn as they turned over, the entire construction swinging passionately. Awkwardly, she turned toward Gabriel as she crossed one leg over the other.

"You enjoyed the lemonade?"

Her voice was low and husky; the voice of someone who has just awoken from the warm, twin comforts of sleep and dreaming.

"Very much, thank you."

When she clambered from the hammock and stood on the veranda, Gabriel cast his gaze downward. She was short and full of figure and he felt he shouldn't be looking upon her nakedness. Instead, he scrutinised the doors in great detail, paying attention to a butterfly that was flexing its opalescent wings, quivering in contemplation before pushing skyward. "Would you like some space, to get dressed?"

"I don't care for clothing, no need here," she replied, "though your respect is noted."

"Okay then," he said as he half-turned and looked past her. "My name is Gabriel."

"Yes, it is. Gabriel Randall Lowry. Welcome, you may call me Tallulah."

"Tallulah?"

"That's the name Momma gave me..."

Before either could say anything, they both jumped at an almighty clatter behind Gabriel. Mr. Bliss, in tackling the steps to the veranda, had bumped into the table, upsetting the glasses. Gabriel and Tallulah watched him wrap his arms around everything to stop it crashing to the floor.

"Oh Ivor," Tallulah carped, "what *are* we going to do about your latest fiasco?"

"I just caught the table, nothing's broken," he replied testily as he came and stood behind Gabriel, not looking at Tallulah.

"Not the table," she continued, rearing suddenly taller than Gabriel had imagined possible, her presence immense. "I meant this – you here with Gabriel. Your recent –

"Let me start by saying how much I respect you, Tallulah, how sorry –

Tallulah yawned, making no attempt to cover her mouth, the sound like wind cutting through a derelict building. "Do stop fawning Ivor…and as for your 'resignation', don't even get me started on that rigmarole!"

"This, is your…boss?" Gabriel asked, looking from one to the other amazed.

Mr. Bliss nodded and Gabriel saw something he'd not seen before – fear in his eyes. As the three of them stood in the hot sun, it was Tallulah who broke the silence, in a tone that suggested only a fool, and a brave one at that, would interrupt her.

"Whilst I appreciate the countless years of service you've given, your recent behaviour with Gabriel, is unacceptable. I wouldn't mind, but it's not the first time, is it…"

"But, but I –

Tallulah raised a hand, eyebrows knitted fiercely together. "Do not talk over me." Turning to Gabriel sharply, "And will you stop fannying about with that fucking mango. Give it here."

Gabriel tossed it to Tallulah who caught it in one hand without looking. Moments later, the tough skin removed, it sailed back through the air, landing as a sloppy, juicy handful. Gabriel nodded in thanks, greedily licking his fingers.

"Where was I? Ah yes, you," she said giving Mr. Bliss a firm stare. "You'll be taking time out," then turning to Gabriel as an aside, "which means I've got to piss about with agency staff."

She beckoned Mr. Bliss with a finger. "You can think about your choices whilst you're away. Approach."

Mr. Bliss took a faltering step, as though expecting an invisible barrier. Tallulah rolled her eyes and clicked her fingers hard. A rapid gust of wind blasted from nowhere, hurling him forwards, a second snap of her fingers stopping him just before they collided.

"In a moment, you will be leaving. A guide will accompany you, but once you've arrived, you will be alone. Think of it as like, a retreat. Only longer – and without fluffy towels, those dreadful reed diffusers and middle-aged white men with dreads."

Gabriel stepped up to Mr. Bliss and put a hand gently on his shoulder, scooping him into an improvised hug. "We've all been there matey, we all fuck up. Take this time for you."

As Gabriel released him, Mr. Bliss stared with calf-eyes, silently pleading for him to intervene. Gabriel pressed the mango stone – which still had a chunky ring of flesh on it – into his hand. "For the journey. Happy healing!"

Mr. Bliss opened his mouth, but before he could speak, he vanished. One second, he was there, staring at a keenly gnawed mango, then he wasn't. Gabriel turned to Tallulah with a look two-thirds awe, one-third surprise.

"Where did he go?"

Tallulah smiled warmly as she settled back into the hammock, stretching her hands behind her head, wiggling this way and that until she found the sweet spot.

"Oh, you know...betwixt and between."

"So, no talking animals here?" Gabriel said with a wink, stuffing another slice of watermelon into his mouth.

Escaping the sun, they had moved into the hut. It was sumptuously furnished in multi-coloured throws, soft cushions and hanging tapestries in a revolution of colours. On a low round table between them was more lemonade and a red china platter of sliced mango, watermelon, papaya and some wonderful berry he'd never seen before; it looked like a bright-green strawberry, but tasted like bubble-gum.

Each sprawled comfortably on a plush beanbag, the low table within reach. It was much cooler inside, a gentle breeze winding in through the open doors, tinkling glass wind chimes now and then.

"This isn't Disney, fortunately," said Tallulah. She popped one of the green fruits into her mouth, chewing it quickly.

"Humour's your favourite defence, isn't it?" she remarked after swallowing.

Gabriel felt exposed, then considering where he was, who he was with, he laughed, realising there were no secrets here.

"It is," he answered graciously. "I'm trying to get better at not hiding behind it."

"Enough. That work is not my concern. That'd be like a parent doing your homework for you."

"Right..."

"I'm not your parent, but you know what I mean."

Gabriel nodded and reached for another handful of fruit, which he fed steadily into this mouth, waiting for Tallulah to say more.

"Talking of parents, Daisy will need you. You'll have to go back," she said matter-of-factly. "I can't make you younger – or more attractive – and certainly no less prone to fucking up, but I've given you longer..."

"You have? Thank you so much, that's hugely appreciated."

"That eagle, don't lose it. You'll need it to get back."

So, that's how we got here, he thought. He was sure there was more he had once known about it; even more he had forgotten.

"And remember, it's only on loan."

Gabriel nodded and stood up. He walked over to where Tallulah was sat, legs tucked under her, curled into the beanbag.

"May I give you a hug?"

Tallulah strained up toward him, "Of course."

The two of them hugged in a medley of heat, fruit juices and nudity that was beautiful – with only a sticky moment of awkward. As they separated, he felt energised. Freed of the malignancy that had been lurking in his cellular nooks and crannies. "I feel wonderful! Forty years younger!"

"That's lovely, Gabriel. Now get back to Daisy." She slid off the beanbag and stood next to him. "Help yourself to fruit, but please don't overstay your welcome, there's a new Anthony Chene documentary I'm looking forward to watching."

Gabriel grabbed a couple of slices of watermelon in his free hand, the other clutching his jacket. "Thank you, Tallulah. It was a pleasure meeting you."

"Just head down the steps then follow the path to the right. You can leave the door open. When you come to the tiger, turn right."

Dripping beads of watermelon juice along the veranda, Gabriel looked for the path. It was there, worn into the knee-high grasses. Looking back at the hut, he called out to Tallulah.

"Thank you, Tallulah, you look after yourself!"

From the doorway, Tallulah watched the thin old man fading into the distance. Straining, she called out, not sure whether he could hear her or not.

"Left! I meant turn left at the tiger..."

Chapter 5 – The Shove

By the time Daisy got away, Arwen and Morfydd had kept her talking for ages, Morfydd insisting on making her cheese on toast before she left – though munching into it, she had been grateful the moment it hit her stomach.

Walking back, she'd thought about where her keys might be, when suddenly she was there – his forlorn cottage, tangled ivy vibrant despite the cold and smears of stubborn snow.

The door was unlocked and having turned over the lounge, lifted cushions, moved the chair and the settee – revealing a crust of dust and withered insects beneath both – she still hadn't found them. Slamming the furniture back in place, she took the stairs two at a time. There was no reason whatsoever for her keys to be in the bathroom, less so either bedroom, but she moved from one room to the next increasingly frantic.

It was only when she sat in the armchair by the fire, that she found them on the cushion, though she was certain they hadn't been there earlier. She'd only intended to sit for a moment, but fell asleep for almost two hours and when she woke, was furious with herself. Scrolling through her phone as she headed to her car, Suni's status still read Enjooooying Jalabeaños. They had invented Jalabeaños years ago, one bleary-eyed dawn in Manchester. It had seemed pioneering at the time, adding chopped Jalapeños and pepperoni slices to cheesy beans on toast. Right now, he wasn't enjoying Jalabeaños, but she really wished he was.

She drove quickly, barely registering the sea beside the road, churning under a sky pulled low and grey. Spring would come, catkins and tightly curled buds already showing on some of the trees. March would bring her birthday, but the way things were, she couldn't make plans; not with her birthday having a Suni-shaped hole in it.

It was like any other hospital: identical meandering corridors with a sharp odour of disinfectant. People in various states of living and dying; blood, panic, gowns and aggressive, drunk men roaming A&E, bellowing at no one. Pandemonium that faded slowly, the deeper she burrowed into the labyrinth of magnolia paint and advisory posters.

Eventually, having spoken to a kindly nurse at a desk buried under files and used paper cups, she found a wipe-clean board outside a room, his name written in blue marker pen. She was surprised to find Mrs. Panchal and his auntie sat beside the bed.

"Daisy, thank you for coming. We've just arrived," Mrs. Panchal said as she gave her a fleeting hug. Daisy had never seen Suni's mum in a tracksuit; pale blue, with a tatty black cardigan over the top. His auntie was as overdressed as always, her expensive perfume swamping the smell of antiseptic.

"They've spelt his name wrong," Daisy grumbled. "On the board outside. How is he?"

Mrs. Panchal shook her head but before she could respond, her sister piped up. "He's going to be fine, not right away, but in the long run."

"They said that?" Daisy asked hopefully.

"They didn't say that, no," Mrs. Panchal cut in before her sister got there, "there's no change."

"She's always like this," his auntie said to Daisy, "said we'd need hours to get here. We didn't. My right foot, I think, must be far heavier than my left."

Turning to her sister, she continued in the same boisterous manner. "We can view Sunil's situation through optimistic glasses, or through darker ones," she droned, in a tone Daisy was finding haughty. "I know which I prefer. Sunil is young, fit and healthy. He'll be right as rain."

Daisy brought a chair over to the bed and sat down. "I hope so. He looks so lost lying there."

Taking his hand, she couldn't remember the last time she'd done that; maybe at junior school. For some reason she had expected it to feel cold, but it was warm, the fingers slender and unmoving. She squeezed it gently, like she'd seen in films – at which point the person in the bed would squeeze back, or open their eyes as they blinked themselves home. There was nothing.

"Can I talk to him?" Daisy asked.

Mrs. Panchal nodded. "Please do. One of the nurses said it can help."

When she started talking, it was like trying to get his attention when he was on his phone. She wanted to talk normally, like they were just catching up, but catching her voice it sounded high and wavering, that tone some people use when someone is sad, or when explaining something to a child.

Leaning across him she spoke softly to his mum – as though whispering might prevent him from hearing. "Have you spoken to Mr. Panchal?"

"I've left messages," she replied ruefully. "When he's away, he isn't often contactable."

"Not even in an emergency?" Suni's auntie cut in with a look of disgust.

"He calls, but hasn't for a few days. Poor signal," she said vaguely, then as though it wasn't sufficient explanation added, "in the woods, or some remote place he isn't able to talk about."

As Daisy let out a big sigh her breath lifted Suni's fringe. It was the smallest of gestures, but one that hinted at life beyond the bleeping monitor. All three of them saw his hair move. No one commented.

As her conversation with Suni drifted, the three of them talked listlessly of weak coffee and icy roads. No one wanted to be the first to name what was happening; to say out loud that he might stay in this state for a while, or worse, indefinitely.

It was Daisy who moved things on, something tickling her ear having brought her back to the conversation, suggesting they should stretch their legs and get some fresh air. It had taken some reassurance, Daisy reminding Mrs. Panchal she had her phone number and would call if anything happened.

With them gone, she stood beside the bed. She focused on reliving the moment with her dad, when the energy had jumped from him. Whatever that was, she needed to be able to feel it now. Give it to Suni, if that was even possible.

Taking a slow deep breath in, she held it as long as she could, exhaling slowly. Then again. Closing her eyes, she tried to let her breathing be, rather than control it. Cautiously, with both palms side by side, she placed them on his chest. Feeling his heartbeat faintly through her hands, she tried to visualise energy coming out her, through her, but even as she did, she had no idea what she was doing.

Try as she might, nothing happened. Her hands grew hotter as she kept them there hoping to feel something. Getting angry, Suni still unconscious, she gave up, just as the booming voice of his auntie could be heard echoing down the corridor.

What had she been hoping to do? Get him going again, like jumpstarting a car?

Gratefully, she took a cardboard cup of coffee from Mrs. Panchal. Gratefully, that was, until she tasted it: sour instant coffee made from roastery sweepings, robbed of its liquid content then blasted with who knows what. Coffee for lazy people, with all the caffeine of a rusty nail. Two sips in and she was scanning the room for a bin.

She was annoyed, wondering what she'd hoped for laying her hands on him like a Texan preacher. Her mind played over the numerous times Suni had put his life on pause to listen to her vent – about situations and people that now, sat by his hospital bed, were completely insignificant. She felt utterly helpless; it was too much to bear.

"I'm going. I'm not helping."

"You being here, is helping, Daisy. I appreciate it, I know Sunil would."

"Yes, you bring...a brightness to the proceedings," his auntie said, in the absence of anything else she could think of.

Daisy looked at them and smiled half-heartedly. "I can stay?"

Even as it came out, she knew it sounded hollow. She would stay though, if it was what Mrs. Panchal wanted.

"It's fine, Daisy," she replied heavily, "I'll call you, if anything changes."

"When," chimed in his auntie. She grinned, as though they were saying goodbye after a delightful afternoon tea. Mrs. Panchal turned away from her sister. Before leaving, Daisy gave each of them a quick half-hug, before leaning in awkwardly to kiss Suni's forehead.

"Take care, I'll come back soon."

By the time she was back at her car, having passed departments with unpronounceable names, dodging a right-hand corridor that led to the morgue, she was glad to be outside. She rolled a cigarette and slouching against the car-park wall, smoked frantically. If Morfydd, or Arwen, had seen *this* coming, they might have mentioned it, given her some clue on what to do.

She grimaced seeing she was almost out of tobacco. A distance away was the illuminated livery of a chain of corner shops, down a narrow alleyway that pressed between the hospital and the buildings opposite.

Indistinguishable buildings loomed on either side, the alleyway darker and narrower than she'd thought. She hurried past rusting security doors and barred, cobwebbed windows. She could smell damp and cat piss, layers of ancient litter pasted along the edges; an empty can rolling over the ground.

She heard them before she could see them: three male voices, with southern English accents. Each competed with the other as they talked nothings, the loudest braying about a girl he'd met in a bar.

"Nah man, she aint my girlfriend. Just some girl I'm fucking. Check these out..."

From their voices, she could tell they were at the top of the alleyway, near the shop. She heard them jeering, over what she assumed was photographs the loudest was showing.

"Great tits."

"Did she swallow?" a different voice asked, sniggering like a teenager.

"Yeah," the first voice snorted, "easier when you don't give 'em a choice."

Daisy felt sick. With the end of the alleyway a few feet away she quickened her pace. She was almost there, just as the men turned the corner, blocking her way.

They were dressed identically: pale blue skinny jeans, checked shirts and brown brogues. Estate agents on a bender. She paused mid-step, then holding her head high walked toward the man in the middle, the tallest.

"Oy-oy, look what we got here lads!" he said as he cupped his crotch with his hands, advancing on Daisy.

"Fresh meat! Fresh meat! Fresh meat!" another of them chanted. Looking at the other two to join in, his words fell away when they didn't.

She snaked around the tallest man and was almost free, when he side-stepped and barged her with his shoulder. Losing her footing she smacked into the wall. She whirled round to face him. "What the fuck!" she hissed. "Get out my way."

It was the smallest of them, short and angry, that stepped up, bloodshot eyes glazed as he sniggered, blowing smoke in her face.

"What makes you think this is okay," she snapped, "trying to stop me getting past? Fucking move."

"Because we can," said the little man, not backing away.

"Get...the fuck...out...my way," Daisy snarled looking down on him.

She heard something behind her as the taller man closed in. She backed herself against the wall and spun round, nostrils flaring as she tensed, her mind racing as she tried to work out what to do.

"Here we are, trying to be friendly...and you go all full on, like some bitch."

He moved in, reeking of stale alcohol. Daisy felt her legs shaking as her eyes darted around, sizing them up. As she felt their eyes on her, her heart pounded and adrenaline flooded her as she tried to work out if she could outrun them, assuming she could even find the space to turn and run.

"Leave it man," said the less talkative of the men, "she's fucking ugly."

"No," the taller man insisted, spitting on the floor in front of her. "She needs to learn some respect."

Back to the wall, Daisy tried to stand taller, make herself bigger than she was, as she fixed him with an icy stare. "Please, let me pass."

"You talk too much," he sneered, forcing her against the wall as he started to unbutton his jeans. "I'm gonna put you on mute."

That was when she felt it, rising up inside of her. Travelling like lightning, it was in her palms; hot and powerful.

Daisy steadied herself as she put her hands up in front of her, then in one rapid movement shoved the taller man in the chest as hard as she could, her hands sparking as they made contact. He flew through the air, slamming hard into the wall opposite. His look of shock turned to confusion when he tried to stand, his legs buckling. The other two men froze, like automatons awaiting a command. They stared at the fallen man, then at Daisy, who turned on them, palms in front of her.

She stood her ground, tensing her legs in an attempt to stop them quivering. One of them broke ground, stooping to help the man on the floor. Daisy willed them to leave as she fought to catch her breath, her entire body ringing with a fierce intensity that felt wildly out of her control.

After what felt like an eternity, the three of them headed away in the direction of the hospital, the taller man limping with the assistance of one of the others. When all three looked back, saw her fixed to the spot palms outward, the short man was certain he saw light glowing from her hands, dismissing it as a reflection brought on by the street lighting that had not long blinked on at the top of the alleyway.

Daisy waited until they were out of sight before sagging against the wall. She sprinted from the alleyway toward the shop. As she grabbed for the door handle, her palms twitched, still hot and itchy.

Along his journey of surprises, one of the bigger ones Suni discovered, was that although no one could see or hear him, it turned out, he could still feel emotions. Seeing his mum and auntie huddled by his bed, unable to make his presence known, his mum looked small and lost; like she had dressed in the dark, her cardigan buttoned in the wrong holes.

"I've brought him ten pounds, for when he wakes up," his auntie announced loudly, glancing over her shoulder before lowering her voice. "And grapes, but they confiscated those," she folded her arms huffily, "apparently, they're not allowed. Pity, they were M&S."

Turning to her sister, his auntie unfolded her arms and opening her hand, revealed ten shiny coins in a sweaty clump.

"One, two, three, four, five – oh shoot these ones are stuck together," she paused to separate them then went on, laying them in a line on the bed. "Six, seven, eight, nine, ten!"

Mrs. Panchal wanted to say Suni would appreciate them, but the words wouldn't come. She smiled thinly as her sister picked up the coins and stacked them on the beside cabinet. She never could sit still. Mrs. Panchal grabbed them, the stack looking like some kind of tip, dropping them on the bed. She could hear her sister talking without really taking it in.

"He can buy himself something nice. Talking of which...did I tell you about my new birdbath? John Lewis."

At that point, seeing Daisy arrive, he'd been elated. She was flustered and her furious look, one he knew well. Her eyes were narrowed, dimming their light, her face set. She would be grinding her teeth too. Watching her trying not to swear in front of his mum and auntie entertained him no end, knowing how much of a challenge that would be.

As the three of them sat by his bed, there had been a brief, unspoken tussle over holding his hand. In the end, Daisy had held one, his mum and auntie taking turns with the other. Suni had moved closer and attempted to hug Daisy, then his mum. Even his auntie, who had flinched and looked around sharply. It was as though they weren't there, his empty arms closing around thin air. Leaning in as close to Daisy as he dared, he had expected to smell her shampoo, but couldn't. He had whispered into her ear: Eight letters, three words, one meaning. Words he had wanted to say to her before, but each time, a hot panic had overtaken him. She had flicked a hand at her ear, as though waving away a fly. He had hoped that once those words were finally out, there would have been fireworks. There hadn't.

When his mum and auntie left the room, he watched Daisy lay her hands on his chest and for a second, thought she was going to unbutton his gown. Whatever she was trying to do, she kept her hands on his chest for the longest time. When she eventually gave up, it was only as his mum and auntie returned.

Daisy had left first, leaning in and kissing his forehead before she had all but fled. After she had gone, the two women folded into one another, heads together. They stayed that way for a long time, watching the steady rise and fall of his chest.

"Right, it must be time for another drink," his auntie had declared unexpectedly, easing herself from the chair with a low moan. She had stretched out her back, before resting a hand on her sister's shoulder. "Come on, let's find something to eat. I need crisps."

As they headed out Suni saw his mum glance back repeatedly, as if leaving might alter something she didn't want to miss.

With the room to himself, he lay on the bed. It was an odd sensation, settling down next to himself. He thought about sleeping – which is all it was, thoughts about sleeping. He wondered how his dad was. Him being here would have meant the world to his mum.

In a place that wasn't sleep, but did feel hazier and heavier, his awareness drifted...and he saw himself at the campsite with his dad. It was like watching a film of the night they had seen the light in the sky. At the point when his dad had rushed for the privacy of the trees, Suni discovered he was able to leave himself stood by the river and hear his dad on the phone, his words forced out between shallow breathes.

"...and we're not ready."

What he couldn't hear, was the person on the other end of the call. Suni had never seen his dad this agitated before.

"I'm fully aware of that, Wordsworth," he said bluntly. "The calculations were incorrect. Do you understand, they're all wrong!"

"Of 'course I'm ready, I already was. Now, it's imperative..."

After the call his dad had frantically rubbed his hands through his hair, staring at his son. The memory pulled apart until Suni could see and hear nothing more of it.

Sensing a presence in the room, he assumed it was his mum and auntie. Opening his eyes, neither were there and the room was in darkness. The light from the corridor was subdued, dimmed for night-time. Lifting his head, he looked for Daisy, even the small boy, Loki. He hadn't seen him again and had questioned whether he had been there at all. In the corner beside the chair was a floating light, like moonlight slipping the gap in the curtains had become trapped in the corner.

He lay back as best he could, watching the light as it formed into the shape of a figure, edged in an exquisite white light that was fringed with a finespun corona of the sweetest blue.

As the shape approached, two more figures formed, either side of the first. Although separate, the shared light bordered them as a trio. They moved to his left, close by the bed. The glowing light washed the room in a profound warmth that he felt at his essence; a cloud of love; perfect and unconditional.

The central figure was around five feet tall and female-looking, the others shorter, their gender less clear to him; all three were adults. They lacked precise definition, drawn from light and shade and Suni thought of holograms, how they look solid at a distance, but increasingly translucent closer up.

They each wore a hooded gown of forest green, fastened at the throat with a silver ribbon. The gowns looked weighty; wonderfully warm on a chilly night. The two smaller figures drew back and the middle figure laid her hands one over the other against her stomach. As she looked at both versions of Suni on the bed, she smiled serenely and he beamed back.

She looked older than him, mid-thirties perhaps, though being of light rather than fully formed, it was difficult to be sure. Her marble white skin, combined with pronounced cheekbones and a high forehead and hairline made her eyes – a deep autumn brown – seem larger and darker. Her mouth was small, but when she smiled it revealed delicate dimples. Spilling down to her waist, her hair, even in the dimmed room, shone like burnished copper, woven with magnificent tints of russet, chocolate and sunset. Suni thought her the most unusual woman he had ever seen, possessing an inner radiance that belonged to moonlit glades and leafy bowers; to fireside tales of enchantment. He was about to speak, when the figure put a finger to her lips. When she spoke, it was soft but sure.

"Lie down, Sunil."

He wiggled down until he was flat, beside his other self. The figure bent over, so close he could feel the light fizzing with potential; with a vitality of hope. She placed one hand over his heart – on the Suni with a fractured skull – moving her other hand to the heart of his other self. She was intoning something under her breath: a soft, rapid sound that made him think of fluttering moth wings. Warmth poured from her hands, steadying the rhythm of his bodily heart as it soothed his spirit. A short time later she moved her hands, placing them around his head. Straining to reach she passed through him – and it felt incredible. Like being touched by stars.

When she had finished, she removed her hands from his head and spoke to him. "You are well. You can tell people about this, about us. We have always been here. Tell everyone, Sunil. We bring the Kindness, but we are not the only way."

As Suni returned to his body – like two identical images overlaid one over the other – the three figures blended into one. The light flared intensely and the figures were gone, leaving behind a tiny glowing white ball that hovered above him. He heard her again. "Tell everyone, Sunil."

Had his mum and auntie come back seconds earlier, his auntie returning with enough crisps to see out a siege, they would have stopped in their tracks, at the sight of a shining, spinning ball of light over his bed. The instant they entered the room, the light shrunk to the size of a pea, then rocketed upwards, passing through the ceiling and the walls, as though they simply weren't there.

Chapter 7 – Somewhere Close By

Tossing items into a basket as though the world was ending, Daisy came away with two bottles of vodka, hair dye, a multipack of Tangy Toms, a cheese and onion pasty, a frozen pizza and the only thing she'd actually wanted, tobacco. Sprinting down the alleyway, she'd locked her car from the inside, sagged onto the steering wheel and cried.

She smoked two cigarettes, still queasy with adrenaline. Her hands itched, but it was easing. Swallowing down waves of fear, a fury raged inside her. Women faced oppression, intimidation and assault from men like that on a daily basis. So many women, the world over. A certain type of man, daubing his insecurities through sustained bullying, control and violence; rising octaves of abuse. Wiping her eyes, she hurried out of the car-park. She needed to lock the doors, shut herself away.

The following morning, Daisy felt like shit. The time-honoured combination of too much vodka and too little sleep. When she had come back the previous night, she had checked everything was locked, closed the curtains and cooked the pizza, tearing into the pasty as she waited impatiently for the oven. She had drunk vodka and chain-smoked until she passed out in the armchair. Sleep, such as it was, was broken by images of the men, sickening intentions glazing their eyes. Having drunk a strong coffee with quivering hands, she knew she had to do something; take any action that might act as a distraction.

Leaning toward the mirror plucking a crooked eyebrow hair, then another, she wasn't sure the red worked. She had wanted deep crimson, but in her haste had picked up dye the colour of post-boxes. Her phone blasted out music as she dyed her hair.

Bikini Kill's Rebel Girl had started it, Fresh had followed and by the time Teenage Bottlerocket's Bloodbath at Burger King came on, she'd jumped around the bathroom, bounced off the sink, then tripped and dyed the greater part of her forehead and the mirror. The room looked like a murder scene. Wiping up, she could imagine her mum pointing out how the red made her look paler; did nothing for her eyes. Rarely one for make-up (naturally beautiful was what a tipsy Suni had called her more than once) she'd poked a cotton bud into each ear, rubbed at the dye on her temples and cleaned her teeth.

Feeling a little brighter she set out for a walk, but reaching the road the sky cracked open, Welsh rain tumbling like nails. Even hurrying back to the cottage left her drenched. Changing her clothes moodily and with nothing better to do, she'd stoked the fire and sat staring into the fire, ruminating. Although her birthday was a couple of weeks away still, she couldn't shake the worry that Suni might not be better by then. He had been there for all of them since they had met (no one had got it when he bought her a giant Oxford English dictionary when she turned thirteen, a gift she had loved then and loved now), bringing birthday adoration and of late, inventing fine birthday games, excelling himself the year before with his *Ancient Aliens* drinking game[2].

~

Outside, February was spinning out its days, the gorse at the end of the drive tight and spiny, refusing to unfurl its petals. There were hints of spring, in the roadside bluebells and clusters of shining daffodils around the trees that hid Morfydd's cottage from the world. Daisy picked a few, binding them together with a fern before moving on.

---

[2] Pick any episode of this glorious TV show and drink a shot each time the phrase "ancient astronaut theorists" is used.

"This is a nice surprise," Morfydd said heaving the door open, its groan of protest louder than Daisy remembered, "come in, Daisy."

Morfydd was dressed comfortably as usual, a baggy green jumper, more holes than jumper, tatty blue jeans and barefoot. Forcing a smile, Daisy held out the flowers.

"Thought you might like these...you got coffee on?"

"I will have – and thank you, that was thoughtful."

Lifting a sleeping Charlotte from the armchair, who gave her a look of disgust before scuttling upstairs, Daisy sank into it, the cat heat and the blazing fire welcome after the nippy walk.

"Love the hair by the way!" Morfydd called from the kitchen.

"Meh. I'm not sure. I was angry, a bit pissed too."

Having dug out an empty jar for the flowers Morfydd forced it between everything else on the mantlepiece. Pouring the coffee, she asked about Suni. Unable to keep it in, everything came spilling out. Hearing about the three men Morfydd had become angry, but saw Daisy needed her to listen and did her best to. At the mention of the Shove, Morfydd had raised her eyebrows briefly, but not pushed her on it.

Morfydd told her she was doing just fine, when Daisy asked, reminding her that her garden, her cats and the woods were more than enough to keep her busy. If she had remembered her birthday was coming, she made no mention of it and Daisy felt a sting of disappointment. Morfydd asked her if she was planning to return to Manchester, or whether she felt ready to spend time with Gwen.

"Not now, with Suni as he is. With Dad missing."

"I get that. You want to be able to do something, something practical?"

"Yeah, I do. Sitting around doing nothing, is driving me mad."

"If you spent time with Gwen, you could learn more about what we do, about the energy you've told me about?"

Daisy sighed and shook her head. Morfydd's persistence was beginning to grate. Whatever the hurry was, it made no sense to her. "Can we leave it. Like, does it have to be now?"

It really does, Morfydd thought, but with Daisy all frowns and fidgeting she kept it to herself. "Magic can help when we're struggling," she urged, like it was the most natural thing in the world. "Does that make sense?"

"I guess."

Daisy wanted it to be like it had before, when she and Morfydd had just hung out. It felt like she had an agenda, which if Suni and her dad had been okay, perhaps she wouldn't have dismissed so quickly. Tossing her cigarette into the fire, she drained her coffee and got up, setting her mug down noisily on the table.

"It's been good to see you, Morfydd. I'm staying Dad's, in case he comes back there. Call round if you like, or we could have a walk on the beach?"

"I'd like that. I'll call soon, Daisy."

Daisy shut the door hard. She was still annoyed. Morfydd meant well, wasn't one to struggle to say things and she found her vagueness trying.

A few days later, which Daisy had spent sleeping, reading and listlessly trying to clean the cottage, there was a knock at the door. She had not long returned from the hospital, still trying to conjure up an energy that made no sense to her. Heading down the draughty hallway she had expected Morfydd and was surprised to find Arwen outside.

"Hello Daisy. I wanted to see how you are, please may I come in?"

Daisy shrugged. "Yeah, if you like."

She was about to ask after Pol, but Arwen beat her to it, filling her in as she painstakingly unbuttoned her grey overcoat. "Pol's with Morfydd, fixing her outbuilding. I've nothing to offer when it comes to repairs, and thought it'd be nice for us to catch up." Looking around for a coat hook, she carefully hung her coat over the banister.

And no doubt, push me into spending time with Gwen, Daisy groaned inwardly.

"I've got coffee or tea? Vodka, if it's one of those days?" Daisy

"Tea's good. Black please, no sugar."

"Go through to the lounge, just to the right after the stairs, there's a fire going."

When Daisy brought the drinks in, Arwen was leaning from the armchair warming her hands. Her long silver hair was tied back, her slender frame hidden by bulky, warm clothes she began to loosen, feeling the heat from the fire. She sat back and reached for her tea, "How are you, Daisy?" she asked blowing on it.

"I'm not bad," she started. "Actually, I feel useless. I can't do anything for Suni, and I'm struggling with Dad disappearing."

Arwen nodded slowly as she sipped her tea. Daisy could feel her looking, knowing she rarely rushed anything. "You'd think I'd be used to that by now," she added despondently.

"It's bound to be hard, Daisy," Arwen said in a voice soft as clouds. "One of those would be difficult. Both together must be really tough. Would some reassurance, about your dad help?"

"Yes, it really would," Daisy said as she turned to Arwen quickly. "Can you give me any?"

"You remember the day on the cliff?"

Daisy nodded. "I'm not likely to forget it in a hurry."

"The light, that's where your dad has gone."

"And where does that go?" snapped Daisy.

She liked Arwen and was trying to keep her tone friendly.

"Imagine a gate at the end of the garden. One that can take you somewhere close by, but very different."

"Okay, so it's like a gate?"

"The one at the cliff, it's not the only one. There are others, quite a few actually. Between places. Is this making sense?"

"I believe that you believe it," Daisy replied unenthusiastically.

"Beyond that particular light," Arwen continued unperturbed, "is a place similar to here. Similar, but not the same. A place fully open to the Kindness. Free of fear; of the reluctance to believe in magic we often find here."

"What," scoffed Daisy, "like some kind of Utopia?"

Arwen put her mug down gently. "That's not a bad word. Imagine feeling positive, connected to nature and to the cosmos...can you imagine that?"

"Uh-huh."

"Beyond the light, it's like that all the time. Pure, loving spirit without ego...without those interpersonal dramas people tend to get stuck in."

Daisy thought of her mum and sighed. "I know about those."

"We can remember, if we want to, that we are more than this," Arwen gestured toward herself and Daisy, "more than the people we are, currently. That we are energy in its simplest, most beautiful form. Everything interconnected."

"How do you know though, for sure?"

Arwen smiled at Daisy as she leaned closer, her eyes twinkling.

"I know, because I've been there. Many times."

"And you get to come back?" Daisy demanded excitedly.

"I'm here with you, aren't I!"

It made sense, what she was saying and Daisy felt herself relax. It fit with things her dad had talked about; Morfydd too. Despite that, she felt herself shutting out what Arwen was saying. She wanted to experience it for herself, not just hear about it.

"Can you take me there?" she asked abruptly.

"Perhaps. The way through isn't always visible, or accessible. Sometimes it needs a certain celestial event, a totem. Someone who knows magic."

"You know magic, right?"

Arwen nodded, giving her a warm smile. "I do. You remember on the cliff, when we made a circle of sound?"

"I do. It vibrated, inside of me. Low and bassy, like standing by the amps at a gig?"

"I was using our combined energy, our intention, with a very old charm, to open the gate. Your dad wasn't meant to go through, nor the other man."

"That sounds like my dad!" Daisy snorted nervously.

"I was supposed to," Arwen said wistfully, "and not doing, has altered the balance of things."

"Altered the balance?"

"For now, yes. There'll be a way, there always is. I wanted to tell you, so you can know your dad will be safe until he returns."

"How do you know he'll return?"

"Because he's not meant to be there."

"But, when?"

Arwen reached over and gave her hand a pat. "I don't see it all Daisy, I'm sorry."

"Thank you, I've been dead worried. I do appreciate it. What about Suni, anything you can tell me, or do?"

Arwen shook her head. "I can't help with that, unfortunately. You might, once you've learned more; experienced the Kindness for yourself."

"And let me guess," Daisy said with a moan, "that means spending time with Gwen?"

Arwen laughed. "Gwen's not so bad, she just takes a while to thaw!"

"Any tips you can give me, I'm all ears!"

Chapter 8 – We Three

Gabriel followed the path between lush greenery. Having ambled cheerfully for a while, lingering over unfamiliar fruits and unusual blooms – freezing on the spot for a plump black scorpion – the trees and plants thinned. Walking through a long field of wildflowers, he thought it odd having seen no one else.

Without the tree cover it was baking hot and he wished he had more of the lemonade or fruit. Where before the path had cut through knee-high grasses and flowers, now it was baked earth. He had kept his eyes peeled for a tiger. *Had she meant a real one?* Exciting through it might be, to witness a real tiger up close and personal, he had little to offer beyond a friendly greeting and a respectable distance.

Sketched into the horizon was a collection of buildings arranged into a street; what looked like a tiny civilisation. Still some way off, it was unexpected, the deep forest leading him to believe that there was nothing here, besides Tallulah and her hut. That, and creatures rarely seen outside of a documentary. *Looks as good as anywhere*, he said to himself as he headed toward the buildings.

Drenched in sweat he travelled along the track as it meandered toward the settlement. And still no tiger.

When the tiger did come, he was disappointed. Whilst it was a stunning rendition, carved life-size from a chunk of gleaming black rock, it was not a real tiger. Granted, the stripes were realistic, as were the paws – neatly together in front as it lay flat to the ground.

Introducing himself he patted its nose, which was warm and smooth. He picked some flowers and fashioned them into an indiscriminate chain he placed on the tiger's head; the blue, purple and red exquisite against the wind-polished, black boulder. The path he had flowed paused at the feet of the tiger, splitting into a distinct left and right.

What was it Tallulah said? Had she said right, or was it left?

Usually, when faced with a left or right, Gabriel would take the left-hand path every time; feeling westerly even when it wasn't. He made for the left-hand path, then remembered she had said turn right.

Swinging his jacket over his shoulder, he took the right-hand path. This new track was gravelled and followed a neater line: a track that felt like it wanted to lead somewhere, having worked up to the idea for some time. Wherever it led, he hoped they had lemonade.

It was a street, with simple buildings along the left-hand side of the road. He saw storage units, a closed café and old-fashioned offices with opaque windows, nestled together in the shadow of a vast, dusty red mountain. Opposite, was a yellowed grassy area with a wooden bench overlooking a sweeping estuary.

Further out, shy dolphins glided underwater. The sea swept in boldly, funnelled through a modest harbour; a collection of unassuming wooden and tin huts that formed a small quayside. Wooden vessels with peeling paint and creaking sails bobbed in the sun. Happily, a breeze peeled off the water, the first cool sensation for some time and he welcomed its tickle on his skin as he made for the bench.

At the edge of the grassed area was a wooden sign. Stout legs had been driven into the dry earth and it was painted in watermelon colours, the board pinky-red, lettering in a dark green edged neatly in black. In the bottom corner, a tiny signature that looked like it read, Freyja. He thought it a quite beautiful sign:

Welcome to Grayling Junction

Population: Some

The bench stood out amidst the faded grass and bleached buildings. Crafted from pieces of fishing boats no longer in service, frequent sitting had worn it to a smooth and remarkably comfortable condition. With three wooden boards nailed to seasoned wooden blocks, the rear was bowed at an angle perfect for reclining.

Gabriel sat down. Taking in the harbour and buildings, there were people; no twitching curtains. At the foot of the mountain, he saw a few more buildings, squeezed into the middle of which, was a tiny wooden hut, with a simple sign that looked like it read 'Mayor Bolt'. There were houses, also in wood, with intricate timber gables; a stoop here, a hammock there. No obvious cowboys. Further off, where the mountain curved out of sight, was what looked like a higgledy-piggledy collection of flats with an estuary view.

At the end of the road, where it curved around the base of the mountain before climbing higher, was an impressive building: The nineteenth-century railway station had been the crowning glory of Grayling Junction, officially opened by the then mayor, Rusty Crouch[3]. All had gathered for the opening (which had included rudimentary, and it must be said fairly dangerous, fireworks) and it was spoken of fondly, for many generations.

At a T-junction on a wonky diagonal from the station, was a lone house guarding the sapphire tail of the estuary. Skirted by a veranda and built from a darker, sturdier wood than its neighbours, its presence loomed large; surly almost.

---

[3] For a longer adventure in the town, the *Grayling Junction* series by SJ Howarth will be released in due course.

Retrieving his tobacco from his jacket, he let the peacefulness of the town wrap around him as he contentedly rolled a cigarette. He cocked his ear – there it was again. A steady clicking sound. He'd thought it was a boat engine, but dismissed it. It didn't sound like a bird or mating call. Smiling, he hoped it might be the Dik-dik. When he turned and looked behind him, he saw that it wasn't.

Making his way from the harbour, at a pace a snail would find embarrassing, was a man moving with two wooden sticks that clicked over the ground. He wore an oily grey and green plaid shirt, canvas trousers and walked barefoot. Gabriel smoked as he watched the man centimetre toward him. His face was a heavy hide, like the cover of an ancient book. Judging from his deeply lined weathered skin, creased and parchment dry, the man must have seen seventy winters at least. As he neared, Gabriel saw nut-brown eyes screwed deep into the sockets, that sparkled with mischief and vitality. He waved lazily and the man replied with a nod, not letting go of his sticks.

When he reached the bench Gabriel saw he had gaunt cheeks knotted with burst vessels. His features lacked soft edges, as though chiselled by a rough hand. Furrowed merriment had pulled the skin tight across his skull and silvery whiskers grew from his face like Pampas grass. His hair was dark, shoulder length and unkempt. Maybe it was just the estuary gently spooning the pair of them, but to Gabriel, he bore the countenance of a man of the sea.

"Good morning," said Gabriel cheerily, sliding along the bench to make room.

The sitting process had begun: the man swinging his weight onto one of the sticks, as he laid the other against the bench. "And to you," he replied. With a slow revolution the man swung from the other stick and onto the bench, setting it down with a flourish; fluid movements with a long history.

As he relaxed, he let out a contented sigh. "Twenty-three minutes, from cabin to bench. Personal best I think." His voice didn't fit his appearance, it was feathery and light; youthful.

"Congratulations. It's a beautiful day for it. I'm Gabriel."

"They usually are," said the man gazing across the estuary. "Good to meet you Gabe, I'm No-Shoes-the-Fish."

Gabriel grinned. *No chance of forgetting that.* "You too. It seems like a lovely town, Grayling Junction. Don't think I've been here before."

"It IS a lovely town, and you're very welcome. Ron will be along soon."

"Ron?"

"My very good friend. We always meet here, start the day together. Usually, we are three, but Tam can't make it."

"Oh...right."

"Still," No-Shoes-the-Fish said laying a hand on his shoulder, "today, we are three."

They both turned, at the clatter of a straining engine coming along the main road, having bounced and skidded down the sweeping mountain pass. An ochre cloud of dust parted to reveal an old workhorse, a '69 Ford F100 truck in powder blue paint and chrome – a lot of chrome.

"Here's Ron now."

As the truck slid to a halt on the threadbare grass, the door swung open before the vehicle had come to a complete stop and Ron Backwards arrived with a prancing canter.

"Gentlemen!" said Ron.

He looked at No-Shoes-the-Fish, then jerked quickly to his right...this was not Tam Flint.

"Oh, a stranger...hullo, stranger."

"Hello, I'm Gabriel."

Ron Backwards was a good man, a popular man, with white hair plaited down his back and a drooping, snow white moustache. Built from an economy of skin and sinew, he looked like a man manufactured from an indestructible, lightweight alloy. His habit of wearing black shirts and black trousers lent him an air of a preacher – though nothing could be further from the truth, not least the nocturnal predilections he regularly enjoyed with Davina Crosby.

He slid in beside Gabriel and nodded expectantly at No-Shoes-the-Fish, who grinned as he squirrelled into his pockets one by one, eventually raising aloft a glass bottle with no label. Trapped within was a riotous liquid; like sunset tricked inside.

"Gentlemen, it's time for our daily salutation!"

Unscrewing the cap, he brought the bottle to his nose and inhaled deeply. Exactly where No-Shoes-the-Fish acquired his rum, none could say. Rumours stole through the sandy streets – effusive murmurs concerning a tangle of homespun distillation hidden in a seldom-used shed. It is a rare drop indeed, however, one that can put a person on their back – even a person with the monumental stature of Tam Flint – with swift and graceful ease. No-Shoes-the-Fish stood meticulously, holding on to the bench as he lifted the bottle skyward:

Bless this morning bright,

Bless this drop,

Bless we three a 'right,

That we may never stop!

"That we may never stop!" echoed Ron.

Regretful not to be taking part, Gabriel licked his lips. Swallowing, he could taste a vague memory of rum.

"I don't, anymore," he said nodding toward the bottle.

Ron smiled graciously and handed the bottle back to No-Shoes-the-Fish. "What brings you here Gabriel, to our charming little backwater?"

"It's something of a tale...but simply put, I'm lost!"

"Lost, is rarely lost," drawled No-Shoes-the-Fish as he drifted into the bronze liquid.

"I'm on my way back to Wales."

"Not far. In certain ways of moving." Ron nudged Gabriel gently with his elbow, "You should go see Lalo Morrow, he'll help."

"Grants wishes, he does," added No-Shoes-the-Fish.

"I would love some lemonade. Some directions, too. This Lalo, where do I find him?"

"Big house, over yonder," replied Ron and No-Shoes-the-Fish at exactly the same time. They looked at one another with surprise, linking little fingers as each made a silent wish.

Ron pointed a wiry arm at the large house at the T-junction. Gabriel got up. "Thank you very much, for passing the time of day with me."

"You're very welcome," replied No-Shoes-the-Fish.

"Most welcome, you are," Ron added. "You'll always find us here, by all means call again..."

With that, Gabriel crossed the yellowed grass, shielding his face from the roaring sun with his hand, as he made for the low house that presided over an unassuming, yet superfluous, T-junction.

Chapter 9 – Exhibition for One

Closing the door Daisy called out, then remembered he wouldn't answer. Each time she came back, she found herself holding onto a brittle hope he might have made his way back unseen.

Having made coffee, washing pots as it percolated, Daisy took the armchair beside the fire. He was everywhere. The arms were worn bare from him sitting there. She could smell him, his unique blend of cigarette smoke, old age and antique roll-on deodorant. Sunlight coming through the window picked out a patch of dust, ash and tobacco strands on the floor.

The last week or so, she had been ignoring calls from work. The frequency had ramped up, then peaked, culminating in an email (written in robotic HR-speak) informing her she was no longer employed. It also made it very clear that there were no circumstances under which she was permitted to keep the branded polo shirts provided (were she to die whilst employed, it stated that 'a suitable family member was expected to launder and return them at their earliest convenience').

Jobless at almost twenty-four and clinging to a measly amount of savings, time at her dad's cottage offered a far better chance of avoiding opinions about what she should do with her life; the isolation increasingly palatable. She had logged into her ASMR channel, with a vague idea of using the cottage to record a new video, but she remembered her recording equipment was back in Manchester.

As she had sat thinking about fetching some of her stuff from Manchester, her mum had phoned. She had left it ringing a long time. Her mum had been frantic, demanding to know where she was. As she gave short answers, her mum announced that now was a natural time for Daisy to move out.

She had been taken aback and as her mum repeated herself, Daisy sensed wine was the foundation upon which this idea and her call had been built.

"Whatever. I'll come for my stuff then, at some point."

Having obviously got what she wanted, her mum changed the subject, droning on about a new group she'd joined. Refusing to ask about any of it, Daisy had tugged at a loose thread in her jumper; somewhere in the distance, a long, meandering account of bible study coffee mornings. Daisy caught something about end times, her mum insistent she prepare for the second coming. It was all so ridiculous. She could picture the scene – her mum fanatically arranging short-dated sausage rolls, carrot, celery and dips. Holding court in the living room, whilst drinking herself further and further away from the salvation the group claimed to offer.

Daisy cut her off, telling her to leave her room alone, and hung up. Sat in the freezing cottage of one absent parent, she questioned what it was she got from either of them. How she had managed to become wedged, yet again, between their respective dramas. He was no better, falling into nowhere as soon as they'd found one another again.

Coming out of the bathroom later, she had popped her head into each room, in case he'd snuck in and gone to bed. His bedroom smelled stale. Tangled sheets and a thick dust over everything. Forcing open a window, she left the room as quick as she could. She figured she might as well nosey around the two spare rooms. They had talked about clearing one of them out for her, something she'd be needing sooner than planned.

The first room, the smaller of the two, was filled with bin bags of old clothes, mismatched furniture and what looked like equipment from his TV days – shiny outfits, boxes of props and tucked away in one corner, albeit completely inaccessible, was a six-foot gold-coloured cage.

With filing cabinets along one wall, the second room had a simple wooden school desk covered with books, more books, magazines and newspapers stacked from floor to ceiling along the wall opposite. Opening drawers at random, she found household bills and bank statements, all unopened. She tugged at a plump red folder poking out, which burst its contents as it came free. She found old photographs of her as a baby; at junior school. Every one of her school reports was there and amongst them, pictures and cards she had made. She slid out a photograph of herself around age seven. She was laughing and, if she did say so herself, looked decidedly cheeky. She put it one side, to show Suni when he had recovered.

On top of the filing cabinets, newer stacks of books had been started between pots containing plants no one could reanimate, piles of rocks and stones, a bowl of what might once have been apples and another galaxy of unopened post – originally stacked, but having slid to the floor at some point.

Both rooms were daunting and neither bore any resemblance to what might be called a bedroom. She paced from one to the other, trying to visualise each room empty (or at least emptier). With a heavy sigh, she started on the smaller one, the slightly less chaotic of the two.

Having lifted and dragged box after box, swearing at most of them, she had reclaimed a narrow gulley just inside the entrance. She had coughed through clouds of dust and dead insects and rearranging the boxes, discovered a top hat, the same one possibly from the video clip of her dad she had watched so many times. It fit perfectly, and she pranced along the landing, waving her arm out as though wielding a wand. Despite the august history of the hat, and a few laps of the landing waving an imaginary wand, Daisy didn't feel magic and put it carefully away in one of the better boxes.

With the boxes stacked on the landing, tucked against one wall protected by grubby blankets, she found canvasses. Most were similar in size to a record sleeve, one or two were larger; longer than they were high. There were nine and Daisy propped them against things as best she could. The smaller ones were neatly rendered images of birds she didn't know and fruit she did. They seemed older than the largest picture. It was more ambitious – a garden scene brimming with plump pink roses and trailing plants. It dawned on her, looking at them again, they must have been painted by her grandmother. Picking them up one at a time, working out where to store them safely, she felt like she wasn't alone in the room and she turned more than once, certain someone had slipped in behind her.

After a few hours shifting boxes, most still on the landing as she tried to make a plan, Daisy was done in. She had found a single bed, hidden under boxes and even then, all but filled by a mannequin reclining on a trio of robes in lurid colours. She carried it into the bathroom, catching its arm on the doorframe, then slipped the top hat onto its smooth, faceless head and left it watching over the bath.

Sifting through decades of junk on her own had turned her sullen. She'd pictured them clearing out a room, together. Music blaring, endless coffee, lots of laughing and as the room took shape, the gulf between daughter and father gradually reduced.

As another bulging tower of boxes toppled, emptying the contents into the only space in the room, Daisy ground her teeth, muttering bitterly about being used to doing things without him. In the mess, she found notebooks and journals in different colours, all about the right size for a cardigan pocket.

Grabbing one, it was filled with his uneven handwriting, and colonies of doodles; a sporadic footnote here and there. Flicking through it, her heart caught as she saw her own name.

He never joined up the capital D, a short line floating within the curve, making it look like a fish head; the elongated tail of the y trailing over multiple lines. A five-letter word made so much grander.

Once she'd got the fire downstairs going again, made more coffee, she rolled a couple of cigarettes and settled into the chair to investigate the nine journals in more detail.

She was forced to accept, from the first of them, that hoping for any kind of order to the entries, was futile. He had written in each notebook on numerous occasions, sometimes in biro, sometimes ink; pencils of varying leads – even a couple of pages in what looked to be chunky orange crayon. It was obvious the journals had been around longer than she thought, had travelled further than Ceredigion. Very few entries were dated. Some of the entries were written as though he was talking to her – one, a long and winding account of how the cottage had come to be his, Daisy grinning as she pictured him and the estate agent, freezing from room to room. Many were indecipherable, written too small or too hastily, and she could hear his gruff tone in her mind. In a navy-blue journal, interspersed with pages of what looked to be random lists, she found a detailed entry charting the origins of Randall's Relishes, the company her grandfather had started.

Picking up on that was bottle-green and leather-bound, she turned it over in her hands. It felt different. It had heavier pages, of a finer quality; the other ones picked up cheaply enough anywhere. The patterned leather was warm, as though it had sat in the sun. Opening the first page, her expectations heightened. His handwriting filled every page, squashed sideways into the margins, impenetrable diagrams spreading over multiple pages:

Quscu, Peru, September 18th '71

Midday, the events of last night still on my mind. It has been hellish hot, for weeks. I slept woefully, waking drenched in sweat. The mattress is hard and uncomfortable, though I am indebted to DeSouza, for giving me a corner of his shack to make temporary shelter.

The man intrigues me. I'm learning everyday about the power of illusion. Of the manners and magnitude of magic. He scares me. When I'm with him – and often when I'm not – there is an energy about him, an influence within him; in his riddles and non-sequiturs. Behind his milky white cataracts is a confidence...no, more than that...a knowing, that he is able to do whatever he wills – to compel elements. I have seen him bring energy from dry, baked earth or pull it down from the sky. With one gesture of his arms, I have seen him stop rain.

Undergoing more of what he laughingly refers to as my tutelage, last night was unlike anything I've experienced. More profound even, than the meditations I practiced over and over in Rishikesh (where I first felt a connection to, for want of a better phrase, a vast, cosmic consciousness, broader and deeper than any ocean. It proved inconsistent, for I am easily distracted. Even so, I knew then, I am more than this body...a timeless awareness; a single droplet in an infinite sea of bliss).

Last night, however, was interdimensional. That is, beyond conventional dimensions. I left this existence behind...this body (?). My soul (?), my spirit (?) went to another time and place entirely; I went beyond. Trying to capture it now, to relive it, to find (chase?) that sensation again, I realise –

Daisy turned the page, impatient to find where it continued. She found a recipe for Mole sauce, another for enchiladas and a string of detailed sketches of what she thought might be coriander; a series of unfinished poems addressed to someone called Tanechka. Wading through the journals, she was unable to find anything else about Quscu and the enigmatic DeSouza, or for that matter Rishikesh. Returning to the bedrooms she upended boxes, rifling through them again for more journals. There was nothing. Each time she seemed to get closer, she was left with a brutal truth: how little she knew about this man, about the fifty-odd years before she'd been born.

Worn out, she realised she hadn't eaten and flopped into the chair by the fire with a handful of crackers. She went at the journals again, trying to be systematic as she folded back corners as a way of highlighting sections, making a pile of the ones she'd been through line by line. Then, distracted by an entry about fish, she was off again, albeit in an entirely different direction...

Chapter 10 – The Red Herring Chapter

Today there is less pain and I even beat the sun to the garden. There were so many stars still out, Daisy. I wonder if you remember me showing you the stars? Such a long time ago now.

I think at this point, I want to tell you about fish. Something of fish, at any rate. I cannot think of fish without thinking of DeSouza – his beard like a hawthorn in first frost, his greedy, stubby fingers messy with fish and hot sauce.

I am back in those hot nights, before (any of) you were here. At night the air filled with such a dizzying commotion – sizzling food, exhaust fumes and more often than not, gunfire. A ton of Mezcal too, as above us lidding the city, brooding purple clouds oozed in from the broken mountains.

The word mackerel is an inaccuracy. In actual fact, the word is used for a variety of different species of fish, mostly belonging to the family Scombridae. The largest of these – when left to their own devices – can achieve well over a metre and a half in length. A natural gift for sparring and rapid movement keeps them lithe (I do like to imagine one or two lazy bloaters in the depths, idling away their days). They are content to tickle their fins in cosy tropical waters and more moderate seas. Rarely do they bother themselves with coming close to shore, having no interest whatsoever in the narcissistic affairs of mankind.

It is reckoned a female mackerel lays around half a million eggs at a time (I can barely imagine). This is done with a sense of duty, unable (unwilling?) to accept that her numerous offspring, greatly prized for their oily meat, will end their short-lived days hoovered into the gaping maw of a fishery.

Elsewhere in the water, lives a distant cousin oft removed. Far closer in relation to the herring, the offspring of the family

Clupeidae, or, to you and I, the sardines and the pilchards. The island of Sardinia, once home to a sprawling family who lived abundantly, gifted us the name Sardine.[4]

These fish are plump to the gills with fatty acids whose qualities, regularly usurped by advertising people, have been discovered to assist in maintaining a reliable heart, regulate blood sugar levels and even slow the progressive advance of mild to moderate Alzheimer's disease, though I suspect any of this is consolation to the fish themselves.

Whilst happy for these benefits, I enjoy these fish because the small rectangular tins with neatly rounded, appealing corners, are very cheap indeed, weighing in at 89p or less. In order that they be consumed direct from the tin, nowadays having a much more convenient ring pull than the previous key mechanism, these fish have travelled a long way. A remote cannery having sealed them in their aluminium coffin, prior to heating them to an inconceivable temperature within the highly pressurized environment.

I believe, it was owing to the efforts of one Robert Ayars, that in 1812 the first American canning factory opened in New York City. A dependable succession of wars swelled the demand for economical, non-perishable food, marching armies expected to be ready, willing and able to kill at a moment's notice. Companies quickly learned the knack of manufacturing in bulk and many was the young soldier cut down with a full fishy belly, in order that I might subsist on a diet relying heavily on canned fish.

Even before war became the unremitting enterprise it is today, it was at the insistence of Victorian Britain that food was able to be kept at home for longer, without the necessity of

---

[4] Scientists have generously provided a general rule to assist fishing folk in categorization: a fish 4 inches or less answers to the name 'sardine', whereas a hulking brute 4 inches or more will raise a fin to the cry of 'pilchard'.

visiting local providers as often, that produced an inflammatory increase in the availability of tinned goods.

This nationwide sprawl toward sloth, first sharpened the blade that would eventually gut the livelihood of innumerable grocers, butchers and fishmongers. With the blade still winking, a virulent bacterium – supermarketius inflexibilious – spawned unchecked; a chronic contagion that felled one independent retailer after another.

Despite all of this, Aberaeron (not far from me) still boasts fresh fish – a cheery person in a bloodied apron inhabiting a fishy caravan on the harbour. Whistling away three days a week, the folk of Ceredigion form regular queues. The leisurely wait is a chance to swap tall tales, small stories and reasonably good-natured gossip – and you will often find me there, for I am no exception to that, Daisy.

Chapter 11 – Waiting Water

Daisy was woken by a loud knocking at the door. As she got up from the chair she had slept in, again, wiping dribble from her chin with her sleeve, something fell to the floor. It was one of the journals. As she stooped to retrieve it, she thought of fish.

Resenting the interruption, she headed for the door planning to send whoever it was away. Before falling asleep, she had decided she would go to Aberaeron. However unlikely it might be, her dad could have ended up there. At the mercy of the sea or a passing fishing boat.

Morfydd stood outside, in a dress Daisy thought a little too summery for February. "Hey, what you doing here?"

"Hi Daisy. I wondered if you're free?"

It sounded like a question, but her flinty gaze suggested otherwise. Daisy took a step back, the door only partially open.

"Err...I'm kinda in the middle of things," she lied. "Clearing out one of the rooms..."

Morfydd nodded slowly. Her silence left Daisy uncomfortable and she tried to take control. "I can come over later. After I've done, I'm nipping to Aberaeron, you need anything?"

"Gwen's at mine. She'd like to see you – *we* would like to see you." Before Daisy could reply, Morfydd said, "It's never wise to keep Gwen waiting. Perhaps I could come back and help you tidy another time."

Daisy was unconvinced. The longer Morfydd eyed her, waiting for her to respond, the more difficult it was to say no.

"Fine," she said with a huffy shrug, "I guess Aberaeron isn't going anywhere."

Patting down the pockets of her coat for her phone, she realised she couldn't find the lighter her dad had given her. Morfydd was already halfway down the drive, her hair whipping in the wind as she stared at the cottage, face pinched.

As Daisy ferreted a hand down the side of the cushion, she found it. There was something else...another journal, crumpled for having been sat on. Flicking through it as she headed for the door, she saw an entry from 1973, another dated 1987. Stuffing it into her bag she wondered if there could be an order after all; a map only her dad could read.

They walked over to Morfydd's in silence. As soon as they stepped inside, Gwen hoisted herself from one of the chairs, her beady eyes fixed on Daisy.

"I trust you're ready, Daisy?"

Daisy saw Gwen shoot Morfydd a look of annoyance, at which she raised her eyebrows and held out her hands. She sensed tension; embers of a recent quarrel.

Daisy shook her head. "No. And ready for what?"

From what she had seen and heard of Gwen, the way they usually deferred to her wisdom and blunt will, left her oddly apprehensive. Although she had met some of the Sisterkin, she knew nothing about how the group was organised (*if it even was?*) or what they did. Searching online hadn't brought up anything, which Daisy found even odder.

It was Morfydd who answered, tersely. "We thought you could spend time with Gwen, help you come to terms with things."

Daisy tried her best to remain impassive. The last thing she had had in mind was spending time with the nowty old woman, who was beginning to remind her of a hatchet-faced, chain-smoking teacher from junior school.

"What is it you think I need to come to terms with?"

"With what happened to your father," snapped Gwen without a trace of care.

"He's gone missing. And he's actually, like, died before," Daisy said rudely. "He'll be back," she added, looking to Morfydd. Morfydd smiled, but behind it, there was something else Daisy couldn't reach.

She felt Gwen's hand at her elbow and jerked away. "What are you doing, I'm not a child!"

If Gwen was bothered by her outburst, she didn't show it. She stood hands on hips, staring at Daisy with one eyebrow cocked.

"You finished?"

"Gwen has her boat, for the two of you..."

Daisy looked at Morfydd, then at Gwen, then back to Morfydd. Being cornered left her raging. She could do whatever she pleased – and spending time at her dad's cottage, visiting Suni and trying to work out what to do with her life was more than enough. She stood on the spot scowling. Choosing the least shit option from a short list of shit options, wasn't much of an option. She turned and headed for the door.

"I'm not going, not with Suni –

Before she reached the door, Gwen was behind her, placing her hands over her temples, her skin rough and cold.

"What are –

Daisy tried to talk but her words faltered. Her mind was fogged, her head pressurized as though Gwen was squeezing it. Feeling Gwen's breath on the back of her neck, she heard her murmuring.

Gwen no longer held her head, but it felt like she did. Daisy wobbled, reaching for the back of a chair, an image filling her mind. There were two coffins, side-by-side. She was unable to see any surroundings, just the sleek, dark wood, each bearing a brass nameplate: one for Suni, one for her dad.

When Gwen spoke again, it was without the full extent of her hardness, though by no means with anything approaching warmth. "It's not just about what you want, Daisy. There's a bigger picture, far beyond trivialities like your father and your friend."

"Trivialities!" barked Daisy, outraged.

"What I've just shown you," Gwen said, "is an outcome, not *the* outcome. Come with me to Tor's Leap. It'll help you help Suni, maybe your dad too, I assure you."

Daisy glared sulkily, finding little of value in her any assurance Gwen might offer. "Tor's Leap? What's that?"

"We can talk on the journey."

"Great", Daisy muttered under her breath, *"more time with this woman."*

"Doesn't seem I have much choice, does it."

"You always have a choice," Morfydd chimed in. "If you wish to spend more time with us though, time at Tor's Leap has to come next."

"Fine. But I'm going back to my dad's, I need to pack stuff."

Lingering in the doorway, she fixed Gwen with a stony look as she pointed a finger at her. "And if anything changes with Suni, or there's any word on my dad, I'm gone. Even if I have to fucking swim back."

Part Two: Travelling Songs

Chapter 12 – The House of Wants

Since the start of Grayling Junction, the Morrow house has been more than just a wooden building held together with rusting rivets and crowned with a stoic roof of local tin.

This is the House of Wants and the sole responsibility for keeping house lies with Lalo Morrow. By way of exchange, the house has looked after Lalo, his father and his grandfather all of whom, like the determined *Echinopsis pachanoi*, thrive in twilight: flowering in the blue hours, growing tall by melodies of the moon; requiring no more sustenance than the roots of home.

Lalo, a name of Spanish origin meaning bringer of prosperity or luck, is the eldest of three. His sister Maya lives beyond the cresting span of an ocean, where she enjoys a life patiently arranged in tidy layers, cosseting three children and a diminutive husband who lives behind large, greasy glasses. Tio, his brother, having briefly sampled the lurid lights and swarming streets of city life, chose to join an eldritch monastery a world away. This collection of hushed chambers is surrounded on every side by sharp rocks clinging doggedly to the spine of Tibetan mountains. Sporadic letters arrive from both siblings.

Born under a 1960's moon, Lalo was an intuitive, sensitive child who found happiness in water, books, solitude and trees. Fortunate enough to have loving parents, his development lacked any definite tragedy. As a young child, his grandfather (whom of late he was growing to resemble) had explained, peering through his jade-green cloud of pipe smoke, that, "the Morrows tend to avoid the ire of the deities", a curiosity Grandfather Morrow put down to their honourable work keeping house.

Shortly before passing, Grandfather Morrow had been entertaining a young Lalo with fantastical, lightly exaggerated glimpses of the Grayling of yesteryear. Without warning, a backlog of coughing had agitated the green smoke and with a broad grin Grandfather Morrow had slouched backwards in his chair. His final gaze passed over little Lalo's head, radiant with the unabridged joy of witnessing the long-awaited return of a lover. With a final sigh, his head had sagged backwards as his eyes closed. He was 117.

The Morrow house is a late 19th century wooden construction of one storey, with a sloping tin roof. Extending from the front, the enclosed veranda has wooden railings and straight-edged supports. A while back, Lalo acquired an old teak rocker and enjoys sitting and watching the sun doing what the sun likes to do before bed. Sometimes, Bethany-of-the-Tears will join him, her regular sobbing topping up the estuary. Neighbourhood cats use the veranda to shelter from the sun, paw prints criss-crossing the dust; old fur cushioning the rocker.

A high fence of nailed wood panels protects the rear of the property. Inside this fencing is a tremendous helping of spaghetti verde, made of knotted vines, flowers, shrubs and adolescent trees that form a thorny blanket tugged up tight to the fence on all sides. Despite the weatherworn wood, a roof stippled with coruscation and a faded countenance, anyone passing does tend to admire the building – time having given it the patina of a well-worn heirloom, rather than the forlorn air of a palace that has exchanged splendour for delinquency.

Gabriel stopped and read a document pinned to the outside of the door – ancient paper in the hand of Grandfather Morrow, waterproofed within a modern plastic sleeve:

The House of Morrow – Terms of Payment and Exchange

1. Payment is made by an act of exchange – something wanted, for something of value, for example, a horse, a child, a precious gemstone, lock of hair and so on. The value of goods tendered will be judged by the Keeper of the House. Ownership of any exchange transfers immediately & permanently to the House.

2. Payment may also be made with the surrender of years of one's life: The Keeper of the House to calculate the cost in years. Customers should be aware that years surrendered may not have already passed and there is no guarantee when they be taken; they may be taken from prime years remaining. The ownership of years transfers immediately and permanently to the House and will be held in clearing until re-distributed to worthy causes.

3. All and any wants will be accommodated provided exchange or payment is agreed and accepted. All decisions of the Keeper of the House are absolute. No refunds will be given.

Inside, it was darker than he had expected, slatted wooden window blinds limiting the daylight. Blinking, he tried to get a sense of the layout. To his left were three low sofas, arranged around a ceramic-topped coffee table in a comfortable U, each upholstered in a worn burgundy fabric with a scatter of black cushions. He could smell incense, traces of smoke plaited into the air. Adjacent to the sofas, a simple wooden cabinet held a coffee machine, coffee, filter papers and a cluster of mismatched cups. Touching the jug, it was hot. He poured himself a mug and took a deep draught. It was marvellous – woody, with hints of cedar and tobacco; heavy-bodied.

"Hello?" he called out, peering through the gloom at what looked like a counter at the back.

Wandering over supping his coffee, he found a counter with a giant, ancient cash register at one end. In the centre was a hefty ledger the colour of midnight and a collection of black pens in a mug with a design showing a pair of bemused, cartoon fish headed in opposite directions. Next to that, a half-empty ashtray and a half-full bottle of Fitou.

Behind the counter was a black leather office chair of lapsed splendour close to a wooden desk. The surface of the desk had been abandoned decades ago, unremembered under a pile of paperwork that grew and grew without being trimmed. Somewhere there is a fountain pen, a writing pad and a late 1930's Bakelite telephone – reluctantly intersexed at some point to accept modern cabling.

Having called out again, sounds of movement could be heard beyond a wooden door marked 'Privado', that opened moments later.

Lalo Garcia Morrow stepped confidently into his kingdom. Average height, with swept back jet-black hair and a widow's peak that lent him an air of refinement, his collar length hair was greying at the temples. The gaunt angle of his jaw, softened with frosty stubble was at odds with his brooding introspection, for when not smiling, he closed himself off like a bank vault. Watery green eyes gave little away. In the past, he had been referred to as handsome, the compliment usually diluted, with the hasty addition of, but somewhat detached.

"Yes?" said, Lalo briefly looking Gabriel up and down.

"I'm Gabriel, good morning to you," he said as he held out the empty mug to Lalo, who just stared at it. "Ron and No-Shoes-the-Fish said you might be able to help me. I'd like some lemonade, please – and some directions."

As he set the mug down, the door crashed open and a man rushed to the counter as though Gabriel wasn't there. He explained breathlessly how he had travelled from a settlement behind the red mountain, having reached a point in his life where he could no longer continue to live hens; many, many hens. He wanted to collect eggs, already had names in mind for his hens and was ready, willing and able to spend time on his hands and knees, cluck-cluck-cluck-cluck-clucking.

Effortlessly, Lalo flipped open the ledger and uncapped a pen. In no time at all, the man had exchanged five years of his life, for 101 hens – hens that would be delivered in three days, courtesy of Ron Backwards and his stalwart truck. Before Gabriel could fully comprehend what he had just witnessed, the hen man was gone, leaving with the same haste he had arrived.

"Apologies, Gabriel, we will get busier..."

"No matter," Gabriel replied. He slouched against the counter, thirstier than ever. "About that lemonade?"

Lalo nodded. "Lemonade is no problem." He went through the door behind the counter, returning a few minutes later with a glass jug of lemonade clinking with a flotilla of ice and a large glass. Setting them down on the counter, he motioned to Gabriel. "Please, help yourself. The lemonade isn't free though, just so you know."

Gabriel grabbed at the jug with both hands and filled the glass. Draining the contents in one go, he filled the glass again. It was ice cold, sharp and delicious. Smoothing down his velvet jacket, Gabriel offered it to Lalo. "Perhaps you'd take this, in payment for the lemonade and the coffee?"

Lalo took the jacket in his hands, held it up, turned it around, checked the lapels and the collar. "The coffee is free, by the way. I will accept this, it's in good condition. You might want to empty the pockets though?"

Freed of the jacket, Gabriel took the lemonade slower than before. Finishing another glass, he felt refreshed and with a hiccup, thanked Lalo. He was about to ask for directions, when they were interrupted.

A bearded magician with razorbill fingernails and a paint-stained tracksuit arrived at the counter, in desperate need of a trio of confident, experienced and accommodating rabbits – adding wearily that he would take hares in a crisis.

Immediately after he had left, a married couple made of papier mâché floated to the counter on a gentle breeze. Gabriel stared through them, as they exchanged an exquisite silver teapot and a Lalique vase the colour of tears, for a lifetime of waterproof solidity.

"It *is* busy," said Gabriel. Wanting to give the customers privacy he had helped himself to another coffee and meandered back to the counter trying not to spill it.

Lalo shrugged, "Trust me, this is nothing. So, you said you're in need of directions…?"

Gabriel gave Lalo a summary of his travels, explaining he was fairly sure he'd taken a wrong turn somewhere, hence finding himself in Grayling Junction, rather than Wales.

"Three years."

Gabriel frowned. "Three years? I want to go now, please."

"Three years, of your life. As payment."

Gabriel weighed up how far he might get without Lalo's assistance. It would be easy enough to pass more time in Grayling Junction, but after, having no idea where he was, even *if* he was, he was unsure. Passing through the portal of light, he had clearly gone somewhere else and finding his own way back to Wales neatly, could take a long time. Longer than three years.

"Two?" Gabriel suggested hopefully.

"Five?" Lalo replied unsmiling.

Gabriel offered Lalo his hand. "Three it is."

Lalo shook it hurriedly, then bent over the ledger, detailing the transactions for the lemonade and the directions. Closing the ledger and folding his arms, he gave Gabriel a thin smile.

"When you're ready, go out the door you came in...and you'll be exactly where you need to be."

Chapter 13 – Tor's Leap

Morfydd had waved them off, standing alone on the shingle until they were out of sight. Gwen had urged the boat over the water as though Daisy wasn't there and she hadn't spoken to Gwen, or offered help. As Daisy imagined it couldn't possibly get any darker, the sky pressed down harder; the distant glow from the cottage swallowed by the night.

Pitching on the black water, clasped within the fist of night, the boat felt much smaller than it was. Freezing spray slicked the deck, determined to spend more time inside the boat than out. It had soaked into her trainers a while ago and her toes were numb, the fitful heaving motion having left Daisy queasy from the moment they set off. As the seething water tossed the boat high on the waves, before slamming it back down again, Daisy was unable to see anything clearly. What kind of boat it was, she had no idea. It had an engine and a roofed area around the wheel, where the two of them could stand, at least partially shielded from the biting cold. Gwen, however, was unperturbed, whistling to herself as she navigated the whitecaps with ease. When she did call out, Daisy was on her phone and it took her a moment to realise she was talking to her.

"There's fog up ahead. Be sure to keep everything inside the boat."

"Where else would it be!" Daisy muttered under her breath.

"Daisy, if I ask you to do something," Gwen said glancing over her shoulder, "it's for your benefit."

Daisy flinched. She couldn't possibly have heard her, not over the sound of the engine, the waves and a rising gale.

"Whatever."

"What is it with your generation?" Gwen grumbled. "See nothing beyond your own dramas."

"And so many of *yours*, write us off, just for being young. Like you've –

"It's nothing to do with age," bit Gwen. "It's those devices you carry around. So many of you, effectively gazing in the mirror all day, every day. Try looking up once in a while."

Daisy hugged herself tightly as she tried to level her temper – her phone didn't even seem to be working anyway. This woman, clearly respected by Morfydd and Arwen, was seriously starting to annoy her. There was a lot Daisy wanted to say, but unable to see any landmarks and with a thick fog advancing, she marched off instead, putting distance between her and Gwen. She paced the deck head bowed against the spray, settling on a raised wooden platform at the far end; not quite a bench, but flat enough to sit on. She tried to roll a cigarette, but it was too wet, too windy.

Gwen hunched tighter over the wheel and squinted ahead. Let the girl do whatever she wanted. Entering the fog, the air changed from a raw cold to something clammier. In one strike it engulfed the boat. Daisy could no longer see even outlines. Waving a hand in front of her face she was relieved to still see something of it, even if it was floating in mid-air, connected to nothing.

The fog thinned, but traces remained, reluctant to give the boat back; a mêlée of air and water, whose tussle for equilibrium paid no heed to her or Gwen. When the final release came, its fingers curled back into the dark beyond the stern, as though pulled underwater.

"We'll be arriving soon Daisy. I may need your help…"

Hearing her, Daisy sighed. She crossed back over to where Gwen stood. "What do you need me to do?"

"Nothing yet, but there's a tunnel coming up…"

A tunnel? In the middle of the sea?

Daisy peered out across the water but couldn't see anything.

"It's the safest way onto the island. There's a wooden pole over there, can you grab it, please?"

Daisy saw a pair of wet wooden poles that had rolled to one edge of the boat. Grabbing one she found it was long, seven feet or more, and much heavier than it looked. Grasping it in both hands, she grinned as she imagined using it to flip Gwen overboard.

As Gwen slowed the boat, Daisy saw a vast expanse of rock jutting high and savage from the water. Sharp edges began to show, then vague contours and suddenly, loomed the remains of a once mighty castle. She tensed as Gwen steered the boat directly toward a sheer rock face, crumbling battlements high above.

Gwen lit a lantern hanging from the roof of the wheelhouse. Faced with the relentless dark all around, its low light gave up nothing of the castle, but did expose the faintest hint of a narrow opening in the rock. Fetching the other pole, she pointed to the side of the boat she wanted Daisy to take, taking her place opposite. "Sometimes we get a little stuck in the tunnel. If you take the starboard side, push us off the wall, I'll take the port."

With the engine stilled, funnelled by the water the boat glided into the tunnel. Daisy tugged her coat around her, keen to push away a solemn, subterranean chill that dug into her marrow. The measureless volume of rock seemed to swallow the boat. Looking back, she could see nothing of the sea, the tunnel mouth, a liminal space; a breach between one world and another.

In the end, the poles hadn't been needed and bumping against a sand bank the boat stopped. Gwen set down the pole and unhooked the lantern, before stepping out and mooring the boat to an iron loop set into the ground. Daisy followed. The ground was stony and sloped toward the water. The air tasted salty, it was bitterly cold and inside, Daisy was urging Gwen to hurry up and show her the way.

Although the lantern illuminated the low, shallow entrance, it wasn't enough to reveal the full depth of the cave. Taking in the craggy walls, testing the wet ground with a foot, Daisy realised it was more than a cave. As the light puckered, perspectives shifted; corners came and went, rock formations appeared and disappeared. Further ahead, was a wide opening in the rock crammed with more darkness. As Gwen shuffled over, the lantern revealed three cells beside the opening – cells gouged from the rock eons ago, each barred with rusted railings.

"Is that...a dungeon?" Daisy asked, wandering over to look.

Closing her hand around one of the bars, it was icy cold and damp. Although she couldn't see clearly, it was obvious anyone left in the cells would be unable to stand upright – and given the proximity of the water, could be in danger of drowning.

"Once upon a time, perhaps. We don't use them," replied Gwen impatiently. "Grab your stuff and let's go and get warm."

Daisy clambered back into the boat, retrieving her rucksack from the covered cabin and slung it onto her back. "Anything else you need me to carry, Gwen?"

"Not for now, thank you. Follow me."

Gwen waddled into the opening, the swinging lantern stretching shadows across the cave as they headed through an archway. "It can get slippery, be careful."

Gwen went first, Daisy staying close enough to not get lost in what turned out to be another cold, dark tunnel; crooked, with a sharply rising incline. When it levelled out, she was beside Gwen in a long, narrow hallway, beyond which it was impossible to see anything else.

"By the power of flame, let light show us the same…"

Gwen raised a hand and cast her words into the blackness. With a snap of her fingers, five torches lit simultaneously and the full reach of the hall was clear. Daisy turned slowly on the spot. *What was it with these women and making fire appear from nowhere?*

Where before, they had been deep underground in a natural cave, now they were higher – and the temperature reflected it: still cold, the air lacked the moistness of before. A stiff wind pushed in, barrelling through the hall and Daisy flipped up her hood, shutting out the chill on the back of her neck.

Stretching into the distance, the hall carried the sound of dripping water and all but filling the room, was an old, round oak table and seven chairs. At the centre was a complicated silver candelabra, encircled by a garland of cracked leaves, long since brown and rasping.

"What *is* this place?" asked Daisy dumbfounded.

"This…is Tor's Leap. We should rest, it's late."

Daisy was tired, but too restless to entertain sleep, but Gwen's tone implied it was not up for discussion; that resting was all that was on offer right now.

"You're in with me. It's up here a way…"

Great, Daisy thought to herself, *just what I've always wanted.*

Gwen moved around the table and along the hall, stopping further up. Bringing a heavy set of keys from her pocket, they clinked together as she looked for the right one, echoing eerily throughout the cavernous passage. She disappeared into the darkness and Daisy heard a key rattling as a lock turned, followed by the scrape of a wooden door over stone. She wasn't about to wait on her own in the hallway and hurried to catch up.

As Daisy walked into the room, Gwen was setting the lantern down on a crudely chiselled ledge. Minutes later a fire blazed in a simple hearth, bringing much-needed heat and light. Daisy stood as close as she could, no intention of moving until she could feel her feet again. Either side of the hearth were low beds – recesses cut from the ground in which one might sleep, if one were not overly choosy. From where she stood, she could make out a small opening high in the roof, one that the smoke was yet to reach, the wind moaning as it blew in.

As the fire became too hot, she examined the nearer of the holes. Inside were rolled up blankets. As she pulled out an armful, a long, low whistle made her turn. It sounded like it had come from the opening, but glancing at Gwen for a reaction, there was nothing. Folding herself into the hole fully-clothed, she bound the blankets around her as tight as possible, grateful for fire. As Gwen extinguished the lantern, Daisy heard a screech. Turning over, wriggling this way and that, she grinned as she realised what she had thought was a whistle, must have been a bird beyond the opening. Nothing more than a combination of tiredness, cold and travelling through the night, she told herself. It was with images of castles, owls and of darkened seas whirling about her head, that Daisy was asleep within minutes.

Chapter 14 – Going Dark

Not much troubles the Celtic Sea. Not much that is, besides the invincible mass of Tor's Leap. An island that forces the sea to work that much harder, jammed into the water like a stopper.

It began like many an island: a serrated lump fashioned from cooling fire, sculpted by wind and water. It was birthed before names were recorded. For centuries, it has gone by the name Tor's Leap. Some call it The Island and for a few, it is known as Ynys Bendigaid[5]. To most, it is simply not known at all, appearing on no maps and in only a handful of memories.

Then came a single seed. Carried by sea or air, dropped by a gull or Red Kite; perhaps a determined Ptarmigan venturing out from Iceland or the Faroe Islands. It was a seed of the *Betula pendula*, or silver birch. Contained soundlessly within its husk, was the past and future of all birches.

The silver birch is a pioneering tree that grows quickly. Once established, it nurtures the company of other species; abundant fungi snuggled into nooks and crannies, not least its closest ally, the *Amanita muscaria* or fly agaric – majestic toadstool of many a fairy tale[6]. From this single seed came the first trembling silver birch, followed by offspring spreading merrily between the wind-tousled heather; bursting from fissures in the primordial rock.

Happier in a pack, it is an uncommon birch that grows alone. One tree becomes a village; becomes a world. Something of a chatterbox across mycorrhizal networks, the birch is generous,

---

[5] Welsh: Isle of the Blessed (loosely).

[6] Before you start wolfing down mushrooms (of any kind), study them in detail. Be absolutely certain they will not kill or injure you. NB: due to Draconian drug legislation in the UK, selling/preparing fly agaric for human consumption is illegal.

giving itself to earth and air, fire and water and allowing taller, slower growing neighbours to take their light. When a birch falls, it offers sustenance for fungi, insects and animals alike.

With the waxing and waning of many a moon, came blackthorn and its thorny guard. Then hawthorn and its eager enchantment. Gorse arrived later, tangling between blackthorn and hawthorn. Over time, the combination of thorn and gorse made the north-easterly edge of the island impassable to hoof, foot or boat. Healing ash and intuitive elder joined after a while, as did enduring oaks, resilient sycamores and much later, a peppering of nurturing, shining-leafed beech. As the island reclined in all weathers, besieged by violent, creamy waves, it was more than content holding the dense woodland.

And so may it have remained, had man not arrived in boats. Scored blood into rock; felled trees and extorted the earth. Mothers, sisters, daughters and aunts followed and with them a deeper respect for the land; for all the beings calling the island home.

It was the cudgel of man that brought the Norman castle. Originally built around 1185, on the site of an earlier wooden construction, which itself had been perched on top of an ancient, chambered temple dedicated to the moon. Like many a Norman castle, it followed the prevailing fashion of motte and bailey construction – the motte the result of the digging out of a deep, protective moat (reclaimed by the sea a long time ago), the bailey the central area inside. The fifty-foot curtain walls were dotted with arrow loops and crowned with crenelated battlements. Although naturally defended by the sea on all sides, a perilous wall walk within the battlements looked out to sea and down to the bailey, safe behind walls thicker than the length of an average arm.

Before the sea gnawed away the edge of the island, entrance to the castle was through a vast gatehouse on the eastern side.

Fortified with a jutting barbican, the gatehouse gave on to a large chamber, which in turn allowed access to a vaulted stone archway to the keep and the bailey. The wall walk was reached from the top of the keep, up a tight, spiral staircase.

That was then. Now, the greater part of the battlements has fallen. Only a crumbling south-easterly portion of the wall walk remains, still connected to the stairs within the carcass of the keep. The outline of the gatehouse remains, but the original landing area lies under the sea. It is not known when the tunnel was dug to allow boats to enter – experts are in disagreement, some insisting it was part of the original construction, others convinced it came later.

It was within the dormant heart of this castle, that Daisy awoke, having slept blanket bound for a long time, the fire having sighed itself out. Yawning and trying to sit up in the rough chamber, she had automatically reached for her phone, only to find it had no service. Slouching in the bed she saw daylight through the opening, the ribbon of pallid light suggesting an overcast day.

Having stuffed the blankets into the hole, she called out to Gwen. Getting no answer, she left the room and followed the dim passage. This rubbled corridor ended in an archway of dark stone open to the elements, pools of rainwater reflecting the daylight. Beyond the archway was the central courtyard. After the dimness of the caverns, Daisy squinted in the light.

Although a few patches of snow remained, it was a clement day. A barely blue sky dotted with pewter clouds, the air fresh and briny. To the left of the archway was the keep, which having lost its roof and most of its walls, still retained an air of importance, despite being bound by ivy and lichen. Immediately to her right, a small orchard of tightly clustered fruit trees reached to the exterior wall, green shoots budding on some of the branches.

A hundred feet opposite was the westerly wall. The majority still intact, save for missing battlement pieces like gapped teeth. This wall squared a corner to continue to the keep in the south. Close to the westerly wall, all the way around to the orchard, the bare earth had been sectioned into squares for vegetables. In an adjacent patch was a herb garden, the delicate plants showing signs of returning, save for a large, thriving rosemary bush, that had braved the winter without flinching.

Keen to investigate, Daisy across into the courtyard, catching the scent of something herbal. The presence of the sea was everywhere, crashing against the outer walls, as squealing gulls circled overhead. At the centre of the courtyard was a large, tiled circular area, mismatched wooden chairs and tables giving it the feel of a rustic retreat. The majority of the tiling was gleaming white, with a five-pointed star set out in bold black tiles. Weaving around the tables she made for the herb garden, stroking the tender, feathery shoots coming through. She found clumps of oregano, and what looked like it might become mint. Smelling the herbs on her fingers as she went, she wandered toward the north-westerly corner, where she had seen a shallow alcove in the wall.

It looked like a doorway that had been filled in. It was the shape and size of a doorway, but the large single block of stone plugging the gap was of a different kind to the castle walls; smoother and flatter, as though picked specifically. The alcove was around a foot deep, six feet high and three feet wide. Stepping inside, Daisy placed her hands onto the stone. It was smooth, as though through regular touch; warmer than she had expected. Despite its vast size, it looked like all it needed was a shove and some unseen mechanism would allow it to open. She leaned her weight into it and pushed with both hands...and nothing happened. Puzzled, she started to feel around for some kind of opening, when she heard a long, low whistle behind her.

This time there was no mistaking it – it was definitely a whistle! The kind that can often erupt from a pack of men, too insecure to attempt anything as straightforward as conversation. She bent her ear to the wind, determined to track the sound, which seemed to have come from the orchard.

She ducked into the orchard, a light wind rustling the smaller branches together like cricket legs. Between the trees she found nothing that could have whistled – no people, no obvious animals or birds. Making her way around the orchard, peeping behind trees, looking up into the higher branches, she heard the whistle again...louder, as if closer by.

When she was little, her dad like to whistle – not that she'd ever heard him wolf whistle. She knew too, that she wasn't someone who tended to hear things that weren't there.

"Dad?" she tried hopefully.

She looked for a tree she could climb, for a better view, when she heard her name being called. She turned and saw Gwen approaching the tiled courtyard carrying a tray. At least she thought it was Gwen. She had done a double-take, for this woman was not only smiling, but was dressed in a simple gown and sandals, white hair spilling over her shoulders.

Sitting at one of the tables, Daisy looked her up and down. She was transformed, in the same way a statue can develop from a block of marble. "Was that you whistling at me?"

Gwen looked at Daisy with surprise. "No, Daisy, I've not been whistling at you!"

"I've heard whistling, last night and just now..."

"There are sea birds and the like, maybe there's one makes a sound like a whistle? The wind can play tricks here, too?"

Daisy wasn't convinced. Not for one moment could she imagine Gwen whistling – at her or anyone else – but found it hard to accept it was a bird; it hadn't sounded like any bird she'd heard before.

"Would you like some coffee, Daisy?"

Daisy nodded eagerly. "I would LOVE some, thanks."

Gwen pushed the tray carefully across the table. There were two steaming mugs of black coffee, sliced apples and pears, a bowl of nuts and a homemade loaf and vegan spread. Looking around the ragged castle Daisy asked, "There's coffee? Here?"

Gwen laughed. "Of course there is. Trust me, I've made coffee in far more complicated places!"

"But how –

"I have rainwater and I have fire. I don't need more than that," she answered proudly, "apart from the coffee, obviously."

Daisy sipped at the coffee. It was hot and wonderful – a strong, dark roast with a reasonable body and a passing hint of cherry.

"It works, whatever you're doing!"

Gwen reached for a handful of nuts and fed them into her mouth one by one, her crunching loud across the bailey.

"You look...different?" said Daisy as she smeared the spread over a thick slice of bread.

Gwen smiled – something else Daisy wasn't expecting – showing worn, stubby teeth and shook out her hair. "I love Tor's Leap. I'm me here, completely."

"Are you high?"

"Not in the sense I suspect you mean, Daisy. Blissful, yes."

"Blissful?"

"Yes. Slow down Daisy, let this place soak into you."

"I've had a wander around. The herbs smell good...and I love being able to hear the sea."

"Tor's Leap is a very special place, Daisy. Outside of..." Gwen gazed across the gardens for a moment lost in thought. "Outside of the usual world."

"This is a different world here?"

"Very much so, Daisy."

"So, who is – was – Tor?"

"No one. It's old English for high rock or tower."

"And the leap?"

Gwen spat out a piece of shell and shrugged. "I suppose someone jumped from the walls at some point."

Daisy couldn't tell if she was joking. This was a changed Gwen – one she found far easier company. She looked younger, even more spritely. The smiling, however, would take some getting used to.

"So," said Daisy swallowing down bread, "what's the plan?"

"The plan? You're here to learn more about us, about..." Gwen paused, raising her eyebrows theatrically, "about magic!"

"What, so I'm like, The Worst Witch?"

Gwen laughed, a booming sound that seemed to burst from deep inside of her, shaking her shoulders; her entire body.

"Not quite. This is magic that comes from a connection to the elements, to –

"To the Kindness?" Daisy interrupted, eager to try and meet Gwen halfway.

"Exactly. See, you're on your way already."

"Will I really learn about magic?"

"You will. We're not only about magic. The Sisterkin preserves the old ways, for sure, but we do more than that."

"More than magic?"

"One step at a time, but yes. As for magic, way back lots of people knew it. It was how we connected to the earth, to the sea, the sky and to the flame," Gwen adjusted herself in the chair, crossing on leg over the other as she leaned closer. "Before this frantic addiction to science, alienated us from nature. Tell me, when you went to school, I'm guessing Jesus featured?"

"He wasn't in my class. We had a Joseph though…"

Gwen frowned and waited for Daisy to continue.

"Yes, my junior school was Church of England, so there was a lot of bible stuff. Always more stick than carrot, from what I remember."

"And I bet you were taught nothing of pre-Christian faith, nothing of the Celts, of earlier beliefs…Goddess culture?"

"The Celts got a mention."

"So, you could say, as an education, it was at best incomplete, at worst, heavily biased?"

"I guess," Daisy said, reaching to top up their coffees.

"There was a time, many centuries in fact, before this false – not to mention deadly – notion that we are superior to nature. This ridiculous belief we are separate from it...that it's nothing more than a larder we can plunder as the fancy takes us. Back then, people understood, we *are* nature and nature, *is* us."

"Good to know," Daisy said dismissively. "When do I get a broomstick?!"

"You think we literally ride broomsticks?"

"I don't know, do you?"

Gwen looked herself up and down. "Can you see me keeping this body on a broomstick? I think not! I have my staff though."

"I've seen you make fire with a click of your fingers, Morfydd too, so I figured anything's possible."

"You joke a lot, don't you, Daisy. When you feel uncomfortable, or don't know enough about something?"

Daisy looked taken aback. "I don't know enough, about anything. Sometimes, I'm not even sure why I'm here at all."

"You are relevant, Daisy. You need no one's permission to be yourself. Not here, not anywhere."

"Not even yours?" kidded Daisy.

Gwen sighed and folded her arms. "Hide behind the humour if you wish. It'll still find you."

"What will?"

"Everything you're hiding from."

Chapter 15 – Winter in the Wood

With a nod to Lalo, and a final glass of lemonade, Gabriel headed for the door and stepped outside. What before had been a wooden veranda of paw-prints with an elderly teak rocker, was now a woodland. At night. Gabriel turned to go back inside and question Lalo, but the door had gone. As had, in fact, the Morrow house and the entire town. Moving slowly forward, hands out in front of him, he tried to feel his way through darkened trees...

An hour later, having been assaulted by a grunting animal – which although he only saw briefly, had looked like a white wild boar – he was forced deeper into the woods by its angry (and somewhat invasive) snout. Without his jacket, he was freezing cold. Snow clung to the trees bending them low, knee-deep as he trudged between them. He was convinced he had seen the same shadowy clearings, the same snowy trunks over and over and had to accept, reluctantly, that he was completely lost – again.

~

I have been here a long, long, long time.

Rain-lashed and snow-bound, windswept, sun-blessed and lightning-savaged; more times than I can recall. I have roots reaching so deep into the earth they defy measurement.

You may know me by the Latin name, Quercus robur, but common oak, pedunculate oak, or simply oak will do just as well (you are very welcome to add mighty).

I am unashamedly plump – two metres around my middle and if you were to cut me open and count my rings (and please don't) you would find that I am 355 years young.

Once upon a time, we were wild meadows here. Fringed with birch trees, acres of flowers ruffled by breeze and tempest alike, heads bowed for the sweet rains of spring, before opening with untamed delight for the long days of summer, falling for autumn and sleeping for winter. That was when I was small, a sapling lacking the confidence to be seen and heard. I am accustomed to standing alone, stretching my boughs wherever I may, my bottle green crown titled skyward. There has been more aloneness than even I imagined, many of my kin snapped and felled, their limbs taken far away. I have been nicked, kicked, licked, and worshipped.

Some point, one spring (nine winters since?) the woman arrived. She was younger then, yet very old. From whence she came, I couldn't see. Within a short space of time, she had scraped out a clearing, stamping down a patch of earth, pacing back and forth day and night. Then, relying on my cousins, she constructed herself a dwelling. I've not built that kind of a dwelling – having no need for such a thing – but she did it with confidence (and swearing) which I took as not her first attempt. That's not to say she didn't make mistakes, didn't have to adapt as the dwelling wobbled up from the earth.

She is a seer, able to view these woods for what they are – strong, indubitably alive and magical; balanced between there and here. Like winter, she can be bitter and disrespectful at times. Few visit this woman; even less find her cabin. Those that do, I have never seen leave. What happens inside I cannot see, once they have stepped over the threshold. I picture bones and burning, have heard rattling chains, the rise and fall of an axe; muffled cries. The unusual smoke, piping its way from her chimney.

Before the next sunrise she will have done it again.

~

Deeper into the woods, it was darker and damper as the gnarled trees closed in. *Where was he? If there was an award for taking wrong turns, it was time to clear space on a shelf.*

It felt darker than it should be; niveous shapes of panic reeling at the edge of his vision. There was movement, rustling; snow cascading from the higher branches. Each time he looked, there was nothing there. Without warning, his bladder picked then and there to painfully remind him he had drunk a lot of coffee and lemonade, and Gabriel rushed between two trees to sort himself out.

Up ahead was a large flat stone slicked with moss and grooved with ancient cup and ring marks. He sat down as night knotted around him. Soft shut ferns, creaking branches; a paling moon struggling through the canopy. He smoked a cigarette as he contemplated his next move. It was getting colder. Once he started shivering, it became difficult to stop it.

As his eyes grew more used to the tenuous light, he thought he spied a gap in the trees. It was past a ring of birches, between dark shrubs. Fixing his gaze on the gap he headed toward it.

Stepping over fallen trees, across a spongy carpet of mushrooms pushing through the snow, he did his best to avoid stepping on the pointed caps. Reaching the gap – or at least the point in time and space where it should have been – he discovered to his dismay it had gone. The trees had snapped shut, squaring up to him shoulder to shoulder. Pushing his hands forward in an attempt to get through, he was forced back.

He felt panic. Not yet breath-robbing or able to root him to the spot, but enough to increase his heart rate; fog his mind with images of falling, then ebbing away to nothing as he ran out of leaves and berries to eat. Squinting back into the dark, he searched for the stone...that too had disappeared when his back was turned. He whirled on the spot, impatient to see something – anything – that looked even slightly like a way out.

He cursed and then, it burst out of him. Before he knew it, he was calling out the trees, in the way one might call out an inept manager, or a partner who has taken one's heart and kicked it around like a football. Forged in fear, his words turned venomous and disrespectful, as he called the trees every name under the moon. The angrier he got, the closer the trees moved in. As he darted to his left, a branch swung into his face and knocked him down. Moving on his hands and knees, stones poking through the snow and his trousers, he launched himself at a trunk and hoisted himself up. It was icy and he slipped and landed on his knees, his head bumping hard against a silver birch.

As he took a moment, his forehead resting within a dimple in the papery bark, a vivid image seemed to come from the tree, filling his mind: He was at home with Daisy. They were sat by the fire, talking and laughing. Their mouths moved, but the vision carried no sound. He saw himself give Daisy an envelope and a small, wrapped present. This had not happened yet. As he tried to hold the image it faded, leaving him bemused as he tried to join the dots.

Having got up, he stepped forward and with only a split-second to realise what was happening, sank to his waist in a sucking, icy bog. He tried to twist round, but the wheezing mud gripped him tight and he sank deeper. The more he struggled, dragging his hands over the marshy ground for something to grab, the faster he sank – as though something unseen held his ankles, pulling him down...down, deeper and down.

Quickly exhausted, with the mud approaching the top of his chest, he slumped forward. He realised he was going to drown – painstakingly slowly, but surely. He let out a long, slow breath.

If this was how it finally ended, so be it!

As he surrendered, let himself sink with acceptance, without resistance, his mind filled with the vision. If he had seen an event yet to come, one so real, then it must still be possible...and he clung to it, with a renewed determination that this swampy hole would not take him.

He felt himself lifted, by what felt like strong hands under his armpits; plucked like a ripe fruit. A loud, wet sound gave out as he was tugged free and set down on hard earth, the mud pouring noisily into the space left behind.

Slicked in sour-smelling ooze to his chin, the weight of the mud was an exorbitant load that left him panting for breath. Scraping mud from his chest and arms he flung handfuls over his shoulder until he had removed most of it. Shellshocked, he stumbled for a splash of light in the near distance. Loping over plants, hands catching on cold bark and crashing into trunks in the darkness, he scrambled for the glow.

He could smell burning wood. Up ahead was a small, wooden cabin. The light was faint, a scrap of moonlight mingling with a carroty glow from the only window. Squeezed between trees, ferns and nippled fungi, it was around twelve feet square, with a steep wooden roof furred with lime-green moss. Smoke spiralled out of a metal chimney balanced precariously on the roof. Darker logs had made the walls, with a low, plank door the only way in – or out. It was a cabin built from axe, saw and determination, the gaps between the logs plugged with moss; held together with moonbeams and magic.

Standing outside he could smell roasting meat and a fragrant, herbal smell. He knocked, with his rumbling stomach in mind, having had little more than fruit and lemonade in recent memory. His teeth clattered together as he rubbed his arms to try feel warmer.

With a creak the door opened, a wave of heat engulfing him, revealing a woman so old he wondered how she could still be alive. He rubbed at his eyes, as though that might send her away; somehow make her younger.

She was dressed in a heavy, black mourning dress and leaned against the doorframe, eyeing him with suspicion. She looked well over a hundred years old, more even, as he studied her withered face. Her hair was grey and wild, matted strands clumped down her back. Beyond heavy lids and crooked brows there was a brightness to her eyes – a striking spring blue. As she stared at him, the brightness hardened.

"Hello, I'm Gabriel. Please forgive the imposition, but I am lost and hungry..."

The woman shifted to the opposite doorframe, still eyeing him warily. "You should have turned left. You'd be home now."

"Left?" echoed Gabriel – then he remembered the tiger.

"Few call here, even on the right path. How have you found this place?"

"Honestly? By accident. I sank in a bog and having got out of that, was trying to find my way out of these woods."

At this the woman gave a cackle. A shrill sound of no warmth revealing teeth either stumped or dying. "A way out? Tricky that."

"It is. I've been here ages, I think. I wonder, if you might be able to help?"

"That depends on what you seek, Gabriel?"

She stretched out his name in a mocking tone and he offered what he hoped was his most winning smile. Whatever was cooking came stronger now and he felt empty down to his toes.

"I was hoping you could give me directions...and if you can see your way to sharing a little food, I'd be very grateful."

"You seek my help, my sustenance...yet you stand there gurning, having not even asked my name?"

"Apologies, that was ill-mannered," he responded, hoping he sounded contrite. "As I said, I'm Gabriel. Pleased to meet you. And you are?"

She gave an exaggerated bow, one he sensed wasn't entirely genuine. "Stillwater. I would say at your service, but I'm not."

"Stillwater, it's good to meet you."

As he offered his hand, he wondered if she had a first name, unless Stillwater was her first name? As she took his hand a chill passed through him and he jerked it away.

"Is it now."

Gabriel waited awkwardly for an invitation to come inside, recognising he had already caused offence. "If you must," she said unprompted. Her movements were slow and careful, like one in pain. He followed at a distance, ducking for the low doorway.

At first, he couldn't see anything. The cabin was thick with smoke and a raging heat from a fire in the centre of the room. Peering toward the flames he could make out the rim of a firepit dug into the earth and hanging over it, from a three-legged iron contraption, a sooty cauldron. By the light of the fire, he glimpsed a thick, greasy liquid bubbling away furiously.

"Sit yer'sen."

He heard her but couldn't see anything to sit on, nor could he track her movements. In the absence of anything else he sat on the ground cross-legged and shuffled closer to the fire.

"Not on the earth, fool."

A foot high log landed beside him with a thud, having fallen out of the smoke. He sat, with his knees close to his chin. As he tried to make out more, he heard the rattle of something metallic, followed by an opening appearing in the roof, the smoke snaking upward slowly revealing his surroundings.

The first thing he saw was Stillwater, closer than he had realised, watching him like a rat leering from a sewer pipe. She was slouched against a wooden table near the doorway, its surface cluttered with glass jars – the contents of which he could only guess at – decomposing vegetables and a lump of raw meat surrounded by old bones.

As she shifted position she scratched lazily at the folds of her dress, a cloud of flies darting into the roof. Against the wall opposite the firepit, was a collection of filthy blankets he assumed was her bed. Still watching him, she jerked her head sideways and hawked up phlegm, spitting it into a shadowed corner.

Adjacent to the bed was a wooden cabinet crammed with tatty books, curled on top of which was a threadbare black and white cat, that seemed even older than Stillwater. It was impossible to tell whether the cat slept soundly dreaming of scurrying through the woodland, or was the work of a gifted taxidermist.

Scanning the rest of the room, he saw a series of ropes and chains suspended from metal loops in the roof and an image of a butcher's cold store came to mind. He shook his head quickly turning in the direction of Stillwater.

"I appreciate your hospitality. Where exactly am I, Stillwater?"

Stillwater chuckled, which fast became violent coughing that bent her double. She spat once more into the corner, then straightened herself out slowly, hands on the small of her back.

"In the woods," she replied with an air of finality.

"Am I far from Aberystwyth?"

"Yes, you are."

She shuffled over with two wooden bowls she had retrieved from the table. Setting them on the floor, she leaned forward and peered into the cauldron. Taking up a large wooden ladle in both hands she gave the contents a stir. Carefully lifting a full ladle, she was about to empty it into one of the bowls, when she dropped it back into the cauldron. "We have a guest," she said with a sneer. "Where are my manners?"

She wiped the inside of the bowl with her elbow, smearing fresh grime over the greasy patina. Unceremoniously, she emptied the ladle into the bowl, then another, splashing it onto the ground, some reaching the fire with a hiss.

"Hare stew," she announced handing him a bowl.

He took it gratefully and sniffed at it. It was the same aroma of he had smelled outside and it smelled good. Having filled a second bowl, she handed him the ladle.

"You're the guest..."

Gabriel filled the ladle, blowing on it before taking a slurp. It tasted like meat gravy made in a pan; heavy and hearty. There were chunks of what might have been potato and carrot, wild garlic and what he thought could be tarragon. Chewing over a chunk of meat, he had no idea if it was hare, but was so hungry, he would have eaten a lightly buttered chair had she offered it.

"This is great," he nodded as he chewed, "thank you."

"Leveret," she said with her mouth full, "probably."

He watched her lift the bowl, sucking noisily before wiping her sleeve across her mouth. Neither spoke until they had finished, heads back in unison for the last of the stock. A stomach full of hot food felt wonderful. The stew had been tasty and he found himself feeling very sleepy and putting down the bowl he stretched contentedly. He was sweating and moved further back from the fire, still shivering now and then.

"What have you for payment?" Stillwater demanded abruptly as she strained toward him. The fire cast shadows over her face, blackening her eye sockets; her mouth thin-lipped and stroke-curled.

"My mistake," he offered civilly. "I meant to ask about money and must have –

"Money is useless to me. I take silver and gold. Iron, or a precious stone, in a pinch."

Gabriel glanced down at his hands and wished he were a man who liked to wear rings, bangles – any kind of jewellery. *If only Davey was here, he could have bought the entire cabin.*

His pale hands stared back at him and still she eyed him, her gaze more inscrutable than an OFSTED inspector. He had taken the stew thinking it was a gift and now the atmosphere felt very different.

"Let me see what I have…" he said rifling through his pockets. "I have some copper coins, some tobacco…those any good?"

Stillwater answered by spitting into the fire. As she dragged her log over to him, shuffling with it beneath her, it was the first time he had caught her sharp, fusty odour. His mind raced as he tried to find something to offer her. He felt the carved eagle safely hidden under his shirt – he was not about to give that up for hare stew, however tasty it had been.

With surprising speed, she reached into her dress and he saw a glint of metal as she whipped out a short dagger, brandishing it close to his face.

"An eye, seems a fair exchange…"

Gabriel leaned backwards, keen to put distance between his eye and the tip of the dagger. "It really doesn't," he countered. "I didn't realise I needed to offer payment. Perhaps there's something I can do for you, chop some wood? Fix something?"

Stillwater rocked back on her log and hooted, a sound somewhere between rusting metal in a winter wind and a scream. "Do I seem like someone who needs a man to chop, or fix things for me?"

Gabriel looked at her ancient frame, the fetid dress and was about to answer that actually, yes, she did. It was not the time for it, her dagger still within eye-jabbing distance.

"I didn't mean to offend. Let me come back, bring whatever you like as payment, if you tell me which direction to take…"

She shrugged as she returned the dagger to the folds of her dress. He was relieved, but didn't take his eyes off her. She reached once more into her clothing and brought out her hand, balled into a fist.

"I'm sure that you would like to leave. Filled your belly, haven't you. My stew settling in your gut, still not paid for…"

Gabriel leaned toward her open-handed. "I haven't anything on me, but I promise I'll come back."

In a flash, she brought her fist up to Gabriel's face and opening it, blew sharply. A corn-coloured dust clouded his face, a bitter taste in his nose, at the back of this throat. Seconds later, he fell backwards off the log, out cold.

Stillwater rose painfully and shuffled over to where Gabriel lay on his back.

"Coming back is thee," she sneered as she kicked at him with her boot, checking he wasn't about to get up anytime soon.

Had he still been conscious at this point, the next sound Gabriel would have heard as she moved away from his body, was a frightful rattling and clanking of chains...

Chapter 16 – Splattlements

Daisy picked up the tray and followed Gwen through the keep and into a small cave beyond. The only light came through the entrance, with large unlit candles on every surface, sat in pools of hard wax. There was a firepit of smouldering embers; a series of sooty pans and assorted trivets on a low shelf cut into the wall nearby.

"I'm guessing there's no fridge?" Daisy said looking for somewhere to put down the tray.

"Not as such. We do have this…"

Gwen crossed the room and squatting down, prised a wooden board from the ground to reveal a small, square pit.

"See, we have our own fridge. Our own way of most things."

Daisy handed her the leftovers, which Gwen carefully wrapped and added to the hole. Returning the board, she stamped it down with her foot. Wiping her hands together she tucked an apple into a pocket of her gown and walked into the keep.

"Right, perhaps I can show you around?" Gwen suggested as Daisy caught up with her.

"Can we go up there?" Daisy asked pointing to the battlements.

"Why don't we do down here first, we can finish with the battlements. It's an incredible view."

Gwen walked her around the gardens, explaining it was her who had originally developed them; others in the Kin taking turns to stay and work the garden, ably supported in the early days, by intermittent groups of handpicked WWOOFers, who would pitch their tents in the courtyard. Although there wasn't much above ground, Gwen pointed out onions, potatoes, cabbages, carrots, garlic, spring onions, excited for the summer months, for peppers, chillies and tomatoes; olives some years. The herbs, she told Daisy, were for culinary, medical and magical use and there were few she didn't have. In the passing of three moons, there would be plants trailing across the ground, as others wound up homemade trellis structures to be closer to the sun. As they sauntered away from the gardens, Daisy tugged at Gwen's arm.

"What was there?"

"What do you mean, what was there?" Gwen replied plainly as the two of them reached the alcove.

"It looks like an entrance, that's been filled in?"

Gwen eyed her carefully. "Then that's what it must be. An entrance, that's been filled in."

"It doesn't feel like it," Daisy frowned, running her hands over the stone. "It looks like it should go somewhere?"

"Perhaps."

"Perhaps? Are you not going to tell me?"

"Like any door, there's a key. Do you need to have all the answers at once?"

"Answers? All I ever get is vague half-answers!" Daisy grumbled. "I thought I was here to learn?"

"Lighten up, Daisy," Gwen responded flatly, "this is one chapter, not the whole book."

Drawing an obvious line under the subject, Gwen left her in the alcove. Daisy kicked at the stone, hoping it might do something. When it didn't, she reluctantly followed Gwen into the orchard.

Gwen introduced her to the different trees like a proud parent. There were apples, pears, damsons and if Gwen was to be believed, a pair of cherry trees and three spent-looking olives. Stopping beneath an apple tree, Gwen rearranged her gown as she sat and crossed her legs.

"Here's a good spot…"

"What for?"

"For your first lesson, if you're ready?"

Daisy nodded eagerly and sat opposite Gwen. "Ready. What we doing then?"

"Magic relies on three things, Daisy. Connection, respect and intention – and each has its own challenge. I thought we could start, by getting a sense of your connection."

"So, what do I do?"

"I'm going to lead you through something. Are you comfortable sitting, or would you rather lie down? I can fetch a blanket?"

Daisy tried lying on her back, the ground cool, but dry. "I think lying down's good. I don't need a blanket, thanks though."

"We start by getting rid of your clutter. Those pointless thoughts that have no purpose. I want you to close your eyes and say out loud what comes to mind. They are just thoughts, pictures in the brain, so don't judge or evaluate them. Just say it. Let it come, let it go…"

The moment she closed her eyes, her mind filled with images:

"Suni, in hospital."

"Try and take slower, deeper breaths. It will help you connect. Breathe in for the count of four, hold it for four...out for four, and count four before the next breath in..."

Daisy almost made a crack about not expecting learning magic to include maths, but remembering what Gwen had said, thought better of it and let it go – "A joke about maths!"

After a while, as she became more aware of her breathing, it did feel easier; her body keeping count without her needing to.

"Let it keep coming, whatever enters your mind..."

"Oranges...the cinema where I work – used to work."

"This is good, Daisy. Be gone clutter! I suspect there's more..."

"My dad...Morfydd's cottage...her cats...her typewriter...the feeling of the breeze on my face...the fact we can have coffee here!"

"Each time you say one out loud, try and see the words drifting into the sky, carrying the thought away. Emptying yourself of everything you don't need."

"My mum..."

"The Winter Gardens in Sheffield..."

Daisy snorted. "Pound coins, shiny pound coins!"

As they came one after another, she pushed herself to really visualise each word or phrase, to see it hovering in the air before drifting up, up and away.

"A beautiful woman I saw in a dream...I didn't know her."

"Did it feel important, the dream?" Gwen cut in.

Daisy was not about to expand on it, the recollection having left her neck hot. "No," she lied, "I don't think so."

"My MOT," she continued, "and when that's due..."

"What I'm going to do with my life!"

"A purple jumper I lost at Uni..."

"ASMR..."

"Suni's mum..."

Gradually, she realised her mind had slowed, the images coming less and less frequently. She *did* feel emptier. It left her flustered; it was something she couldn't remember experiencing before.

"What's happening, Daisy?"

"The images have stopped...now I can see colours. Like lights in the distance."

"Any particular colours?"

"Pink...no wait, white. Hang on, it's pink again..."

"See if you can fix on the light, whichever colour."

Daisy begrudged Gwen speaking – as each time she did it was just as she was trying to do exactly as asked. With her eyes shut, it felt like she was seeing through a new eye in her forehead. There was light an arm's length away – and it was beginning to expand. As she tried to concentrate on the light, she noticed lilac at the edges, a deeper violet pulsing at its middle. She *felt* it – a growing connection to the light. It was soothing, but energising at the same time.

"I think I've got it! It's out in front of me – getting bigger and bigger..."

Gwen clapped her hands together suddenly and the light vanished, blackness taking its place.

"What did you do that for?" Daisy demanded, opening her eyes.

"That light is an impression of the Kindness, so if –

"*That* was the Kindness?!"

"An element of it, yes. It's a hopeful start, Daisy."

"It is? What is the Kindness though, like, actually?"

"Love. Limitless, loving source energy at the heart of the universe. We're all made from it, me, you – everything."

"And that's the same as magic?"

"Not the same, no. Magic is…a bit like the Kindness given voice, or form."

Gwen beamed at Daisy with a satisfied look. She was pleased to see Daisy trying, having privately wondered whether she would have been able to concentrate. "What you've just done, you can practice, should practice. Learn to clear the clutter faster, connect easier."

"And is *that* magic?"

Daisy had expected more, her mind now back to racing with ideas; of invisibility, of flying, seeing into the future.

"It's a beginning. For now, I think it's time for refreshments, yes?"

Daisy felt exasperated. Gwen stopping her, was like being dragged out of the cinema as the film started, having sat through countless adverts and trailers. All she wanted, was to close her eyes and get back to the light. She sat up and shrugged. "I guess. Need any help?"

As Gwen got up, she shot Daisy a mysterious look. "I'll be back." Smoothing down her gown she marched off towards the keep.

Daisy leaned back on her hands, whilst trying to stretch out pins-and-needles in her feet. Closing her eyes, she looked for the light. Instead, her mind swam with unbidden memories: wild nights at The Dove and Rainbow in Sheffield...a top hat...a narrow country lane she didn't recognise...her childhood bedroom window caked in condensation...Suni's hair wafting in his hospital bed...her dad beside her bed in the dark, unfolding one of his curious tales...a sky heavy with stars...

Gwen, arriving with coffee, interrupted her thoughts. Handing a mug to Daisy, she sat down and watched expectantly as she took a sip. Daisy spat it out to one side. "It's cold!"

"We'd better warm it up then!"

Gwen leaned forward and balanced her mug on the earth, placing a hand either side. Daisy watched her close her eyes, her chest rising and falling slowly. A few minutes passed, during which Daisy all but imploded with unasked questions and then, a single bubble broke the surface of Gwen's coffee...then another. Then, a series of bubbles, not long after which steam started to spiral. As the coffee started to froth, bubbling over the lip of the mug, Gwen removed her hands. Picking it up, she sipped at it and swallowed, letting out an exaggerated sigh. "Perfect!"

Daisy let out a nervous giggle. Before she could make a joke, or ask Gwen about what she had just seen, she indicated with a nod of her head for her to have a go. "Your turn."

Setting her mug down Daisy twisted it back and forth until it stood solid. She dipped her finger into the coffee. Still cold.

"So, I just put my hands on it, yeah?"

"Clear the clutter. When you see the light, imagine it embracing you. Coming down your arms into your hands. If it helps, see it as coming down from the sky, in through the crown of your head and up through the earth."

"And that's it?"

Gwen bit her lip and took a deep breath in. "Just try, Daisy."

Daisy stared at the mug in front of her: dark blue, with a faded pink peace symbol. She closed her eyes solemnly. The words and phrases came softer this time. Gwen was right, it did feel easier, as though there was less accumulated clutter.

The light reappeared and she saw it as part of a broader light all around. Placing her hands on the mug, she concentrated on the violet light travelling down her arms, attempting to control it – the last thing she wanted was to shatter the mug, or catapult it across the orchard. No, that wasn't true – the last thing she wanted was cold coffee.

As her hands grew hotter, they felt like they had in the alleyway, only more under her control; less frantic. Opening one eye she glanced at the mug...there was a bubble! Right at the moment she had opened her eyes, a bubble had broken the oily surface...then another! She let out a squeal, almost knocking over the mug. "I did it, Gwen, I did it!"

Gwen smiled but said nothing. She had seen the bubbles, but needed her to experience them for herself. Daisy dipped a finger cautiously into the coffee...

"Fuck's sake!" she exclaimed, sucking tepid coffee from her finger. It was slightly warmer, but by no means hot and she fought an urge to write it off as no more than wishful thinking.

"It's your first attempt, Daisy," Gwen responded, with the stiffness Daisy was used to. "Could you drive your car, the first time you got behind the wheel?"

Daisy thought about her driving lessons and felt annoyed with Gwen; with herself. Not only that, but she had barely-even-tepid coffee to drink, which did nothing to ease her irritation.

"Why are you always so sharp, Gwen? Like an old Greta. Like everything's a protest, always a battle?"

"Trust me, Daisy, the world dearly needs Greta and all the others like her. I doubt you'll know about the women of Greenham Common either – the world needed them too. Needs people who stand up for what matters: Greenpeace, Sea Shepherd, hunt sabs, all the individuals, the groups – everyone who cares about the earth and the people on it," she went on, rummaging into her gown for the apple she'd stowed earlier.

She bit into it chewing thoughtfully. "As for me, I've spent so long protesting," she added around a mouthful of apple, I'm not sure I know how to stop."

Before Daisy could reply Gwen put up a hand. "Enough magic – and enough of my opinions. Shall we go up the battlements now?"

As they entered the keep gulls bolted skyward with a loud beating of wings. A handful remained on the walls, eyeing them keenly for scraps. Gwen tossed her apple core upwards, a gull soaring forward and taking it mid-air.

The staircase to the wall walk was an immense chunk of stone with rough cut steps. Had the keep not lost its roof – not to mention the wooden joists originally separating it into floors – the staircase might have looked less like a wedge of stone that had simply grown up from the earth. Gwen led on as they climbed higher. Daisy looked down and her stomach turned over. Fixing her gaze on the back of Gwen's legs she took each step carefully, careful not to look down. By the time she reached the top, Gwen was leaning against the battlements looking out to sea, Daisy out of breath as she stood beside her.

The wall walk was barely two feet wide and movement in any direction felt risky. Daisy wrapped an arm around the hefty battlements. Gwen, however, was far more comfortable leaning her weight into the wall as she gazed out to sea.

"Well, here we are."

"It's...really...really high," Daisy said shakily.

Keeping an eye on the wall walk whilst clinging to the battlements, took most of her focus, conversation something of a luxury right now.

"It is. Imagine running up those stairs under attack! Do take care, it's very narrow up here."

As Daisy felt her legs spasm, she tried to forget she was standing on a hazardously thin strip of stone with a deadly drop behind her, and concentrate instead on the view. She noticed an accumulation of more bird droppings than she had ever seen in her life. The battlements and wall walk were covered with patches of black, white and grey, splashes of squeaky green here and there, the successive layers having hardened over time.

"That is a lot of bird shit!" Daisy exclaimed as she tilted her head to look at Gwen — something that made her instantly dizzy.

"Yes, it's everywhere. Covers the battlements...splattlements, you might say!"

Daisy shot her a pained look, laughing too hard, too long, as she tightened her grip on the stone. She wasn't ready for jokes; she had barely settled into Gwen smiling.

Peering over the battlements the sea churned far below, whirling furiously where water and earth met, waves slamming into the walls as foamy spray shot high into the air. Further out she saw the soupy ring of fog the boat had passed through; the sun unable to push through, a sea breeze unable to move it on.

"That fog's weird?"

"It's a glamour. Keeps us safe from passing boats and prying eyes."

"A glamour?"

Gwen nodded. "An illusion, to make people see something different, or to conceal something – in this case, an entire island!"

There was pride in her voice, rightly so Daisy thought.

"Wow. So, we're completely hidden."

Not entirely, Gwen kept to herself. This was a subject she had discussed with Morfydd frequently, with disagreements about whether it was adequate protection.

Daisy released her grip and edged along the wall walk. The view was stunning and she side-stepped cautiously as she took more in. Wherever this island was, glamour or not, she could see no boats and not a hint of land.

Suddenly, between the sounds of the waves barging into the island, she heard the whistle again. Moving further and further away from Gwen, she wanted to see how far the fog reached – and now, was determined to find the source of the whistle, once and for all.

"Daisy, please be careful nearer the corner, the path –

Gwen froze. As she had turned to look, Daisy had caught her foot on rubble and tripped. Gwen rushed forward, but wasn't quick enough. Unable to right herself, Daisy lost her balance. Flailing her arms she clutched for the battlements, then with a scream that echoed around the bailey, she tipped backwards, arms thrashing in mid-air as she fell from the wall walk...

Chapter 17 – The A-9

When Suni awoke it was surprisingly simple – he just had to open his eyes. He woke to find a plastic tube wedged down his throat. Wrestling with it he tugged it free, gagging. The rhythmic bleeping immediately became a clanging alert and minutes later two gowned nurses hurried into the room. One fussed over him, as the other registered their disappointment at him having removed the plastic tube.

He tried to take a full breath but it was unfamiliar. Eventually, he managed to level out his breathing, feel more like he was breathing and not the machine. Satisfied he was alive enough, one of the nurses scribbled onto a board hung from the end of his bed. A consultant would be round to see him, though when that would be, they couldn't say.

Suni was very thirsty. He was disappointed there was no welcome party around his bed. Had Daisy been unconscious in hospital, he would've been there when she woke up – because he wouldn't have left. Ever. He sank back into the pillows, head throbbing. His chest felt delicate, as though waking from hibernation. He was desperate for everything to feel as it usually did, impatient with himself for feeling sluggish; his breathing still that of an apprentice.

From the corner of his eye, he caught movement in the corridor, saw a figure disappear out of sight. A minute or two later the figure passed by again. It looked like a man, the majority of his face hidden by a cap and a hooded top. They paced back and forth, hands deep in the pockets of a black overcoat.

On the third pass they darted into the room, grabbing at a chair and setting it down beside the bed, before collapsing into it. Suni recoiled. Only when he forced himself to look at the man's face, beyond the straggly beard and cap, did he recognise him.

"Dad!" he cried straining forward and wrapping his arms around him. His dad didn't respond. He smelled of soil and plants; the scent of crushed vegetation.

"Hello Sunil," his dad said softly. "Your mother told me what happened," he added flipping his hood down, but not removing his cap. "How are you feeling?"

"Thirsty, but okay. I was with Daisy and her friends. Then I hit my head…"

"I was so worried," his dad replied, rooting into the pocket of his coat and bringing out a bottle of water. "I'm very glad you're awake – take this."

Suni opened the bottle and took a long drink. It made him cough, water spilling over his chin.

"Slowly, take sips."

"I thought you were away with work?" Suni asked between cautious sips. "I mean, I wanted you here, but didn't think you'd be able to come."

Mr. Panchal dragged the chair closer, glancing toward the corridor. He looked like he was about to speak, but jumped up and hurried to the window.

Standing at the window seeing his only child in a hospital bed, Mr. Panchal struggled to make sense of how everything had led to this: his journey from naïve research student studying quantum theory and mechanics, to his pride at securing his first post-Masters job within a government laboratory. How that job had led some years later to an unexpected secondment – one that had arrived with minimal information, but an incredible salary.

Taking it had changed things, given his family a higher standard of living than he ever imagined. At the time, it had felt like so much security. Over time, he quickly discovered that his work with what was called, The A-9, was shrouded in non-disclosure agreements and a level of confidentiality that was brutally enforced; an environment in which surveillance, threats and vanishings were commonplace. He had stopped looking for a way back a while ago.

Pushing through the gap in the curtains, he gazed intently at the sky for a long time. "I can't be here long," he said as he returned to the bedside. "Shouldn't be here at all. I wanted to make sure you were okay."

His words came in a despairing tone Suni hadn't heard before. "I'm glad someone's here," he said pointedly.

"Your mother will be coming back later and –

"And Daisy?"

Mr. Panchal shook his head looking remorseful. "I don't know Sunil. Your mother hasn't been able to get hold of her."

"She should be here," huffed Suni. "I would be, if it was her in here."

"She'll have a good reason – maybe she's with her dad?" Mr. Panchal offered half-heartedly.

Suni was about to tell him that was unlikely, but stopped. Something had happened at the cliff. Although his recollection was patchy, a feeling in the pit of his stomach told him things weren't right. "Yeah, maybe."

He was desperate to talk to his dad, but it felt impossible. He looked like he had that morning at the campsite. In fact, Suni decided, he looked worse. The beard did nothing for him either, sprawling across his throat like mould; his eyes bloodshot and smudged with heavy bags.

"Dad, you don't look so good, are *you* okay?"

"I was worried."

"Is it just that?"

His dad looked at him intently, as though weighing something up. "No, it's not."

Before Suni could ask anything else, his dad got up and made for the door. Spinning round, he paced back and forth at the foot of the bed.

"They're opening, all over the place," he said gravely.

"What are?"

His father continued without answering the question, as though talking to himself. "We've always known about them – Göbekli Tepe, a sacred well in Sardinia – and that one's the moon – countless stone circles...but now we've tracked them to woodland in Europe and North America...a few days ago, one way out, deep inside a cave in the Middle East..."

"Dad," urged Suni, "slow down. Take a breath."

"Just yesterday, no wait, the day before? I don't know. I found something in the Celtic Sea, but couldn't pinpoint it, with any accuracy..."

"Tracked what, exactly?"

There was so much more he wanted to know, but his dad showed no signs of slowing down, his breathing frantic. "We have to contain them, Sunil," he insisted, rubbing his hands over his face. "Anything could come through and we have to be ready."

"Anything? So, it could be something, good? Something helpful?"

Mr. Panchal grunted. "Highly unlikely Sunil," he snapped. "Statistically unlikely, according to the calculations."

"So, you don't know for sure?" Suni pushed. "Dad, when I was out of it, things happened…I saw –

"Enough Sunil. Please trust me, I know what I'm talking about."

"Dad, wait a minute," he insisted, reaching for his dad's arm. "What's going on? What about fireworks," he started sourly. "The destiny you said I need to step into?"

"I said, ENOUGH!"

Suni fell silent. His dad was not one for raising his voice and never had he seen him so anguished. An intense memory of the beings of light came to mind and he felt the feeling of peace that had come with them. Clear as a bell, he heard their instruction that he tell everyone. His dad would be someone he would usually tell, as a sounding board. Faced with him as he was, it seemed not only foolish to share anything, but risky too.

His dad got up and pulled his coat around him, tugging the brim of his cap down before flipping his hood up. "I have to go. I'm sorry I raised my voice, Sunil. I don't know when I'll come again. Everything's happening so fast."

Suni swept the blanket away as he tried to swing round and get off the bed. His legs felt unsteady as he stood. His dad hovered in the doorway, glancing up and down the corridor. Before Suni could stop him, he was gone.

Mr. Panchal hurried down the corridor. His relief at seeing Sunil awake faded as he strode toward the entrance, head down for the security cameras. Coming to the hospital had been a significant risk; a breach of protocol, for which there would be repercussions and he began rehearsing explanations under his breath.

As he stepped outside, he was startled by a screech of tires. He looked around expecting an ambulance, but seconds later, a black Urban Defender with tinted windows, bounced onto the pavement. Mr. Panchal looked around desperately for a way out and was about to break into a run, just as two men in olive combats, faces obscured by black masks, jumped from the vehicle and grabbed him.

He tried to break free, but stood no chance. He was shoved into the back seat, then pinned between the two men once they were in. As the driver gunned the engine, the vehicle bumped off the pavement and roared out of the car-park.

Chapter 18 – We All Need a Cave

As caves go (and he'd known a few), it wasn't particularly roomy. It was, however, warmer and dryer than most. It came part-furnished too, with a generous assortment of dried grasses and downy vegetation gathered by hands, paws and beaks unknown.

The cave was low and shallow. Its jagged mouth overlooked a narrow, deep valley filled with trees all the way to three distant waterfalls. The falls cascaded a hundred feet to the valley below, glinting in the sunlight. At this height, the crowns of the trees formed a spongy-looking carpet, mist from the tumbling falls meandering through the canopy.

A few feet inside, was a dip carved into the ground with scorch marks. Like many of us, Mr. Bliss had spent time in caves, during those years captured in stone. We remember our time in caves, even when we don't remember. A deep, intuitive reminiscence of dark and fire, of threat and home; a furtive riddle woven into our spirit.

When he had first arrived, once his guide had disappeared – whom in his opinion had done very little beside stand in the cave and beam reassuringly – he had gathered up armfuls of the dry vegetation and made himself a nest, tucking it into a natural hollow at the back of the cave. He had slept well, on the nights when wind hadn't blasted around the cave; the nights when he'd not felt quite so apprehensive.

He had been here since Tallulah had removed him from the veranda, initially whiling away the time licking mango juice from his fingers and gnawing at the stone. Time was harder to catch here; only light or dark. He had scratched a mark onto the wall with a stone each time he saw daylight, but was wasn't sure now, whether he'd remembered to do it every time.

Some days were clear, days when the remote mountains revealed their presence and permanence. Sunlight exploded into the cave, as though it were right outside (very quickly, he had made a dark purple visor appear, to keep the light out of his eyes). Those same mountains on overcast days, disappeared into a shimmering haze that submerged the whole valley, hiding the trees. During the dark time, the trees whispered mysteriously, a rumbling of water further out as the falls danced under the moon.

There had been a day, early on during his time here, when he had inched his way to the edge of the cave and sat with his legs dangling. He had discovered a much smaller, slower waterfall to the left of the cave; a trundler, rather than a gusher. Sitting there, both the waterfall and the treetops felt close enough to touch; close enough to simply hurl himself into.

Within this dwelling of cave and valley Mr. Bliss neither was, nor was not. When the light arrived each time, there was no hunger or thirst, as though such needs had been satisfied whilst he slept. In spite of this, he had drunk rain on a few occasions, lying on his back and wriggling along the ground until his head was outside, gazing up into the downpour.

During the first few revolutions of light and dark he had thought about Gabriel, still irked by the idea of him roaming free with no care for due dates. Slowly, realising there was little he could do about it from the cave, he had begrudgingly started to accept that whatever Tallulah did next, he had no control over.

Accepting it was one thing. Liking it, another entirely. He had been sent here to reflect; forced to come face to face with himself. Like time spent in any cave alone – especially one with no obvious way out – his deepest feelings, those that linger unspoken or bubble to the surface with a sudden bite, he pushed down vehemently, choosing to dwell instead, on the hulking and filthy OVERDUE.

He knew Tallulah well enough to know that she would not permit him to leave, until something had changed in him. And that was it – the inescapable reality of no escape. Unless, the urge to jump won out. It was only the unpredictability of what that might bring that stopped him. He might live, or worse, merely start again inside the cave.

As the turning of light and dark rolled on, sometimes acknowledged in scratch marks and sometimes not, with little to do besides think – and pace back and forth somewhat stooped to avoid hitting his head – Mr. Bliss was forced to think. Not only about events that had led to him being there, for beneath those, was a wretched loneliness that tolled mercilessly. At the heart of this loneliness, lodged in a quiet corner like neglected treasure, was the place where Emmalina Ashton endured. Her smiling face, her soft touch and her loving heart. A gratifying beacon he could never again reach; yet never ignore.

In the year 1665, the city of London was a muddled heap of thoroughfares, ginnels and murky alleyways. Hemmed in by walls abandoned by the Romans, the vast majority ran with animal waste, offal, food slops, blood, spit, shit, semen and rivers of piss and ale.[7]

Even after proclamations from Charles II concerning the state of the city and its ailing construction – unheard or ignored by the many – the majority of buildings still remained flame-ready, made of timber and thatch; packed in tighter than mourners at an open grave. Then, as now, London was a city of gridlock –

---

[7] London nowadays is very different, having less animal waste.

carts, horses, wagons and people battling for space and breath, all piped through the incommodious walkways like living icing.

1665 had seen an unusually dry spring across England, one that brightly unfolded into a warm and pleasant summer. Grasses grew high, mead was drunk, mead was spilled, drinkers of mead fell over and hopes for a fine harvest grew bolder as the dry spell continued. A dryness few foresaw would, in its own way, contribute to an inferno the following year that would engulf the overcrowded streets and buildings of the city.

When that Great Fire did vault free of Pudding Lane the following year, pirouetting from building to building, the rigid city walls only served to make escape more convoluted. Outside the wall, the desolate shanty town (a frequent haunt for Mr. Bliss), did enjoy four nights of unseasonable warmth.

Mr. Bliss had prowled the streets, clad in a black topcoat, waistcoat and canary yellow breeches (a style pilfered from dead French aristocrats the previous year). His hair back then was cleaner, a luxuriant, smoky grey tumbling to his shoulders in tight (and it was said by some at the time, rather effeminate) ringlets. There had been a slim, dark moustache he had been trying out – an obvious and fawning tribute to the then monarch – though he had drawn the line at extending his tribute to fathering numerous illegitimate offspring.

When indoors, for warmth and comfort he favoured a chintz gown in emerald – still very popular having arrived in the country at the turn of the decade. That was when he wasn't assuming the appearance of a peddler, which he adopted as the fancy took him – or the traditional skeleton-and-scythe. High days and holidays he reserved for appearing as a jester. Whatever his appearance, tucked under his arm would be a tightly rolled parchment detailing his collections, delivered each day to his Ludgate garret by a loud, ill-disposed raven at first light.

For a fire of such magnitude, his collections had been more of a dribble than the torrent one might imagine. Returning to the cheerless causeways of the city numerous times since, he had found himself wishing for a second, even a third helping of Great Fire.

A year before this infamous fire lay siege to the city, a triple-bind of Dutch ships, Amsterdam cotton and the ubiquitous *Rattus rattus* had brought bubonic plague to London. Like many a plague or pandemic, it spread initially through exaggeration, lies and fear, before felling Londoners in earnest.

Mr. Bliss had been exceptionally busy, gaining no comfort from the predictability of his days. Recalled to London over and over, regardless of where else he needed to be, it developed in him a lasting disdain for a city of hostility and fleeting and ridiculous trends.

As the plague had burst from the city walls, he had followed the boils and the swellings with collection after collection. All too often, he found himself calling for an entire household waiting on the threshold together – albeit less confused than his collections nowadays, death being far less of a surprise in the 17th century.

In the late summer of 1665, George Viccars – a tailor's assistant staying in the Derbyshire village of Eyam for work – took receipt of a bale of cloth from London. This bale had arrived damp. Muttering to himself, he had opened it out and dried it before the fire, making a mental note to inform his employer of yet another damp delivery. Within an hour or two of the cloth being stretched across large flat stones before the hearth, George had felt himself bitten by a flea – nothing unusual in his trade – followed by another...and another.

By first light of the day after next, following a night of furious headaches and vomiting, George discovered a swelling in his left armpit. Later, another bubbled from his neck. Within a week, panic had swept through the tiny village and George Viccars was dead. Five months later, just in time for Christmas, a fifth of the village had joined him.

When Mr. Bliss travelled north to collect George (amongst others), he had taken a room at an inn on the outskirts of Eyam and settled in. Each time the sun nudged aside the night, the raven arrived with a parchment that grew longer and longer by the day.

Back then, with a lot less people clinging to this precarious orb, although a good many died younger, his collections had felt easier to maintain. Even at the height of the plague, he had been able to give a certain amount of time and care, even reassurance on occasion. He tended to stay longer in each locale, sometimes managing to rest for consecutive days, merrily ensconced within lodgings boasting a roaring fire and more often than not, a steady trickle of ale.

It was during one such extended stay, at the inn near Eyam, on a hot, dry day in the summer of 1665, that his path had crossed that of Emmalina Ashton, and he had been forever changed.

Chapter 19 – 'Look at each other and go bleurgh!'[8]

Daisy watched helplessly as the sky rushed away from her, Gwen frozen on the wall walk, mouth open. It was impossible to judge how long she was falling, had she even been able to gather her thoughts, as she plummeted toward the ground...

Lolling contentedly within the arms of a pear tree was a figure – lithe, shaven-headed and dressed in pale jeans and a rainbow wool jumper. Fascinated, they watched events unfolding. Gaining their attention had been the plan, they hadn't predicted the potential dangers of whistling at someone stood on a high ledge. "Shiiittt," they said aloud, as the young woman tumbled from the battlements.

Swinging down from the tree, they landed perfectly and sprinted from the orchard, clearing the distance to the castle wall in a blur. Faster than the average eye could follow; faster even, than hurt feelings.

They made it with enough time to slow her fall, casting an intention into the air that she land safely. Transforming from thought into energy, it rose upwards; an energetic vibration that altered the density of the air between the woman and the ground.

Daisy felt herself slowing, as though the air had thickened. Still flailing her legs and arms she braced herself for the ground...just as the figure stood strong and neatly caught her. She landed in a slender, yet strong pair of rainbowed arms, a couple of feet from the ground.

She opened her eyes, confused. Looking around, she saw the liveliest eyes she'd ever seen – the deep blue of rock pools – set

---

[8] Thank you, ITV, Nick Wilson and Timothy Mallett.

into a narrow, Elfin face with a delicate mouth, long, graceful neck and a narrow chin.

As she was gently lowered, her legs wobbled like jelly as she tried to process what had just happened. Gwen came waddling at speed from the keep, stopping in her tracks at the sight of the stranger, her expression instantly one of contempt.

"You!" she snapped, visibly unsettled. Her breathing laboured having hurried from the wall walk.

The new arrival stepped back to give Daisy space, cocking their head in Gwen's direction with a superior look. "Old Gwen...you still alive then!"

"You, are not welcome here."

Gwen's unbridled rage unsettled Daisy, but seemed to have no effect whatsoever on the stranger, who continued to stare at Gwen mockingly. They shrugged matter-of-factly, not in the least intimidated. "Nice to know nothing's changed then."

Daisy stepped between them. "You saved my life!" she cried as she flung her arms around them.

As Daisy stepped back bewildered, they chuckled. "And look at you, falling for me the first time we've met!"

"What is it Daisy," Gwen interrupted rudely, "with you and your family, falling off things? I did say to be careful. Are you okay?"

"I think so. I'm kinda shocked, but nothing hurts." Then turning to her blue-eyed saviour, asked "Who are you?"

"I'm Lysh. Good to meet you."

"Lysh?" echoed Daisy. "Short for, Aleesha?"

"Nah. It's short for Delicious."

"Yeah, right." Daisy groaned rolling her eyes. "Seriously, your name's Lysh?"

"That, Daisykins, is for me to know and you to find out!" Lysh replied with an impish grin, before turning dramatically and skipping back to the orchard.

She watched as they took a running leap at a branch bare-footed, scampering effortlessly up the tree, navigating the twisting limbs like a cat, before settling into a crook higher up. Daisy watched them watching her with a brazen stare, that seemed to say, come join me, I dare you!

"I'm glad you're not hurt," Gwen said touchily, "but watch that one, they are not to be trusted."

"How come?"

"Another time, Daisy. But you spend time with them at your peril. I'll be in the kitchen if you want me, want some food."

As Gwen marched off, she turned frequently to look at the orchard. Daisy watched keenly, having seen something in Gwen she had not seen before: a flicker of fear as she'd barked at Lysh.

Daisy crossed to the orchard slowly, her legs still wobbly. She felt sick; unsure exactly what had just happened. It was true what people said, about your life flashing before you – even if it had flashed inconsistently, in an entirely random order.

Reaching the base of the tree she gazed up at Lysh, who was still perched contently. To Daisy, it looked unsafe, but Lysh sat without a care in the world; not even holding on.

Lysh watched her closely, having only managed glimpses at a distance before now. She frowned a lot, narrowing her eyes in a way that made her look guarded. Her baggy blue-black plaid shirt and tatty jeans hid her shape. Lysh thought the red hair jarred with the astonishing green of her eyes.

Lysh grinned at Daisy staring up at her, then pushed out an exaggerated wolf-whistle, eyebrows raised.

"It was you!" Daisy snapped, hands on her hips. Lysh grinned and pouted. "Why have you been whistling at me?"

"I wanted to get your attention."

Daisy laughed awkwardly. "Why?"

"You coming up then?" Lysh called, wiggling over until they sat astride a broad spur, swinging their legs.

"What?"

"Are you coming up here, to join me? I mean, it's the least you can do really, when someone's just saved your life!"

Daisy looked at the trunk, not sure when she had last climbed a tree. Grabbing at a thick limb she had no idea what she doing, struggling to pull herself up as her feet skittered over the trunk. Trying again, she hung suspended until she managed to haul herself up. She jammed herself between two branches, only a few feet from the ground. Now she was stuck.

"You take your time!" Lysh teased. "To your right," they added pointing, "there's a fat branch, grab that..."

Daisy strained her arm over and heaved herself up with all her might. Winding an arm around part of the tree she shouldered in, scuffing her knees on the bark. Huffing and puffing she climbed higher, falling into the spot where Lysh had been sat before, slightly out of breath as she clung on to the tree.

"Fuck me, Daisy, you need to exercise!"

Daisy threw Lysh a scornful look as she repositioned herself, trying not to look down. She was about fifteen feet up, but after the wall walk, it felt far too high.

"I've just fallen off a wall...climbing up here, is a bit much!"

"And yet here you are."

Daisy blushed as the sapphire gaze refused to look anywhere else. Their eyes met for a second and Daisy turned away. She caught the setting sun full on, its pinked copper tones sinking behind the castle walls as shadows slunk in from the corners.

"I need a cigarette to level me out," Daisy said rooting into the pocket of her shirt. "Do you smoke?"

Lysh nodded. "Sometimes. Roll me one, would you?"

Daisy rolled two cigarettes as best she could, balanced in a tree trying not to look down, or at Lysh. Lighting one, she handed it to Lysh, who inhaled deeply and blew the smoke out through their nose. "Cheers."

"Thank you – again," Daisy said clumsily.

She gazed into the bark of the tree, keen to lose herself in the finely grooved patterning. She traced the fingertips of her free hand over its coarse surface; gentler around the benevolent eyes within the knots. Lysh made her nervous, and not understanding why only heightened the sensation.

At the end of the larger bough where Daisy sat, smaller forks fanned out, frailer branches bending toward the ground. Subtle, private nubs swelled from the sprigs; tender beginnings that with the passing seasons would become crisp, sweet fruit.

"My pleasure," Lysh replied suddenly nearer, startling Daisy. "It's not every day such a beautiful person, literally falls out of the sky."

"You're lucky I didn't flatten you," responded Daisy with a loud snort – which to her horror sounded like a pig.

"Yeah, that's some heavy plaid."

"Says you in the rainbow jumper," Daisy bit peevishly. "Anyway, why are you here, at Tor's Leap?"

"Why not."

"Gwen didn't seem pleased to see you?"

"Gwen's rarely pleased to see anyone."

Daisy couldn't argue with that, even if she had seen a different side to Gwen on the island, some of the time. "Fair point," she nodded. "It seems like you and Gwen have some, history?"

"You could call it that," Lysh replied, refusing to be drawn further. "The key to Gwen," they went on, "is letting her help you. Let her be the teacher. Play dumb, play helpless and –

"I don't play dumb or helpless, for anyone," Daisy cut in haughtily.

"Oh-kay," Lysh paused, changing the subject. "So, what about you, Daisy, what brings you here?"

"Time out, I guess. I –

She was about to tell Lysh about her dad and Suni, but recalling what Gwen had said about Lysh, held back. Whilst Gwen was challenging at times – much of the time – she did seem honest, brutally so; not a woman to mince her words or exaggerate.

"You couldn't just go on holiday, like normal people?"

"I'm not normal people."

"Intriguing..." Lysh said flatly, as though suddenly bored.

Swinging a leg over the branch and twisting sideways, Lysh was on the ground. Daisy shook her head, having not even registered them moving.

"Wait!" Daisy cried, becoming tangled as she tried to get down. Stumbling through the tree she landed clumsily, flattening one arm as she crashed against the trunk.

"It's been delightful, Daisy," Lysh called out, in a tone that said otherwise. Lysh was already across the courtyard, Daisy trotting behind rubbing her arm, the distance between them seeming to get no shorter. With the courtyard falling to the shadows, the absence of the sun had brought a chill to the air. Squinting into the pooling dark, Lysh was nowhere to be seen. It was as if they had simply been swallowed up by the night.

As soon as she entered the kitchen, Daisy welcomed the solid wall of heat. She found Gwen bent over a large cast iron pot above the fire, stirring the contents with a wooden spoon. She didn't look up and Daisy wasn't sure whether she'd heard her, or had heard her and was still moping.

"Anything I can help with, Gwen?" she asked loudly.

Gwen looked over her shoulder. Seeing Daisy, her eyes flicked around the room. Daisy walked over, settling as close to the fire as she could. "It's just me."

"Good. Are you intending to eat with me?"

"If that's okay?" Daisy said sheepishly. Why Gwen was directing her anger at her she had no idea, but she didn't want to miss out on whatever was cooking.

"As you like."

Gwen shuffled into a dim corner and returned with a folding wooden chair under each arm, which she put out noisily, delving back into the corner for a small wooden table. This too, was set down with a surly clatter.

"I'll get some plates," offered Daisy as she poked around the stone shelves.

"Bowls, we're having stew."

Daisy found a stack of rough wooden bowls and prised two free, putting them on the tabletop. "Bowls it is."

The meal passed in stony silence, with Daisy quickly reminded that one person cannot make a conversation. Whatever was niggling Gwen, she wasn't about to share it. Any attempt at getting her to talk about Lysh was closed down. The stew – far warmer than the atmosphere – was a tasty, spiced mixture of beans, crescents of red onion and chunks of savoy cabbage.

She had told Gwen as much, hoping it might tease out something more than a grunt here, a sigh there, but that too became an uphill battle, one Daisy couldn't be bothered to waste any more energy on. As soon as Gwen finished, wiping a chunk of bread around her bowl and poking into her mouth whole, she rose from the table. "I'm going to bed," she started, still chewing, "if you could tidy up, I'd appreciate it."

"Of course, and thank you for the food, it was lovely, Gwen."

"Don't wake me when you come to bed."

Throwing everything into a large bucket of soapy water, Daisy furiously rinsed the bowls and spoons, water splashing everywhere. Whatever was going on with Gwen and Lysh, was nothing to do with her. It felt like she had caused some major slight, one she was supposed to guess at, rather than Gwen doing her the courtesy of actually telling her; it was like being at home with her mum.

In no hurry to settle into the chambered bed, nor to share the same pitch-black space as Gwen, Daisy rolled a cigarette and went outside. Sat at one of the tables she smoked sullenly. The day's events had been exhausting, had spoiled the connection she had experienced earlier; the magic. When she had got up that morning, dying had not been part of the plan and sat alone in the courtyard, she thought about close it had come. She thought of her dad, of Suni. Even her mum. Had Lysh not intervened, Daisy reflected with an agitation that made her leg twitch, she would be dead.

Sitting had left her cold and she jumped up and walked around the gardens, to the far end of the bailey. A cracked fragment of moon was barely visible, lost to swollen clouds with no wind to move them on, leaving her little light to see by. Within the soundless cracks in the walls, night creatures crept apace; spiders edged over stones, woodlice scurried into cracks as other creatures advanced. Glancing to the sky, as though scowling might somehow shift the clouds, a thin slit opened to reveal a scatter of bright stars. She recognised them immediately, with a heavy heart. She was almost glad when a sharp crack caused her to turn.

"Lysh!" Daisy called out as she jumped between plants, tripping over a tangle of something she wasn't able to make out.

Lysh stood before the stone, seeming to notice her approach, but not responding. All was buried in darkness and for a moment she thought she had imagined it. It was definitely Lysh though, who cast their arms outward as though dismissing her. Daisy felt a sharp gust of air force her back, preventing her from moving any closer.

"Wait...don't go."

With their back to Daisy, Lysh ran at the stone slab as though it wasn't there. Daisy flinched, then finding she was able to move again, bolted forward determined to follow. She came to a skidding halt, too late to prevent her banging into the cold stone, Lysh nowhere to be seen.

Chapter 20 – "Fuckadoodledoo!"

Gabriel did hear the rattle of chains, much later. When he opened his eyes, he was groggy and confused. His throat ached and his eyes burned. There was one thing he knew with certainty: he was suspended over the fire, which was by no means far enough away. It was searing and the smoke stung his eyes. Trying to turn his head, he discovered that in addition to his ankles and arms bound in chains, a heavy metal collar had been fastened around his neck. For a moment he was taken back to a private dungeon in Mexico City decades before, the only thing missing, a ball-gag in his mouth. Every movement he attempted unleashed an unholy clanking of chains and the squeak of straining wood.

Lifting his head as much as he was able, he looked around for Stillwater. There was no sign of her. Daylight tried to push through the lacquered grime on the window. The oldest cat in the world had moved from the cabinet and now lolled on its back on the blankets. At least he hoped it was the cat. He made a noise – one of those kissing sounds that might persuade a cat to come over; that, or stare indifferently. The cat let out a lazy miaow, before burrowing into the blankets and turning its back.

Gabriel was no stranger to being in chains, tied up, or imprisoned in boxes. That was a long time ago and he struggled to recall how on earth he used to do those tricks; there was usually a feint to them. Many was the occasion he had thrilled *Asss!* audiences freeing himself from lidded barrels, locked boxes and metal cages. Granted, he had relied (mostly) on a cage with a hidden exit; a box with a false bottom. There had been times when he had dislocated a thumb or finger twisting his hands free of cuffs, ropes or chains.

As he tried to twist free, the chains jangled their lament and all he managed was a swinging motion back and forth, side to side as he tried to buck himself into the air and use his weight to pull loose a chain or two. Unfortunately for Gabriel, he weighed very little. His velvet lapels had been the heaviest part of him – and they had caused trouble enough at the cliff. After ten minutes of jerking in the air he was spent, the chains swinging him gently as they slowed.

He needed help, but wasn't about to shout out for fear of alerting Stillwater. Closing his eyes, he brought back to mind his temple guide, put himself back in that place; feel her radiance as he asked if she could help. A draught wrapped around him and before he could open his eyes, he heard a voice he hadn't expected, here of all places:

"What the fuckadoodledoo have you got yer'sen into this time!"

"Davey!" Gabriel said opening his eyes. "Am I glad to see you. Please, do something to get me out of these chains!"

Davey stood off to one side, sporting a too-tight baby pink tracksuit paired with fluffy green sliders, toenails in matching lime. His frosted tips were hidden beneath a tatty purple truckers' cap with a mountain range on it. He pushed Gabriel on the shoulder, chuckling as he swung back and forth. He pushed again, harder. "Have I interrupted some sex thing here?"

"I didn't do this to myself! Stop pushing and help me get free, please!"

"Right, yes, of course. Where's the key?"

Gabriel rolled his eyes. "If I had the bloody key, do you think I'd be hanging here like roasting meat…"

Davey chuckled to himself as he searched the cabin, poking noisily into shadows and peeping into corners. There was no sign of a key, nor anything he might use to break or dislocate the chains. He did find a metal bucket with water in it and emptied it over the fire, smouldering logs hissing as the flames died. Gabriel spluttered and coughed as smoke engulfed him.

Davey, meanwhile, tugged at one of the chains. He pulled harder, putting his full weight behind it and jumping from the ground. With a splintering of wood, the chain ripped free, Gabriel's leg bobbing aimlessly in the air.

"Great! Now the others."

Davey moved around tugging each chain in turn, but none came free as the other had. Both of them turned suddenly (as much as a man chained over a fire can turn) at a sound outside.

"Davey, listen to me, there's this awful woman lives here, if that's her outside you need to do something else – and fast!"

Without hesitation, Davey moved quickly until he stood at Gabriel's feet. "I've got an idea Gabe, but you aint gonna like it..."

Before he could reply Davey crouched, then launched himself into the air arms out like a diver. Passing between the chains he landed squarely on Gabriel's back. The combination of Davey's bulk and Gabriel's featherweight frame proved too much for the chains, yanking them unceremoniously from the roof. With an almighty crash they fell into the sodden firepit, narrowly missing logs which had refused to go out completely. Rolling them over, Davey let go of Gabriel and they scrambled to standing, bumping into each other as they made for the door.

Rushing from the cabin they passed a raggedly blur, neither stopping to investigate. Having returned from gathering wood, Stillwater dropped her basket and looked like she was about to break into a run, but thinking better of it, hurled a curse at their backs.

Gabriel slowed, barely able to breathe, Davey stumbling behind. There was no sign of Stillwater and they'd run far enough that her cabin was no longer visible.

Davey bent over hands on his knees, panting like a spaniel.

"We...are...too fucking...old...for running!"

"We definitely are," Gabriel agreed. "How did you find me, Davey?"

"I was sent."

"I did ask for help..."

"You know me, pickle, always where the action is."

"I just didn't expect it to be you. I'm glad it was," Gabriel said, stopping him with a hand on his arm. "I thought I was done for."

"Nah, you'd got a fair bit of cooking time left...listen, I owe you an apology, Gabriel."

"No, you don't, jumping on me did the trick!"

Davey shook his head, "Not that," he stopped, sadness in his eyes, "That Mr. Bliss fella, it were me told him, where to find you."

"I know that – and I know you too, Davey, you wouldn't have done it without a good reason –

"Dunno about a good reason. He forced me, said he'd not collect me unless –

"Collect you?" Gabriel interrupted, then it dawned on him. "Oh fuck, you're dead, aren't you Davey?"

"As a doornail."

"That, explains the outfit," Gabriel said with a drawn smile, "someone dress you after you died?"

"Fucked if I know. One minute I were having sex – and great sex it must be said – next minute, came harder than I've ever come. At least I thought I had. Turned out, it was a massive heart attack."

Gabriel let out a low whistle. "Shit, I'm sorry that happened to you, Davey. Maybe not a huge surprise…"

"Fucking were to Gareth."

"Have you been able to…see him, since?"

Davey looked away. "He's broken."

Gabriel tried to find something reassuring to say, but Davey waved a hand dismissively. "I feel sad for him, picking up the pieces. There's no sadness where I am…and it's not unfamiliar, given my work," he shrugged. "Souls, playing roles."

"What happened with Mr. Bliss?"

"If I didn't tell him where to find you, he was gonna leave me in between. Only for eternity, like. Fucker."

"And once you'd told him?"

"He let me move on, wi' nowt like a thank-you, I might add. Ignorant twat. Pretty much booted me into the light. Been there ever since. Resting up, catching up wi' folk – no surprise Burgundy Nigel were on me like fucking mould. And lovers, you can imagine how long that took. Then I were asked to come here."

"For what it's worth Davey, even with Mr. Bliss after me, I'm still here!"

As they trudged through the snowy woodland, Davey stopped suddenly. Bending to pick up two large stones poking through the snow, he used them to break the cuffs around Gabriel's wrists and ankles – Gabriel drawing the line at his suggestion he could remove the collar around his neck in the same fashion. Twisting his wrists around and rubbing at his ankles, he told Davey about Tallulah and the peculiar town of Grayling Junction.

"Fuckin' hell Gabe, for a man dying you've been busy. Where's Daisy in all this?"

"Hopefully, still at the cottage with Morfydd. Or at mine."

"How's that been?"

"She's hurt, obviously. I have a lot of making up to do, but it's good. We talk, we laugh. She doesn't mince her words either."

"I can imagine. That could've come from either parent."

"True enough. By the way, do you know where we are?"

"Yes, I do." Davey grinned, with all the pride of a travel-guide about to reveal one of the Seven Wonders. Gabriel waited for him to elaborate.

"Well?"

"In the woods. What you might call parallel, to the part of Wales where you live."

"Parallel?"

Davey nodded enigmatically as he put a finger to his mouth.

"How did I end up here then?"

"Magic. The right kind of totem. Passing through a portal. Fluke? Did you use owt like that, pass through a portal of some kind?"

"Not knowingly. Like I said, after Grayling I ended up in the woods...so what now, Davey?"

"You have everything you need. I was only sent to help with your...predicament."

"I don't feel I have what I need."

Davey tugged at Gabriel's shirt sleeve bringing him to a stop.

"That chuffing eagle, the one 'round your neck."

Slowly, pulled from memory, he recalled what it had enabled him to do. "All this time..." he said softly, as though to himself, then to Davey, "Over there, where I usually am I mean, I couldn't remember, but it did feel like there was something I was supposed to remember..."

Tucking it back inside his shirt, he was about to give Davey a hug and wish him well when he backed away from him.

"Hey wait, will I see you again, Davey?"

Davey stood straight-backed and offered him an exaggerated salute, as he piped up "We *all* see each other again – and again!" With that, he stepped backwards into the shrubbery and disappeared. Now, Gabriel remembered.

With the carving in his fist, he spoke in his mind. Years had slipped by since he had made these sounds. A simple mantra in a language he had never known, given to him by DeSouza. Repeating it over and over, he waited. Up ahead, a portion of the wood began to change, a misty area developing between two birches, the first of a series that formed a short colonnade. He felt a quickening, the air becoming a gauzy haze, not unlike a mirage. With one final repetition, he stepped into the miasma as though breaking a giant cobweb.

Not too far from the main road that runs between Cardigan and Newport, stands a cromlech, or dolmen, largely undisturbed for over 5000 years. Immense slabs of stone, hewn from the same Preseli bluestone as Stonehenge – and by the same entities.

What many have considered a prehistoric burial chamber – the remaining stones originally encased within a mound of earth since eroded or pilfered piecemeal – is a chamber in which no bones have ever been found. Known to the ancient Welsh as The Womb of Ceridwen, goddess of change and rebirth, the site has long been acknowledged as one of a series of portals dotted around the UK and Europe; a crossing place.

It was under this five-metre capstone that Gabriel dozed amiably, a perky breeze billowing through the open sides. He had slept like a hedgehog. Uncurling himself he sat up, realising with a start that the woodland had gone. Inexplicably, so too had the iron collar around his neck. He felt something on his face, and touching it, discovered his face was very hairy. This was no new beard, or temporary moustache for a November hipster. This was an established beard warming his face and diving deep into his shirt. Putting his hands behind his neck, there was long hair and plucking a strand, it was the colour of untouched snow.

How long he had been asleep he had no idea and was unable to explain how he had travelled from forest to stone – nor how sufficient time had passed for him to have become unexpectedly hirsute. He stood up and brushed dust and soil from his trousers.

In the distance, he could make out the silvery, snaggle-toothed Preseli Mountains. Based on that and an undue amount of guesswork, he was about seventy miles from home. A few days walk, less if he could thumb a lift or catch the solitary bus that appeared occasionally along the coastal road.

Having left behind the cromlech, with limited roads to choose from, sometime later he passed through a place called Crosswell. Gradually moving what he hoped was north-east he pushed on, keen to find whichever bend would reveal the coastal road south of Cardigan.

It was cooler over the lower ground, with far less snow than the woods; warmer too. Passing a lay-by, there were three cars collected like secrets. Catching his reflection, he threw back his head and laughed. Between leaving Grayling Junction and waking under the cromlech, he had gone full-on Hollywood wizard: his hair, eyebrows, moustache and beard all the same pristine white; a new man, clad in clouds.

As he admired his new self, he realised he couldn't remember the last time he'd felt any pain. No ache deep in his bones, no burning in his chest. Softly, he gave thanks to Tallulah, to No-Shoes-the-Fish and Ron, to Lalo, to Davey – and finally, casting his gaze across the fields, then seaward and skyward, he thanked the Kindness. This was a day of green lights.

It was standing next to a rusted metal pole showing an image of a long-forgotten bus, that he settled in for a long wait. He had smoked a cigarette, then another. With time to spare, he went through his pockets. His shirt pocket held his tobacco and lighter, his trouser pockets contained the grand total of 29 pence in grubby coins, a pink pebble and in the back pocket of his ancient trousers, an old paper flyer for an anti-Thatcher gathering in Manchester.

29 pence would not get him back home, but the flyer would. Folding it, he tore carefully along the creases to make four identical pieces. He worked from memory, doing his best to make each one the same dimensions as a ten-pound note; blank on one side, a quarter tale of protest on the other.

With his hands together, the paper trapped between, he waited until he could feel energy in his palms. Bringing his clasped hands to the eagle, he spoke words of intention; words of influence. It was some years since he had summoned a glamour, able to alter physical appearance or affect the perception of the recipient. It felt like it had worked, the pieces of paper still blank from his perspective.

The bus hissed to a stop and the door opened. Gabriel greeted the driver – a round man with short blonde hair and a friendly face – and asked for a ticket to Llanon. Handing the driver one quarter of the flyer, he watched him hold it up to the light, then evidently satisfied, tuck it into his shirt pocket. As the machine spat out a ticket, Gabriel leant close to the Perspex partition and gave the driver a wink. "Thanks, keep the change."

It was a small bus of twenty seats and Gabriel took one near the back – the back row taken by a baby-faced man who smelled strongly of wine, his sallow skin and watery eyes hinting at a man who might often smell strongly of wine. The other passengers were two women he took to be sisters – wedged into their seats with a collection of carrier bags and talking rapidly in Welsh – and a teenage boy with headphones on, a tinny thump of music audible.

Tackling a particularly steep hill, the bus wheezed and groaned and for a moment felt like it might go backwards; gears crunched and smoke belched from the exhaust. Straining for the brow, the bus gave a final death rattle and the engine stopped, the driver steering the bus onto a grassy embankment overlooking the sea. Swinging open the partition and freeing his trousers from his crotch, he faced the passengers and announced cheerfully, "Sorry folks, we might be here a bit. Feel free to stretch your legs, take in the view. I won't go without you."

Leaving the door open, he disappeared around the back of the bus. Then came sounds of clinking and clanking before the engine turned over, wailing in pain then shuddering to a halt. Moments later, the clatter of a spanner hitting tarmac.

Having rolled a cigarette, Gabriel stepped from the bus and lit up. He found the driver smoking, looking out to sea.

"Any joy?" asked Gabriel.

"Ach-y-fi! This bus is older than me."

"May I try?" asked Gabriel, squashing his cigarette underfoot.

"If you think you can get it going now, be my guest..."

The driver turned to the sea, fishing a mobile phone from his pocket and turning it sideways, moved slowly left and right. With him absorbed taking photographs, Gabriel peered into the metal hatch. It looked like an engine, but that was where Gabriel's knowledge stalled. What he had in mind wasn't about spanners. He pressed a couple of fingertips to the engine – it was hot, but not so hot it burned. Fanning out his hands he placed them either end of the engine and closed his eyes. Energy spiralled down from the sky, rose up through the earth, with Gabriel as the meeting point; a willing conduit for the gathering energy.

As his hands grew hotter the engine turned over, then stalled. On the third try he changed approach, placing his hands on the battery. Smoke coughed out the exhaust and the engine started...and this time it didn't stop. Lifting his hands free he turned to block the view, as an arc of white light flashed between the battery terminals. Slamming the hatch as the driver approached, Gabriel turned, rubbing his hands together.

"Battery. Seems alright for now, but you should get a new one."

"Diolch!" the man said with a smile, as he extended his hand to Gabriel. As he shook it the driver jumped back.

"Sorry, think I've picked up some static..."

The driver grinned. "Huh, we're both conductors!"

Gabriel returned to his seat. Before, the energy had risen and disappeared quickly, after some kind of human contact, like the walk-in centre; with Daisy. Holding onto the railing of the seat in front, he encouraged himself to release any remaining energy into the metal; earth it.

Leaving the bus at Llanon, the driver bid him goodbye with a toot of the horn. Gabriel waved and ducked into the shop. With two more pieces of paper, he bought tobacco, a bottle of water, a cheese and pickle sandwich and a loaf of bread. He posted the remaining paper and his change into a box for sea search and rescue, the coins fizzing as they left his fingers.

Sat on a weathered bench outside he munched the sandwich happily, the energy in his hands having subsided. Everything was pleasantly familiar; the graceful neck of the coast, the glittering water; his cottage no more than thirty minutes away. Fortified by the sandwich and the water, he set off eagerly. Home, strong coffee – and Daisy – within reach.

The morning after Lysh disappeared, Daisy had got up feeling like she'd not slept at all. She wanted to talk to Gwen about the stone, not to mention push her on her dislike of Lysh.

In her rush to find her Daisy realised she was up earlier than she thought: plants still snoozing inside night frost, the moon low in a dark, puffy sky. Echoing through the courtyard was a rhythmic murmuring; a muffled sea conversation Daisy couldn't understand. When the first light began to bleed into the sky, strands of furious pink strung like bunting, everything felt more alive; her senses heightened.

Passing through the damp keep, she found the kitchen chilly and dark, the firepit just cold ash. She'd wandered the cavernous hallway, re-examined the cells and the watery tunnel. Seeing that the boat had gone made her apprehensive. She was stuck on the island, at the mercy of Gwen and her moods, far more than she wanted to be.

After mooching around a while, she had got a fire going in the kitchen and made some coffee; eaten a couple of apples and a handful of nuts. Having the island to herself gave her chance to explore and if she was honest, an opportunity to nosey into corners without Gwen catching her.

By the time she had trudged the passages again, re-examined the large table – trying different chairs hoping she might notice something new – then wound her way back through the archway to the courtyard, daylight was spilling through the archway, lighting the passage. It was then she saw something she'd not noticed before – a small wooden doorway set into the left wall.

It was such an old door, she assumed it must have been there as long as the castle. Gripping the iron handle, she was not surprised to find it locked, even if part of her had hoped otherwise. Using the torch on her phone she found a large keyhole, but the light gave up nothing of the inside. The door was not padlocked or barred and she set about looking for the key.

Rifling through where Gwen slept, she had checked over her shoulder constantly, jumping at the slightest sound. Running her hands around every inch, apart from a couple of wizened apple cores, she had found nothing. She had lit one of the torches with her lighter, waving it all around making shadows scamper over the walls. She searched carefully, smoke trailing as she pushed the torch into every corner and every crack, startling spiders; minerals in the rock winking as the flame passed by. Dissatisfied, she grabbed her rucksack and stomped back outside.

Coming here, she had packed hastily. Stuffed a couple of jumpers, a shirt and underwear into her bag and not much else. Emptying it onto one of the tables, she'd been elated to find a Double Decker that must have been in there before and gorged on it gladly. Chasing a chunk down her jumper, she found it smeared over her top lip and wiped it with a finger. Maybe being here alone wasn't so bad.

Jamming everything back into her rucksack, the crumpled journal from her dad's armchair fell out of a jumper. With all that had happened on the island, she had forgotten about it. Flicking through it, it was similar to the others: miniscule writing and undecipherable doodles, like a spider had walked over an ink pad, before being given the freedom of the pages.

The entries that were dated, covered 1973 to 1989, each page bearing no resemblance to the preceding one. She was about to stuff it into her bag when she found a drawing that filled the centre pages. Flattening it out, her eyes widened as she recognised it as identical to the light on the cliff. Captured in vaguely concentric, smudged pencil whirls, it had been drawn with what looked like haste and heavy pressure, the dark lines tangled. The margins held notes so small it was impossible to read, even when she brought it closer, tilting it to catch the sunlight. It was only when she had taken a photograph with her phone and enlarged the writing, incomplete phrases were revealed, adding to the frantic feel of his entries:

...a way through? ~~A passing place?~~ – or...if it's likely? – a place for...is this light...and a ~~sacred~~ safe, sacred...for...and...of us...

Stuffing it into her bag, she couldn't shake her dad. Him walking out had changed her as a person. The elusive memory of him scored into her relationships; so many of her interactions. It was in her friendship with Suni – the times she had taken him for granted or tested him; submerged him under expectations. The more she thought about her dad, something struck her: when that man had turned up and attacked him, no one had done anything. Not one of the women, all of whom Daisy knew were capable of magic, had intervened. Anger boiled up in her, a rage it felt easier to direct at Gwen, rather than anyone else, determined to tackle her as soon as she returned.

The following morning, having spent more time tossing and turning and sobbing within the freezing chamber than she had sleeping, Daisy had found Gwen in the courtyard, huddled in a blanket nursing a mug of coffee. She looked tired, though when Daisy settled into a chair opposite, she managed a smile.

"Morning, Daisy. Morfydd sends her love – and fresh bread and vegan wine. There's coffee if you want some, in the kitchen."

"I do," Daisy answered as she got up. "Do you need a top-up?" Gwen shook her head. Daisy returned a few minutes later with a large mug of very hot coffee. "You've seen Morfydd then," she began before sitting down. "Any word on my dad, or Suni?"

"Nothing, I'm afraid. Morfydd's well, looking forward to seeing you again."

Daisy sagged. Whilst the chance of Gwen having news was slim, she had hoped she might know something. It was a stark reminder she couldn't stay here indefinitely.

"How long am I going to be here?"

Gwen glanced at her sharply. "How long? It's not really measured in time, it's –

"Don't," Daisy growled, leaning toward Gwen with a stony stare. "Stop with these mystical answers. I feel so fucking lost. Miles away from the people that matter to me."

"You're not a prisoner," Gwen said bitterly. "You can leave any time."

"I can't. I don't know how to drive a boat!" Daisy barked, battling not to scream at her.

Gwen rose suddenly, leaning on the table for support. "Get your stuff then."

Daisy took a deep breath in and tried to let it out slowly. "I don't mean right now, I just meant – forget it. Can we talk?"

"If you like."

"Are you going to sit down?"

Gwen sat and folded her arms tightly. "Well, what do you want to talk about?"

Daisy launched right in. "Why didn't you help that day on the cliff, do something to intervene?"

"Because I couldn't. Nothing I could have done, or anyone else for that matter, would have changed the outcome. It's beyond me – or my magic, before you ask."

Daisy was stumped, Gwen having anticipated her next question and closed it down.

"How do I get clean here, have a wash?"

Gwen raised her eyebrows. "*That's* one of your questions?"

"I mean, it's not essential, but it'd be nice to know?"

"There's a tin bath in the kitchen. You boil water over the fire. You can work the rest out. If you want one, tell me and I'll give you some privacy."

Daisy couldn't decide whether it felt good getting some answers, or whether she was trying to stave off a growing discontent. If this was magic, it was not what she'd expected at all.

"What about the magic, can I learn more about that"?

"Yes, you can."

"Good. So, what's behind the locked door, near the big wooden table?"

"More magic."

"Can I have the key?"

"No, you can't."

Daisy thought about pushing Gwen, but everything she'd experienced so far made it feel pointless; Gwen, shuttered no less tight than the door itself. Neither spoke for a while, having reached what certain people like to call (in a ludicrously exaggerated French accent), an impasse. The silence was broken by gulls squabbling over ocean spoils, breakers smashing into the island. The limitless patience of water, taking an imperceptible bite from the island each time; gnawing it away century upon century.

"Perhaps we can talk about what might come next," Gwen suggested suddenly. "After we practice clearing your clutter – of which there seems to be a lot right now – about connecting to the Kindness?"

Finally! Daisy thought. "I'd like that. What's next?"

"Respect. Whenever we use magic, it's not just us. It's our connection, our intention, but we rely on the elements, on the Kindness."

Daisy nodded eagerly as she swallowed down the rest of her coffee, hoping Gwen would stay on track.

"It's an exchange of energies. We don't just take, we give back, too."

"Give back?"

Gwen nodded, shifting in her chair until she got comfortable, relaxing as she continued.

"We celebrate nature, everything living. Give thanks. So, when we create magic, we do it for the good of all, not just for ourselves, or what we need."

"Like a gratitude journal?"

Inwardly, Gwen griped. "Something like that, yes. We make gratitude – to use your word – part of our magic. Remember Samhain, with Morfydd?"

"Yes, we gave thanks. Weaved it in to what we were doing. I didn't know that was part of the magic though."

"It takes many forms. Tell me, do you feel the seasons changing?"

"I guess. Like, I notice the leaves turn in autumn, sometimes the flowers in spring...is it bluebells? Snowdrops?"

"And do you feel yourself change Daisy, in line with the seasons? How do you feel, for example, when the darker months come, the shorter days?"

"I love the darker months. They make me want to slow right down. It's hard though, as everyone else gets more and more frantic the closer Christmas gets."

"You feel something shifting. What about when you're with nature, or when you feel the elements? Maybe there's one you feel more than others?"

Daisy sensed a softening in her tone, like she was making headway. "Water, maybe? I like trees too. I know some people are scared of them, well, scared of the woods. I'm not. When I was little, Dad would wake me up and we'd go out in the dark, look at the stars together."

"And how did that feel, looking at the stars?"

"Like there was..." Daisy took a moment trying to find the right words. "Something bigger all around us, cleverer than both of us?"

"Do you remember anything else? How does it feel now, as an adult?"

"Back then it made me feel safe. But that might have been because it was one of the few times with my dad, y'know, just the two of us? I still look for them. Makes me feel connected to him – and to something else."

"You feel connected," Gwen echoed leaning in "Can you describe that a bit more?"

"Sometimes, it feels like me and the stars, are made from the same stuff...whatever that is?" she answered, nodding to herself as if in confirmation. "Like we're not separate, if that makes sense?"

"It does. That feeling, is part of the respect in magic. We're not using the air, earth, water or fire just for our own ends, we're an extension of it – as it is, us. The Kindness is all of that. It is spirit, the heart of the energy within the universe. We borrow from it. We don't own it."

"So, how do we give back? Do we have to...top it up?"

Gwen smiled. "Top it up? I like that, Daisy. I've not heard it put like that. How do you think we might do that?"

"Err...we do kind things? Try not to hurt people or animals. The planet? That seems a bit simple...like if it were that easy..."

"Simple usually works."

Mulling things over, something came to her. "So, when I fell off the wall and Lysh saved me, was Lysh giving something back, using magic at the same time?"

Instantly, Gwen drew back. "That one wouldn't know respect if they tripped over it."

"What is it with you and Lysh?" Daisy nudged, readying herself to push harder. Lysh had been waiting at the back of her mind, like a brightly coloured hat left behind in a bus shelter.

"Much of what we do – what we are – as the Sisterkin, is secret. We don't shout about it. Lysh never got that, always wanted everyone to know what we do, that we –

"I can see both sides," Daisy offered.

"Really?" Gwen responded witheringly. "How much do you know, Daisy, about the way witches – women – have been persecuted?" Gwen said with a sigh.

"Not much. Nothing, really."

"I thought as much," Gwen went on huffily. "You can find it out for yourself, but simply put, tens of thousands of women, hundreds of thousands potentially, were murdered throughout America and Europe."

"What! Why?"

"A systematic genocide; one that is never taught in schools. Men of the church rounding up women of any age, including children. Drowned them, burned them at the stake. Those that lived, were assaulted and raped; criminalised."

"Why don't I know about this?"

"Why would you, it's largely been erased, by men. With religion and legislation. And don't think it doesn't still go on," she added ruefully. "Even if they don't burn us nowadays."

Daisy tried to make sense of everything she was hearing, her head jamming with questions. Before she could ask anything, Gwen carried on, like she wasn't stopping anytime soon.

"Back then, it was the women in villages, and further back in tribal communities that held the knowledge of plants; the wisdom of healing, midwifery and reading the stars. Passed down, one safe keeper to the next. That was who people turned to; who *men* turned to. Then the accusations and the burnings came. It wasn't about or magic, or witchcraft; it was about control. Men clinging to power, terrified by women who wouldn't conform; women who refused to stay silent."

Gwen stood up suddenly and let out a long sigh. "I think I want some wine."

"I've been sat here," Daisy started before Gwen reached the table, "wondering how these things were allowed to happen."

Gwen nodded. "Find out more, when you've left here. You know how I feel, I'm not one to hide it am I. Find out how *you* feel."

Gwen had returned with an open bottle of wine in one hand, two mugs on her fingers and a thin wooden staff in the other. Having set down the wine and the mugs, she nodded at Daisy to pour as she laid the staff down.

"There is one other thing, that I did want to know about?"

"What's that, Daisy?" Gwen replied, smoothing herself down. She leaned back, the chair creaking as she moved.

"That alcove, the stone doorway?" Daisy filled two mugs, sliding one over. "Cheers," she said raising her mug – surprised when Gwen chinked mugs.

"It's a haven," Gwen said, pausing to take a drink. "More than that."

"Is it where Lysh came from?" Daisy asked carefully.

"Pah!" Gwen responded, wagging a finger at Daisy. "That one, definitely doesn't belong there."

I saw her go through the stone! Daisy wanted to say, but Gwen's response was so severe. "What do you mean, by a haven?"

"Where do you feel most safe, Daisy?"

Daisy wasn't sure. Six months ago, she might have said the Panchal house, or the house she shared with her mum, at a push.

"Honestly? Probably Morfydd's house."

"Beyond that stone, is where we all feel safest. An incredibly special, crossing place. Where we connect to our song, to the Kindness. Where we give back, too."

"Crossing place?" Daisy said to herself, thinking of her dad.

"Your father isn't there, Daisy."

Daisy felt uncomfortable; her thoughts, her fragile hopes and fears exposed, as though strung around her like baubles for Gwen to see. "Then show me what is!"

Daisy marched over to the stone door. She stared back at Gwen who watched her with a look of annoyance. "I'm not moving," Daisy shouted, leaning back against the stone.

Bending to retrieve the staff, Gwen made her way over, the tip of her staff clicking across the courtyard. Daisy grinned inwardly; perhaps she was starting to get Gwen after all.

"Step aside, please."

Gwen moved up to the stone and started to hum; a low, deep sound. It wasn't loud, but Daisy could feel its power. Gwen took the staff in her left hand and made a tight circling movement as Daisy felt the air begin to alter. It felt like standing too close to machinery. Gwen tapped the staff on the stone three times, and it vanished. It wasn't a fade, or a gradual movement – it just disappeared. With the stone removed the air cooled, heavy with the smell of damp earth and plants; a strong leafy scent. Daisy stepped closer to Gwen, who moved away. She indicated with the staff for Daisy to step forward, into the darkened entrance.

"You've kept on about it, Daisy. So, off you go. Step over the threshold..."

Chapter 22 – The Witch Whistle

It was the afternoon after the day his dad visited, when Suni woke to find his mum sat by the bed, flicking back and forth through a magazine. She tossed it on to the bed. "Sunil, it's so good to see you awake!"

Mrs. Panchal scooped him into her arms as though pulling a turnip. As they separated, Suni shimmied up the lumpy pillows until he was sat up.

"Your auntie sends her love. She's exploring Aberystwyth."

"Have either of you been home?"

"Here and there. We've stayed at a hotel on the seafront. Very lovely, quiet."

"And Daisy?" he asked quietly.

Fidgeting, Mrs. Panchal chased fluff down her cardigan. The look in his eyes pained her and she was disappointed with Daisy.

"She has been a few times, held your hand and talked to you, but –

"She's not here now."

"I've left messages. They've not sent."

Suni leaned from the bed and opened a small bedside cabinet, craning his neck to see inside. "Mum, have you seen my phone?"

"Yes!" she replied with a smile, bending to dig into a bag beside her. "The battery was flat so I took it with me. Here you go."

Suni switched it on, frowning impatiently as it moved through its rigmarole of start-up displays. "I brought the charger too, so it won't go flat again," his mum said proudly.

There were three unread messages. A boring billing message, a pointless request for feedback and the last one, from a guy at work letting him know they were all out for drinks in Manchester – days ago.

"I'm sure she'll come, especially once she knows you're awake. Why don't you message her?"

Suni fired off a message asking her to call, or come to the hospital. He had started typing that he had two important things to tell her, but deleted that bit.

"Has the consultant been round, Sunil?"

"They're keeping me in for a couple more days, to make sure everything's as it should be. Apparently."

Mrs. Panchal felt herself relax. "Such good news. We can take you back to Manchester, once you've got the all clear."

"Mum, can you do me a favour, please?"

Mrs. Panchal nodded, leaning toward him.

"Please, please can you bring me some food! A big fat pasty of some kind, crisps – nothing healthy!"

"Funny you should say that," she replied, ferreting in her bag again. "I'd brought these in case."

She handed him a giant cheese and onion pasty, a jumbo-sized bag of pickled onion Monster Munch and a bottle of Coke. Suni tore into the pasty, taking huge bites, barely swallowing in between. "Mum...this...is...amazing!"

Slipping the bag onto her shoulder she leaned over, kissing him on the forehead. "Message me if you need anything. I'll come by tomorrow – and I'll keep trying Daisy."

He hugged her quickly before tackling the Monster Munch. Tearing at the bag he scattered most of them over his legs, gathering them up as he checked his phone, his message to Daisy still unsent.

As Mrs. Panchal waited outside for her sister to come racing into the car-park…whilst Suni licked crumbs from his fingers and scowled at his phone, far from the hospital, deep within an underground bunker in the Midlands, Mr. Panchal was in trouble. Serious trouble.

Since being grabbed by the men, Mr. Panchal – or No. 5 as they insisted on calling him – had been held in a windowless room. One of many identical spaces, within one of many clandestine buildings belonging to the organisation that officially didn't employ him.

Arriving through a network of concealed tunnels, the Defender had parked in an open garage area. Retrieving firearms from the boot the two men dragged him out and shoved him past similar vehicles. They stopped at an iris-scanning security door; a single Doc Marten shoe abandoned outside. He was frogmarched along faceless corridors; blank walls and immaculately swept concrete floors. Each corridor, junction and door were identical and without signage; a deliberate design intended to thwart escape.

Artificial lighting droned overhead, the relentless buzz like a first migraine. Heading deeper, any change of direction came as a sharp jab from the barrel of some kind of gun. Mr. Panchal wasn't sure whether he had been to this particular location before, but the room he found himself inside, he had seen countless times elsewhere. Most were holding cells for interview or interrogation; observation. Utilitarian in design, each had a metal table bolted to the floor and two chairs, also bolted down. There were no exterior windows, but one wall was an unbreakable mirrored pane. He had witnessed events from a similar, unseen room behind on occasion, but had not expected to find himself inside of one of these locked rooms.

Wordsworth had insisted on doing the interview. He had held that particular moniker since his student days at an ancient university (where he had squandered a sum of money that could have housed all of the homeless in London), reading Classics, nepotism and assault.

As No.2, he was Deputy Director of the A-9. A thin man, with the deathly pallor of a night creature, he favoured crisply laundered black Dior suits. He spoke in a clipped tone heavy with private education, an everlasting reek of Sobranie cigarettes lingering in his wake. Outside of work, no one knew what he did. He shared nothing, nor invited anyone to join him. A man of abject isolation, he knew as much of care and compassion, as a fridge knows of what happens to the food once removed. At sixty-three, he could have retired long ago, complete with a new identity and bottomless pension. Not for Wordsworth, who stubbornly refused to go, without a bullet or an inexplicable drowning.

Had he gone, he would have been replaced by No.3, or Donne, who was a man of churning impatience, having waited in line year upon year for his inevitable promotion – one that when it came, would be akin to that of a local authority, relying wholly on longevity and hierarchy, rather than productivity or expertise.

Whilst Wordsworth was fully entitled to delegate interview and interrogation to whomever he saw fit, save for No.1, he rarely did. If he enjoyed anything of his role as Deputy Director, it was the queasy delight he took from the discomfort interviews allowed him to inflict.

Wordsworth slurped noisily at a glass of chilled water without sharing.

Wordsworth drummed his bony fingertips on the surface of the table, producing a sound like children escaping.

Wordsworth blew cigarette smoke into scared faces, confused faces and tough faces alike.

Wordsworth brought out a photograph of Mrs. Panchal, encouraging Mr. Panchal to consider how she might look to him, doused in petrol and set alight.

Mr. Panchal had been with the A-9 long enough to know how to conduct himself, his answers unadorned and wherever possible, blandly uniform: "I was visiting my son, who had been unconscious in hospital." He had varied the phrasing, trying not to appear rehearsed, but not the meaning. Knowing they were being recorded, he had maintained even breathing and refused to fill the pauses Wordsworth employed frequently, his glee at using silence to trip him up barely concealed. There were questions about Suni, about how he ended up in hospital, about how he had known he was there. It had not been subtle. There had been questions about Mrs. Panchal, the specifics of her daily routines. Repeated questions phrased differently, peppered with others scrutinising his loyalty to the A-9 and their work; thinly veiled accusations like the pall of stagnant water.

Hours later, Wordsworth having grown bored of the questions, and the judicious responses he was getting, decided it was time for a different tack.

"I think we've been in here enough No.5. I imagine you're hungry?" he asked after another long bout of silence.

"I am hungry, yes."

"Let's take a break."

Wordsworth stood and smoothed down his suit trousers with his hands. Mr. Panchal was not buying the sudden courtesy, if anything it only heightened his vigilance.

As Wordsworth leaned toward a panel at the door, Mr. Panchal got up. The chairs were not designed for comfort and he felt a numbness around his pelvis. He stretched and trying to remain composed, followed Wordsworth down a long corridor that ended with another security door.

This was a communal room, with low sofas and a water cooler in one corner, gurgling periodically. He sat down, welcoming anything softer than the chair. Opposite him, the longest wall was unbreakable glass, floor to ceiling. The room beyond was in darkness, save for a red light that blinked slowly.

He leaned back legs uncrossed and watched Wordsworth fill a paper cup from the cooler. He handed it to him without speaking. As he drank it down, he knew Wordsworth would be watching his micro-expressions, desperate for anything that hinted at something unspoken; give him away.

"Seems there might not be any food, after all."

His words bounced around the room; his tone clear there never would have been any food. Pacing slowly, his delight in having the upper hand was obvious in his gait.

"Come to the window No.5," he said with a sweep of his arm, "there's something I want to show you."

Standing beside him at the glass, Mr. Panchal felt uneasy. Wordsworth pressed a button on a display set into the wall and fluorescent lights in the room beyond crackled to life. It had the same uniform concrete floor, the same unfinished look. Around twelve feet wide and eight feet deep there were cameras in each upper corner. The blinking red light was part of a panel beside double doors at the back. The only objects in the room an empty hospital bed and monitoring equipment close by. The bed was empty, with heavy restraints at points for wrists, elbows and neck. The sheets were dishevelled and peering through the glass, Mr. Panchal was certain there was dried blood on them.

"Now then..." Wordsworth announced, the faintest hint of a smile at the corners of his mouth, his voice higher.

Reaching into his suit jacket he brought out a metal box the size of a mobile phone. Dull matte black with a series of recessed buttons. "The tech guys in Sonics, have been busy of late..."

Mr. Panchal watched the double doors at the back of the room open. Two men dragged in an emaciated woman and left. She was wearing a filthy white gown, her hair shaved to her scalp. Blinking in her surroundings, she narrowed her eyes to the light and paced in a tight circle head down.

"Personally, I think they have excelled themselves this time," Wordsworth squealed. "It works at close contact, but can be drone operated too. Full ops test soon. Consider this...a sneak preview, just for you," he finished with a sneer.

The woman took cautious steps closer to the glass, trying to see through. As she neared, Mr. Panchal saw her wrists and legs were covered in bruises. Her eyes were bleary and between her nose and lip like old jam, was a crust of blood.

"What is this!" Mr. Panchal demanded, turning on Wordsworth, eyes blazing, "Who is this woman?"

Wordsworth shrugged as he examined his fingernails. "She was one of a few caught at Stonehenge, last winter. We thought her part of this Sisterkin, or whatever they call themselves."

"And is she?"

"She said not," Wordsworth replied blandly, studying the nails of his other hand. "Doesn't really matter either way."

"So, she's —

"Enough," Wordsworth said putting his hand up. "Time to see what this can do. Think of it as like a..." he paused looking the woman up and down, "dog whistle. I like to call it the Witch Whistle."

Mr. Panchal felt his stomach turn over. Suddenly, Wordsworth turned to him and laughed. "It's like being in an aquarium...I want to tap on the glass!"

As he jabbed the knuckles of his hand against the glass the woman flinched then froze. Only her eyes moved, scanning the glass. Wordsworth pressed his thumb against the button and held it down.

Mr. Panchal fought a grin...whatever Wordsworth had planned as a grand display of power, had done nothing whatsoever.

Then, the woman fell to her knees. Collapsing on to her side, she clamped her hands over her ears, desperate to shut out a sound that screamed in her head: an intense, high-pitched noise, like metal dragged across metal at an astounding volume.

"Turn it off!" Mr. Panchal shouted grabbing at the remote control in Wordsworth's hand. He sidestepped and pressed his thumb onto another button. The woman writhed on the floor, arching her back as her body convulsed. As Wordsworth pressed another button, her fitting slowed and within moments she had forced herself to sit, legs splayed out to one side.

As she hugged herself, the first trickle of blood showed at her nose. With another jab at the button, she was writhing in pain, mouth gaping as she screamed behind the soundproof glass.

Once more, Mr. Panchal tried to make Wordsworth drop the remote, grabbing his arm and forcing it against the glass. Snaking free, Wordsworth backhanded him across the face, hard enough to knock him to the floor. Staring down one arm of his jacket, he ran his hand along it as though removing lint.

"That was stupid, No.5," he hissed as he swept back his thinning sandy hair.

Stepping over to where Mr. Panchal sat on the floor looking up at him, he kicked the side of his head, knocking him out. "Very stupid."

As Daisy followed a passage between silver birches, behind which stood stiff firs, the ground was soft underfoot. It was dark, the sunlight barely piercing the trees. She felt hidden.

She had not gone much further when the ground dipped, continuing to drop steeply as it squeezed between immense rocky sides, close enough in places for her to touch both sides at once. Vast rocks taller than houses, draped in moss and capped with trees, gnarled roots bulging through the rock in places.

As the soft earth became steps that led deeper still, she took her time, stopping to touch spongy emerald moss, running her hands over the rock, her fingers catching jagged neon-green ferns. Each time she stopped to touch something, to peep into cracks in the rock, it felt like whatever she looked at, looked back. Everything, so alive in this snug, secret gorge.

Faced with a titanic expanse of rock reaching thirty feet above her, she was unable to go any further. An enormous single slab, it looked like it had fallen from the sky and embedded itself in the earth, blocking the path. Glancing back, she could make out the edges of the stone doorway; Gwen's shape in shadow. She turned on the spot sniffing. She had smelled plants and damp earth, the air cooling the further in she went. Now, she caught the salty tang of the sea; strong, as though nearby. She sniffed again, trying to locate it. Following a faint draught, she found sliver of daylight deep inside the rocks, beside the vast rock barring her way.

Feeling with her hands, there was a way through – so narrow she had to shuffle in sideways. Moving hand over hand, she inched toward the light, her nose filling with the flinty smell of the rock. Two-thirds in, she started to panic, convinced it was getting narrower. Forcing herself to focus on the light, the enormity of the rock still carried with it the sensation of being crushed slowly, but intently.

Suddenly, she was free – stumbling from the crevice into a rocky corridor turning sharply left. It was a narrow tunnel with a low roof, still with a gradient, but shallower. Not far ahead was the light, which after the sideways passage seemed so much brighter. It shone through an opening, a shaggy hole in the rock, fringed with grass. Had she been able to reach it, it was too small for her to fit through; for anyone to get in or out.

Daisy let the light wash over her. With it, came not just a briny odour, but an insistent melody; the call of the waves funnelled through the opening, booming down the stone tunnel. She took a few steps to where the tunnel broadened into a circular chamber and found the hole was directly overhead. At the heart of the chamber which was around ten feet across, was a burned area with the remains of charred vegetation and the stump of a candle. Another passage led beyond the reach of the light. It was lower, barely higher than she was and much straighter. She couldn't see a lot, but made out smaller chambers either side. One at ground level, one around chest height and one level with her face. She wasn't about to start poking her hands inside and turned back.

Returning to the circular chamber she realised she was hurrying. It felt like much deeper underground, the tunnel where she stood far beneath the courtyard. The rock was different, no ferns or moss; more like the caverns inside the castle, the room where she and Gwen slept; as old as time, yet oddly homely.

Trailing her fingers along the wall, she jerked it away as she felt an electric shock; sharp and sudden, but not painful. When she placed her palms flat on the rock, it was like plugging into a limitless library. Her mind flooded with memories, fragments of dreams. Some she recognised, like her and Suni meeting for the first time at junior school, when he had sidled over shyly. Others didn't feel like her memories – gardens of wildflowers, a heavy treeline at sunset. An immeasurable consciousness, that felt like it contained everything that had ever been; might ever be.

As soon as she removed her hands, the images were gone. She was about to try again, when she heard rustling behind her. It was Gwen, Daisy having not registered her approaching until she was upon her.

"That's enough, Daisy. Time to go back."

"Oh, come on!" Daisy pouted. "Just a bit more, tell me about the chambers down there…"

Gwen shook her head. "This is sacred space, with a potent energy. It's not a tour."

"But I –

"Please come back with me, now."

Gwen didn't wait. Daisy followed begrudgingly, wondering how Gwen managed to squeeze through the sideways passage – something she was not looking forward to tackling again.

"So, is that another glamour?" Daisy asked once they were back in the courtyard, the alcove closed once more.

"It's just as it appears, a doorway."

Not one I can open, Daisy thought.

"It was incredible in there Gwen. Everything felt so…alive. Are you going to tell me more about it?"

"Yes, why don't we have a coffee, get sat down?"

Before Daisy could answer, she saw Lysh sauntering from the keep in the same rainbow jumper, with baggy green combat trousers and scuffed trainers. Lysh gave her a quick wave before ambling over and hugging her. Realising with horror she had wrapped her arms around their waist and not their shoulders, Daisy bolted backwards, mortified.

"How you doing Daisy?" asked Lysh. "Hello Gwen," she added, not looking at her.

"I've things to do," Gwen said rudely before heading off.

Having recovered herself, Daisy laughed as Lysh glanced in Gwen's direction. "Well, that's my coffee fucked!"

"Good job you've got excellent company then."

Daisy jabbed Lysh in the arm, regretting it the moment they shot her a look of surprise.

"What you been up to then, you and Old Gwen?"

"I've been through there," Daisy said nodding at the alcove, "where you ran off the other night?" she added pointedly.

Glancing at the alcove Lysh shrugged. "Easy, when you know how." Fishing into a trouser pocket they pulled out a half bottle of vodka. "Fancy a drink?"

"Yes, I do. Why *did* you run off the other night?"

Daisy took a gulp and passed it back to Lysh, who let out a loud ahhhh after swallowing. She hadn't noticed before, but when Lysh spoke, there was an accent that reminded her of how people talked in Sheffield.

"It'll be dark soon. Fancy a fire?" Lysh asked, deliberately ignoring Daisy's question. She hesitated, images of Gwen interrupting them, quickly putting out their fire.

"Don't worry about Gwen. She can't bear to share the same patch of ground as me!"

"So, about the other night?" Daisy insisted.

"I just had to go," Lysh replied flatly. "We mekking this fire, or what?"

Daisy sighed. "Lead on..."

As they approached the keep bats scattered, blending into the night, before a long, low howl sounded around the keep.

Daisy stopped in her tracks. "What...was that?!"

"That'll be Muffin," Lysh replied laughing at the panic on Daisy's face, "the castle cat."

With perfect timing, an enormous grey cat strolled from the shadows on gigantic paws. He stopped and licked his lips, then came a low rumbling purr like an idling engine.

"It sounded like he was talking!"

"It has been known..."

"And he looks about a hundred years old!" Daisy added clapping her hands excitedly. Lysh crouched to stroke the cat, who butted his head against their knee, letting out another long, deep meow. "Awww, he's gorgeous!" Daisy exclaimed. As Lysh stood up, before Daisy could approach the cat was away, back into the shadows.

There had been no sign of Gwen and minutes later the two of them were scurrying outside with armfuls of logs and kindling. By the time the sun dipped behind the walls, the last of the light pulled up and over the battlements, Daisy had started building the fire, whilst Lysh gathered stones and shells from the garden, to circle the fire. As Lysh brought two chairs over from the tables, Daisy was carefully arranging the last of the kindling. "Get that lit Daisy, it's freezing!"

"Alright, alright."

"Come on, we can sit round the fire like two old people on their allotment at the end of the day!"

Daisy turned and looked at Lysh, trying to get a read. It was an odd thing for Lysh to have said. "Imagine, you as an old woman!"

"Ouch," Lysh said softly. "Only our second date, and you've misgendered me."

"It's not a date," Daisy corrected bluntly. "And I'm sorry, I didn't know."

"You didn't ask."

Daisy chewed at her finger, bit her thumb nail.

"I'm asking now?"

"I'll be an old, person. You can be the woman, if you like? I'll just be me – them – thank you very much."

The atmosphere had changed and Lysh looked hurt. Daisy wanted things back to how they'd been and reaching over, touched them gently on the shoulder. "Well, you're a *person* I'm enjoying hanging out with."

"Hmm. You're alright, I guess."

Daisy stooped to start the fire with her lighter. "And okay, I'll be the woman." The kindling was dry and the flame rushed at it. Minutes later, the logs were already beginning to smoulder as the flames grew fiercer.

"Do you know what we need, Daisykins –

"Can you stop that, please. It's Daisy."

Lysh swallowed and took a moment. "Sorry, Daisy. We need music, what you into?"

"Err…punky dubby stuff; bassy. I'll take house, bit of ska. Dancey stuff, something upbeat. What about you?"

"Depends. When I'm driving, I like house too, trance as well. Especially on a night drive. For now, I'll put on one of me favourites. It's punky, works any time of day. You got a phone?"

"I have, but the battery's pretty much flat."

"I can fix that, chuck it o'er. Just so you know, if this doesn't have you up and dancing, yer officially dead!"

Daisy fished her phone out. The battery was on 3%, so what Lysh could do she wasn't sure. "You got a socket I don't know about then?"

"Yeah, me."

Daisy watched Lysh balance the phone on their leg as they clasped their palms together and closed their eyes. There was so much she wanted to ask, but seeing Lysh concentrating, she bit her lip. She studied a chickenpox scar at the corner of their mouth, their laughter lines, trying to work out what age Lysh was.

Daisy picked up the vodka and took a drink. As the alcohol made for her bloodstream, she felt a rush; a loosening in her shoulders. Minutes later, a cosy flush spread across her cheeks like daybreak. She sat quietly, if a little impatiently, wondering if Lysh was messing with her. Any minute now, she expected them to snap open their eyes and fall about laughing. Lysh remained in the same position for a few more minutes, face relaxed, the phone between their palms. When they opened their eyes and handed it back, Daisy was astounded, the battery now at 93%.

"Close enough," Lysh said. "Couldn't be arsed to wait."

"How did you…"

Lysh grinned. "Magic. I'm sure you've worked out this whole island is magical – I'm betting you've done the thing with the cold coffee, right?"

Daisy nodded eagerly. "I did – have you done that too?"

Lysh rolled their eyes. "*Everyone* does that," they said enigmatically. "You gotta find your element. Mine's air. So, bringing energy down and into your phone, is easy for me."

"Could I do it then?"

"Anyone can do it. Once they can connect. Those whose element is air, just seem to be able to do it quicker."

"How did you find out, that you're air?"

Lysh looked up at the sky. "You just know, I guess."

Daisy thought about it. Earth didn't feel right to her, so fire maybe? Air she couldn't get her head around at all, which left water. She was about to grill Lysh further, but they grabbed the phone. "Music time, what's your password?"

"Sleepyhead," Daisy replied without hesitation.

Moments later she heard a pounding drum, chased up quickly by a bassline that bubbled like hot soup. Guitar skank strokes chimed in, rising and falling, her foot tapping before she knew it.

"That bassline!"

"Usually, I'd shuffle. But for you, who I'm sensing might be a Dub the Earth virgin, you're getting the whole album: Raving for the Underdog."

Daisy started nodding along with the bouncing rhythm, thinking how much Suni would love it. Lysh was right – she did want to dance. Knocking back more vodka, she got up and began swaying with the music, shoulders loose, hips like a pendulum.

Lysh was up moments later, pulling the jumper over their head, revealing a purple vest top and arms bright with tattoos. Flinging the jumper onto the chair, they shimmied over to Daisy arms in the air, weaving side-to-side like an enchanted cobra.

Daisy giggled. "Well, that didn't take long!"

"I love this music!"

As the fire blazed higher, they danced around it, passing the bottle back and forth until it was empty. Giant shadows flickered over the walls, mimicking their dancing. They laughed and fell about, holding hands as they circled the fire faster and faster, out of time with the music. After a few tracks, Lysh collapsed into one of the chairs breathing heavily, Daisy whirled into the chair beside them, cackling wildly as she sat down.

"Fuck me, Lysh, you need to exercise!"

Lysh laughed, slapping Daisy on the arm. "Touché!"

"Has time stopped? It felt like we were dancing for ages!" Daisy exclaimed, not realising she was shouting.

"Timothy Time Thief, must have the night off!"

Daisy giggled and leaned in to Lysh, the gap between the chairs having mysteriously disappeared.

"I like the way you move, Daisy."

Daisy felt tipsy, fast approaching the point where she had to take a moment to form her words, really think about the order. All she managed was, "You do?"

"Yes." Lysh dug her in the ribs, causing her to jiggle in her chair. "See!"

As Lysh moved their face closer to hers, Daisy jerked back almost tipping her chair.

"What is it?" Lysh asked gently. "Did I –

Daisy sat up stiffly. "I feel a bit sick." Her throat was dry and suddenly she felt dizzy. Lysh tapped a foot fitfully, watching Daisy get up too fast, as though her vision was late catching up.

"I think...I need...some fresh air."

"We're outside, Daisy."

Daisy felt helpless, like she could be sick any minute. Throwing a hasty apology at Lysh, she stumbled across the courtyard, banging into one of the tables before zig-zagging toward the archway. Crashing through the pitch-black passage, she fell a couple of times, legs unsteady. Her mind was spongy and the only idea that made even a little sense, was getting off the island. Before she knew what she was doing, she was on the boat, shining the torch on her phone over the controls. There was a stubby key, which she turned. The engine started and she grabbed at what looked similar to the gearstick of her car.

Had Gwen not brought the boat into the tunnel backwards, all Daisy would have managed was to crash it into the rocky wall where the inlet ended. Somehow, she found herself pitching on the waves just outside the mouth of the tunnel. The sea foamed as it tossed the boat up and down. Daisy doubled over and was sick on her shoes, clinging desperately to the Perspex housing covering the controls. Gulls squawked, but in the rolling darkness she was unable to see them, sensing a large flock circling the boat.

Confused, barely able to see straight, she pulled and pushed frantically at the controls, unable to make the boat do anything. Spinning in a circle at the mercy of the water, smoke belched and the engine died. The boat bucked on the water, hurling her backwards as she lost her grip, sliding along the sodden deck. Her heart pounded as she slipped again, unable to get her footing. Only a few feet shy of the tunnel, with the boat rocking so violently it felt as though it could be slammed into the rocks any moment. As the charging waves ricocheted off the island, the boat rose high on the water, catapulting Daisy further down the deck. As she grabbed for the edge of the boat, icy water poured in. With a final toss, she was hurled into the water, thrashing her arms as she tried to find something to grab at.

Coughing out mouthfuls of water and choking on her own hair she tried to sweep it off her face, floundering in the water, trying to remember how to swim. She got three fingers over the edge of the boat and held on with her all her might, kicking her legs wildly as she dipped under the water; the force of the sea casting her about like driftwood.

With her whole hand now clinging to the edge, she gripped it with the last of her energy, a paralysing numbness spreading through her legs until she could no longer make them kick. Dragging her other arm through the weight of the water, she managed to hold on, but hadn't the strength to haul herself into the boat. The water churned and she felt the boat heading into a spin and she knew she was going to drown. White-knuckled, her icy fingers screamed in pain as they weakened their grip, slipping from the boat.

Under the water, her mind suddenly free of its clutter, she saw the bright violet light, pulsing as a warm glow. It expanded to embrace her and the boat, and inside the raging cold and the swelling of the waves, she felt the energy of the water; a benevolent easing of its power, as though rather than being intent on pulling her under, it now held her. Flaring, the light swept through her and even with eyes closed, she felt the waves and the boat lit by the vivid glow. A burst of energy flooded her body, as a wave scooped her up and over the lip of the boat. It was like bouncing into the boat from a trampoline, and whilst her landing lacked grace, she met the deck gently as though lowered with care.

Spluttering and shivering, she navigated the controls of the boat as though guided. She had no conscious idea of what she was doing. A rising wave pushed the boat toward the tunnel opening, gliding the rest of the way along the inlet.

With the last of her strength Daisy managed to drag herself from the boat, collapsing onto the stony slope. Gasping for breath she crawled forward, still struggling to get completely out of the water. The last thing she was aware of, before blacking out from cold and exhaustion, was a figure scrambling toward her, hand outstretched...

Chapter 24 – Words in Smoke...

Letting himself into the cottage, it felt like he'd not been there in a while. Gabriel called out to Daisy, disappointed when there was no answer. The tidier kitchen, the lingering aroma of strong coffee and countless cigarette ends on the hearth having missed the fire, spoke of her having been there.

He had opened the kitchen cupboards at random and peered behind curtains, before he remembered there was no alcohol in the house. Then, came a creeping dread as he had to remind himself, he no longer drank alcohol. During his time away, apart from sitting with No-Shoes-the-Fish and Ron, the urge to drink hadn't been there. Now, returning to the scene of his grime, an intense craving reared like a predator. Waiting for the dripping alchemy of his Melitta percolator he felt restless; unease spread through him as old patterns nipped at his heels. What looked like his cottage, what smelled like his cottage, twisted itself into a museum of memories; every room heavy with a pervasive association with alcohol.

Sat in his armchair having struggled to get a fire started, he cradled the coffee in his hands, welcoming its punchy familiarity. He drank it hot, savouring every mouthful then smoked a cigarette. He thought of Davey, reflecting on how he had passed – exactly the way he would have wanted it, deep inside the man he loved – and managed a chuckle. It faded quickly as the reality of losing his best friend hit home.

Rooting out an ashtray from beneath old magazines, a scrap of paper wafted to the floor. It looked like a page from one of his journals and reading it, his heart leapt. It was a note, in Daisy's bubbly handwriting with her phone number (clearly, she knew him well enough already to know he would have lost her number – and he had) – Dad, please let me know you're okay as soon as you can. Love you, Daisy xoxo.

He dialled carefully and waited. A polite female voice told him the number he was dialling was not in service. When he asked why, the woman just repeated what she had already said. Grumbling, he had replaced the receiver and tried again, taking even more care. Once again it was the same woman – and still she refused to engage in conversation. Perhaps Morfydd had a telephone that worked better. Before leaving, he scribbled a note for Daisy and left it beside the coffee machine: Daisy, I'm alive and well! (again). With Morfydd, back later. Love, Dad x

Stowing the piece of paper with Daisy's number in his tobacco tin, he climbed the stairs to look for a coat. A stack of boxes filled the landing and one of the rooms had been partially cleared. Changing into his mustard jumper and a heavy overcoat he left.

"Gabriel"? Morfydd asked squinting. The flowing white hair and beard had flummoxed her and it was only catching his eye that she recognised him. "What on earth?"

"Hello Morfydd. I hope I'm not interrupting?"

Morfydd smiled as she stepped back. "Not at all. You can be a good reason to put off weeding."

"You flatter me," Gabriel said grinning as he stepped inside.

Morfydd was Morfydd, hair tied back, happy in tatty jeans, purple house slippers he'd not seen before and a bulky dark green jumper that looked very warm. As Gabriel settled into the chair by the fire, she made a large pot of coffee. He watched her busying herself in the kitchen, humming to herself. "Do you like cheese scones?" she called out, to which he nodded keenly. Returning with a plate of scones fresh from the oven, a pat of butter and a jar of Marmite, she set everything down on the table between them.

Once Gabriel caught up, discovering Daisy was with Gwen, he was relieved she was doing okay, though saddened to hear about Suni; a little disappointed too, hearing it was Morfydd who had encouraged Daisy to go away. She reassured Gabriel, more than once, that Daisy was fine – perfectly well in fact. She explained time with Gwen was part of her learning who she was; learning more of the Sisterkin. As a retired magician, she hoped he would understand better than most.

"She left a sweet note," Gabriel said, remembering why he had called on Morfydd.

"She missed you, Gabriel. She was all sixes-and-sevens after you vanished. Furious too!"

Gabriel grinned as an image of the day they'd fallen over in the snow together came to mind. "But she's safe?"

Morfydd nodded. She could feel his worry in the room. "She is. Why don't you send her a message."

"A message? I said I can't get through to her phone," he retorted, more abruptly than intended.

"And I didn't say by phone…"

Morfydd eased out of the chair and beckoned for him to follow her. "Grab your coat and meet me outside. On the cliff side. I'll be there now, just need a couple of things…and Gabriel?"

"Yes?"

"Be careful near the edge!"

Gabriel stood with the cottage behind him, feeling odd stood on the cliff. They had talked so long it was dark and whispering softly, the sea was smooth and black. He didn't notice Morfydd had joined him. Her footsteps made him turn, the muted glow behind the curtains revealing her outline. "Right, what are we doing?"

Hidden by the dark, he didn't see her roll her eyes as she answered. "I'm starting to see where Daisy gets her impatience from." Morfydd shook out a blanket and let it settle over the ground, getting on her knees and smoothing it out. "Come, sit."

The blanket was thick, fleecy and comfortable. As he waited, he tried to relax. Now his eyes had acclimatised, he saw her kneeling opposite.

"Okay Gabriel, we can get a message to Daisy. Keep it short and simple, nothing too –

"I just say it, out loud?"

"If you let me finish! Short and simple, you're going to write it down."

"It's too dark?"

"It won't be – if you stop interrupting!"

With a snap of her fingers a flame appeared, between them was an indigo candle on a stone saucer. "The colours don't matter too much to me," Morfydd explained, "it's about the intention. That said, purple's a good fit."

She reached into the darkness beside her and he saw her unscrew the lid of an unlabelled, wide-necked glass jar.

"I do like to dress the candle though."

She smiled to herself as she sniffed it, before scooping out a few fingertips of an oily green paste which she rubbed between her hands. "My own concoction", she added proudly. It was deep and earthy, with a cloying floral note that tickled his nose. He watched her pick up the candle and roll it between her palms until she was satisfied it was covered with the paste.

"We're getting there. Take these…"

Morfydd handed Gabriel a purple pencil and a small piece of parchment the size of a business card. "You don't need to tell me the message, just write it on here. And please, take your time."

Morfydd sat back on her knees and closed her eyes. She pictured Daisy at her cottage, holding the image as Gabriel bent over the paper, chewing absent-mindedly on the end of her pencil.

She thought about Gwen's visit the day before. She had been troubled. The two of them had always disagreed on the subject of Lysh – and subsequently, on the subject of Kara and Daisy. Something in Lysh rubbed Gwen up the wrong way and despite her best efforts, she had not been able to smooth that out. Gwen had been edgy and impatient and she'd let her talk everything out in her own time. It had been good to see her, to get an update on Daisy, albeit one coloured by Gwen's dislike of Lysh. Her dreams of late had been vivid and although she hadn't shared that with Gwen, she had shared a growing sense she felt of events quickening – the return of Lysh doing nothing to allay the feeling. Whilst Lysh returning was unexpected and warranted further discussion, Morfydd had wanted to talk about Daisy. Boiling a cup of coffee was standard beginners' stuff – she herself had done it a long time ago – and she could imagine Daisy's frustration. At least the mug hadn't exploded, like the first time Lysh had tried.

Gabriel meanwhile, having mulled over more complicated messages than necessary, settled for short and simple: Be safe Daisy, I'll be here when you get back. Love, Dad x.

He was about to hand the paper to Morfydd but she looked deep in thought and he waited. "Morfydd?" he asked gently a few minutes later.

"You all done?" she responded as she snapped her eyes open.

Morfydd took the piece of parchment from him, catching sight of his tiny handwriting, but not reading the message.

"All you need to do now, Gabriel, is bring Daisy to mind and imagine speaking your message to her. Picture it as smoke winding its way into the air, finding its way to Daisy."

"And that's all?"

Morfydd sighed to herself, shaking her head.

"The tricky bit, I'll be doing!"

He closed his eyes and pictured he and Daisy after their visit to Aberaeron. That had been a good day; had felt like they were growing closer. Morfydd held the piece of paper between her hands and brought them to her heart as she spoke softly, her words barely audible over the murmuring waves.

"Words in smoke, smoke from flame, be with Daisy, speak the same."

"Words in smoke, smoke from flame, be with Daisy, speak the same."

Leaning toward the candle she released the paper. It hung in the air as though suspended on invisible wire, before being consumed by the flame, a puff of smoke as Morfydd repeated the words a final time. The smoke spiralled upwards, winding higher and higher until it could no longer be seen. With a sharp blow into the air, Morfydd clapped her hands together, startling Gabriel.

"Let it be so!"

Chapter 25 – The Crossing

Gwen eyed Lysh across the kitchen. She wasn't about to voice it, but their help with Daisy had been crucial. She was far too old to be dragging an impatient and foolhardy girl out of the sea. Had Lysh not intervened, she would not have managed to get Daisy into the kitchen. When they had, Lysh had refused to leave.

Lysh slouched against the table knowing Gwen was watching. Let the old woman do as she pleases. Daisy, sleeping in a chair by the fire, looked shattered. Lysh wanted to keep an eye on her – and she didn't need Gwen's approval.

After helping carry Daisy into the kitchen, Lysh had found a towel and dried her hair. Gwen had stoked the fire and made a pan of strong coffee. Daisy had not stopped shivering, her teeth chattering together. Water pooled around her, as she babbled to herself, looking bewildered.

Gwen had barked orders, making it clear Daisy needed to get out of her wet clothes. Having stomped from the kitchen she had returned with more towels and an old green jumper and worn jeans – not bothering to explain where she had found them; Lysh left wondering if Tor's Leap had a lost property box hidden in the caves.

Lysh had eased Daisy's sopping jumper and t-shirt, over her head and wrapped a large towel around her. They had done their best to dry her in a way that was business-like, then spread her wet clothes over two trivets to dry. Gwen had been surprised by the care Lysh had shown, crouching at Daisy's feet to remove her trainers, neatly lining them up by the fire. Lysh had asked Daisy before unbuttoning her jeans, talking her through what was happening as they slid them down until they were balled up at her ankles, freeing them as Daisy groaned and kicked out a leg.

Gwen had handed Lysh a fresh towel and they had dried Daisy's legs slowly. Eventually, Daisy was dressed in dry clothes, still confused and still drunk. Her head had lolled forward, as Lysh had tried to get her to take sips of coffee. Sagging in the chair, she was snoring loudly within minutes.

She woke with a sneeze, then another; one more for luck. She had no idea where she was and stared at the kitchen like she had never seen it before, gradually realising she was wrapped in a heavy blanket in a chair beside the fire.

"Look who's back from the dead!"

Daisy moaned as a patchy memory surfaced: she and Lysh had been drinking and dancing around a fire. She couldn't remember much else, but had a dark feeling she had done something bad. What flavour of bad she didn't know, gripped by that panic unique to blackout hangovers; what some refer to as the horrors, or the fear.

"Lysh, I'm so sorry..."

"What for? Snoring like a rhino?" Lysh said laughing, flopping into a chair opposite.

"Sorry...for something? Everything? – and do rhinos' snore?"

"And what about me, Daisy?" Gwen interjected from behind her. "Anything to say to me?"

Fuck, Daisy thought. She tried to face Gwen, but turning made her woozy. "I'm sorry Gwen...what did I do?"

Lysh filled her in before Gwen could, laughing again. "You got drunk and went rogue...stole Gwen's boat!"

After Lysh made coffee, they had all moved outside, Daisy wanting fresh air. If she was going to be sick, which still felt a distinct possibility, she would rather that happen outside.

It was mild and dry out, rainclouds in the distance quietly plotting. Telling Daisy what had happened, her disappointment was obvious. Daisy knew she'd done wrong; disrespected Gwen and Tor's Leap. She apologised over and over, hoping each time it would soften things. All it did, however, was make her apology seem less sincere. It hadn't escaped her notice, however, that Gwen was sat at the same table as Lysh, having not got up to leave, or, so far at least, dismissed them in her usual manner.

"Thank you for apologising, Daisy," Gwen said, and glancing at Lysh added, "Lysh was a huge help, carrying you in from the water. Undressing you."

Daisy blushed furiously. Mumbling thanks she squirmed inside. She couldn't look at Lysh, but felt them looking at her. "Think nothing of it, Daisy.

The three of them turned suddenly, at a noise from beyond the wall – a fast, whining engine, not unlike a Sunday morning hedge strimmer. Whatever it was, the rising volume suggested it was coming nearer.

"What is *that*?" Daisy asked, turning to Gwen as though she would know.

"I've no idea." Gwen replied, her tone less confident than usual.

"It's a drone!"

As Lysh pointed, a lightweight, metal contraption sailed over the wall. It circled the bailey, lower than the walls, but too high for them to reach. Daisy felt her head pounding, just as Gwen clamped her hands over her ears, before falling from her chair and writhing on the ground. Daisy reached to help her, but her head was filled with a shrieking tone; like a nail being hammered into her brain. Clutching her temples, she screamed out and buckled over in the chair, crawling under the table.

Lysh stood rooted to the spot. Their first instinct was to help Daisy, but knew what they needed to do. Connecting effortlessly with the energy of the air, they raised their hands and brought them together, as though taking a huge scoop of the air...

From under the table Daisy was unable to see everything, but heard Lysh let out a loud cry as they pushed both hands out, directing an invisible bubble upwards. The drone faltered, swerving to one side as though hit by a gust of wind. Whoever was controlling the drone, it looked as though it was trying to rectify itself. Lysh sent another wave of energy upwards and this time the drone smashed into the battlements, part of it breaking off. Spinning wildly, it cartwheeled through the sky until the engine cut out and it plunged into the sea.

Daisy knelt beside Gwen and helped her sit. Although none of them had seen the drone hit the water, the searing pain stopped at exactly the same time. Lysh hurried over and helped lift Gwen onto the chair, then Daisy, hands trembling, rolled cigarettes for them both. The three of them sat dazed. It hadn't been said by anyone yet, but whatever had just happened, the drone had shattered the peace and safety of the island, bringing with it a grave threat.

By the time night came, Gwen was back to her usual self, although she had invited Lysh to eat dinner and the three of them had not long finished a hearty onion stew with homemade rolls. A steady rain had fallen most of the afternoon, turning the gardens boggy and they had eaten in the kitchen. Lysh seemed unruffled; they had been less affected by the drone, which none of them could explain.

"Daisy, I've been thinking about today," Gwen began, "I'd like you to go back to Morfydd's. It's not safe here."

Answering Gwen, it was Lysh Daisy looked at. "I'd really like to stay. There must be something I can do?"

Gwen shook her head. "No, Daisy. I realise now, I need to better protect Tor's Leap." Her face creased with concern. "Whatever that was, it's seen us; hurt us. Maybe, I've been complacent, living here like there's no threat," she said ruefully.

"I agree with Gwen," Lysh cut in, "however much it pains me to say it. I can help, in a way that you can't, yet."

"For fuck's sake," snapped Daisy, "why is it always other people deciding for me. I'm a lot stronger than either of you seem to think."

"It's not about strength," Gwen said. "It's about experience, and that, you don't have."

"No-one's saying you're not strong, Daisy," Lysh countered gently. "We just don't want you to get hurt, either of us."

Gwen snorted. "And, however much it pains *me* to say, I feel the same as Lysh."

Daisy folded her arms and chewed her lip. Yet again, she felt stupid, like a child trying to persuade the grown-ups to let her stay up. "Fine, whatever. We going then?"

"I have to check the boat over, I think it might need some attention," Gwen said. "Perhaps you and Lysh can spend time together, before you go?"

"Do you fancy that?" Lysh asked. They had aimed for an even tone, but it had come out desperately hopeful.

Daisy scowled at them both. When she did answer, briefly catching Lysh's eye, it was hard to keep frowning.

"Yeah, why not. But no vodka!"

"Right," Gwen said getting up, "I'll leave you to it. Daisy, I'll see you soon. Lysh, thank you."

Lysh gave Gwen a polite nod then turned to Daisy. "Right, you, s'pose we'd better get your stuff together."

"Did I have to pack right now?" Daisy asked wiggling her rucksack onto her back.

Crossing the courtyard, the air smelled of the sea and although the rain had stopped, it remained wet and slippery; the gardens muddied and forlorn.

"You'll be leaving soon and –

"Gwen said she needs to look over the boat?"

"You're not going by boat," Lysh answered mysteriously. "Come on," they added, offering Daisy a hand.

Daisy took their hand without thinking, but before they were even halfway across the courtyard, she let go of it, feeling awkward.

"You've got small hands."

"Have I?"

"Yeah, they're tiny," Lysh said with a chuckle. "You're tiny."

Daisy looked up at Lysh, who was almost a foot taller. "And how's it up there? Chilly in the clouds?"

Lysh stuck out their tongue and moved quicker toward the alcove.

"Can I ask you something?" Daisy said when they were side-by-side in front of the stone.

"Of course…"

"Last night, did I do something bad? Upset you?"

Lysh took a step closer, pleased Daisy didn't recoil this time.

"You didn't, no. I spooked you, so it should be me saying sorry – so, sorry."

"I'm glad we met," Daisy said awkwardly, moving away. She was glad she had met Lysh and wanted them to know that. What she kept to herself, was how abrupt leaving felt. Lysh said nothing and stepped forward. Placing their hands on the stone, they slid their arms sideways and it disappeared.

"What the…" Daisy said, her mouth hanging open.

"Like I said, easy when you know how." Lysh gave Daisy a wink before continuing, "I'll come with you as far as the chamber. You coming?"

Walking the path in silence, the mossy chasm was wetter than before. Dripping could be heard; a splash as one of them stepped in a pool of water. When they came to the passage, Lysh motioned for Daisy to go first. It was easier this time, knowing there was a way through. In no time at all the two of them were in the stone tunnel, lit by moonlight coming through the grassy opening. As Daisy stepped into the circular chamber underneath, she was disappointed to see Lysh turn back.

"Hey, wait!"

Lysh paused and looked back. "This is me. You need to do the rest, on your own."

"What?"

"Trust."

"Let me guess, another part of my learning?" Daisy said with a sigh. Now it made sense, the new truce between Lysh and Gwen.

"Do you trust me, Daisy?"

Daisy thought for a moment. "I do actually. And I don't trust easily."

Lysh grinned goofily. "There you go then." As they reached the entrance to the passage they called out, "Until next time, Daisy."

Daisy bolted up the tunnel and wrapped her arms around Lysh. Straining on tiptoes she planted a quick kiss on their cheek. "To remember me by!" she said before darting away without looking back. What Daisy didn't see, was having clambered into the dark opening in the rock, Lysh stayed, rather than returning to the passage beyond.

Daisy stood in the chamber unsure what to do. In actual fact, that wasn't true – she did know what to do, but was scared. She had learned enough during her time at Tor's Leap, she thought, to do it. Stepping into the shadowy corridor, she felt around with her hands until she found one of the nooks on her left. The stone was dry and cold. The higher ledge was too high, the low, felt too low. With a deep breath she slipped off her rucksack and scrambled into the middle hollow.

It was long enough for her to lie flat. With the rucksack as a makeshift pillow, she lay on her back trying not to think about how close the stone was to her face. She trailed her right arm out of the hollow, keen to remind herself that she could get out at any point.

She did her best to empty the clutter in her mind, this time feeling as there was a panic in the more persistent thoughts:

"The drone..."

"Lysh…"

"Stealing Gwen's boat…"

"Gwen collapsing…"

"Lysh…"

Daisy heard something and stopped. It was a low, steady tempo, like a beat. Slowly, she realised it was the rise and fall of the waves she could hear; the sea breathing. As her mind started to clear she focused on the crash of the breakers against the island. The bright light appeared, but this time it was a golden white. Allowing herself to drift into the rhythm of the water as it echoed around the hollow, the light began to pulse, in time with what now sounded like drumming.

Boom-boom-boom…boom-boom-boom

Boom-boom-boom…boom-boom-boom

Increasing in volume, the throbbing filled the round chamber, thudding around where she lay. She could feel it in her whole body; the hollow an ancient echo chamber.

Boom-boom-boom…boom-boom-boom

Boom-boom-boom…boom-boom-boom

Louder and louder, it came. Slow and steady, as the spirit of the sea sounded all around. Daisy felt herself swallowed by the light as it coursed through her; the hair on her arms and neck on end. Unexpectedly, she heard her dad, as clear as if he was stood beside her: "Be safe Daisy, I'll be here when you get back. Love, Dad". As soon as she heard him, the words were swallowed by the echoes.

The tolling sound seemed to corral the light into a cocoon around her and she felt lighter and lighter. There was a growing sense of separation, as though part of her could slip easily out of her body. Her mind raced, trying to rationalise what was happening. She grabbed her rucksack, as if holding it might bring some comfort. Still anxious, but trying her best to relax, she gazed deep into the heart of the glorious, glowing light that now filled not just the hollow, but the entire chamber and tunnel.

With the light swirling, she experienced herself as a weightless, limitless energy. She was inside the light, carried upwards through the stone. As the drumming changed, suddenly out of time with itself, the brightness flared, impossibly radiant, as the light on the cliff had. Then with a final flash, Daisy was gone...

Part Three: The Returned

Chapter 26 – By the Boundary Stones

At nineteen, Emmalina Ashton was unconventional in that she was not married. Choices in the village were limited, many marrying distant relations; some marrying closer than that. Her elder sisters Alice and Anne, had married before they had turned eighteen. Alice moving to a farm near Sherwood Forest, Anne remaining closer, becoming the wife of the minister at Abney. Her friends from the village, Elswyth and Maryell, also wed early and catching up with them on market days, high days and holidays, they talked wearily of scrubbing and cleaning, of having babies with little say in the matter.

From 1665, those in the area wanting a marriage with minimal pomp and ceremony, could travel the eight-mile journey to Peak Forest, the minister able to issue marriage licenses without having to record quite so many details – for those with the time and patience to wait as he insisted on reciting his full title each time, that of Principal Official and Judge in Spiritualities in the Peculiar Court of Peak Forest.

Tom, a farmhand from Bakewell, liked to follow Emmalina around the weekly market, held regularly in the nearby town since the 1300s. He would duck his head in her presence, sometimes clutching a posey of wildflowers; hovering behind her as though perpetually on the cusp of an overture.

Then came the one occasion when the stars must have aligned favourably, the day he found the confidence to do just that – thrusting the wilting flowers at her and mumbling into his chin. Emmalina had been gracious, taking the flowers and responding with a polite thank-you, her air of ambivalence leaving him little to work with. If she was honest with herself – and she usually was – she wanted more than a farmhand, keeping herself clean and tidy in the hope of meeting a country gentleman at one of the markets, or larger fairs. A man of law, a wool merchant; even a catchpole would suit her in a crisis, or so she imagined.

And so it was, that she kept an eye on her surroundings, especially the markets and fairs, not to mention each time she passed the comings-and-goings at the village inn. Always a tangled medley of human existence, there would be horses, carts, tradesmen, brigands and soldiers passing through, moving on, or sitting in the sunshine drinking ale and making deals.

It was one such day, a warm June morning in 1666 when she would usually be delivering homemade bread around the village, that she first saw Mr. Bliss. At the time he was going by the name of Edwin, in his finest guise of a respectable country squire; clothes cleaned and pressed by the landlord's daughter at the inn where he took lodgings.

On this particular morning, bright with untroubled sunshine, Mr. Bliss had exited the church graveyard, or rather, the ever-expanding patch of ground rapidly becoming home to the majority of the village. It was not unusual back then, for those awaiting collection to find their way to the graveyard or the church – a lifelong fear instilled in them when alive still lingering – and more often than not, as he was at one of the two locations, they would be at the other.

Rarely did he require help with his collections and rarer still did he accept any, but Marshall Howe knew everyone in the village and miles beyond. Having been one of the earliest to catch the plague, he had survived. Figuring lightning might be benevolent enough to not strike twice, he had offered his services to the village, digging graves and assisting with burying the dead – a role that had regularly brought him into contact with Mr. Bliss.

As the plague moved through the village like an invisible assailant, through the summer and autumn of 1665, there had been talk of abandoning the village and fleeing to Sheffield. Some did, but the majority deferred to the churchman, Mompesson, who had urged the villagers to sit tight and quarantine themselves and the village, in the hope that such generosity of spirit might prevent the plague spreading into the north of England.

Many villagers, including what was left of the elders, talked of this long into the night, those well enough at least, around a blazing bonfire. Maintaining a distance and an absence of human touch, they called to one another under a smoky moon. To say they embraced the idea of quarantine without resistance, would be naïve, yet by the time they were wending their way to their respective cottages, they had agreed it was necessary for the greater good, painfully aware it meant certain death for many in the village.

With the quarantine in place, the villagers found themselves at the mercy of those outside, who would bring food and leave it on the boundary stones that marked the edge of the village. As payment, coins were left in a trough of vinegar, or in vinegar-filled holes chiselled into the boundary stones – an attempt to sterilise the coins and ensure no one bringing food had direct contact with the villagers. Marshall, still immune from a second helping of the plague, took on the task of moving the supplies of food and essentials, pushing them around the village, in a wooden barrow he scrubbed with a vinegar-soaked cloth every night.

Meeting Mr. Bliss for the first time, he had felt a chill as the well-dressed dandy spoke to him. Leaning against the graveyard wall, where it opened onto fields sloping steeply to the tree line, he had been munching on an apple, a safe one from one of the packages left by the stones.

The man had introduced himself as Edwin. He had given Marshall three names and asked if he might point him in their direction. In place of any further explanation, he had offered a gloved hand aglint with silver coins.

Marshall had found little to like in the man. Granted, he was well-dressed and spoke well, but clinging to him was a coldness, even on warm days, as though he had inexplicably stepped out of winter. He had told Edwin two of the names he had not long buried, pointing over the wall at matching mounds of earth; two in a field of dozens. Mr. Bliss had seen more than just those two waiting beside the mounds; some confused, most desolate.

And so it came to pass that Mr. Bliss – whose handful of coins never ran dry – used Marshall as a shortcut. Whilst he never shared his reason for being in Eyam, or his reason for spending more time around the dead than Marshall himself, the gravedigger had his own views. Cheerless opinions that after a tankard or three of ale, he would openly share with anyone who listen and those with no interest in doing so.

Emmalina and Mr. Bliss had been headed in opposite directions along the dusty street through the village. The only two people out despite the warm weather, the plague having shuttered windows and bolted doors. Gardens, however, were thriving, the street heavy with a mingled fragrance of herbs and flowers, the hum of bees weaving a drowsy air into the warmth.

He had seen her from a distance. She moved unhurriedly, a basket on one arm, dressed in a simple linen dress dyed dark green, her feet bare and dusty.

Like any of the best pairings, all that was needed for the sweetest of beginnings was a shared smile. Followed, on this occasion, by a robust "Good Morning Miss," from Edwin, who had stepped aside for her, with somewhat exaggerated chivalry.

Edwin was a handsome man. Tall and slim with strong features and always clad in the finery of the day, which Mr. Bliss preferred in black, and aged around twenty-five. A man to swell bodices and breeches alike.

Emmalina had flashed her green eyes at him and bid him good morning, her cheeks ruby red as he held her gaze with a confidence she had found stirring; his eyes dark and impossible to read. When she had looked and smiled, he had lit up inside. As she passed, he had caught a waft of fresh bread and keen to prolong their meeting was going to ask whether he might buy a loaf, but the moment passed and before he knew it, she was blithely on her way without a backward glance.

He had stood on the spot astonished; no less transfixed than the first time he had seen fire. It was as though she remained and he could still gaze upon her treacle-coloured hair tumbling down her back, fall once more into the shamrock glimmer of her eyes; desperate for a memory of her dimpled smile to lodge forever in his mind. Moving on reluctantly, he had been unable to focus on his collections. Each time he looked at the parchment, or chased down one of the poor souls around the village, his mind was anywhere else:

Those freckles! Drawn over the bridge of her nose, the top of her cheeks, like a constellation as yet unnamed!

How unguarded her smile had been...holding his gaze in a manner that might have been considered by some in the village, as impudent.

He estimated she was around eighteen or nineteen and immediately began wondering whether she would be troubled by their difference in age – a few thousand years at least. With Edwin having the look of a man of twenty-five, that was as much as he would be sharing, should their paths cross again; an event he intended to do everything in his power to make happen.

It was less than a week later, leaving the inn looking for Marshall, that he and Emmalina did cross paths once more. She had woken that day feeling bold and catching sight of him, called out cheerily. Looking around he couldn't see her. On her second, louder call, he spied her leaning from an open window in a row of cottages he had been a regular visitor to of late, only two days since having called for an entire family of seven.

He walked through a wooden gate into a small cottage garden. Threading carefully between poppies, hollyhocks and foxgloves and a modest, yet flourishing herb garden, he had stood beneath the window, with all the burgeoning passion of Romeo beneath that infamous balcony.

"I was going to take a walk up to the boundary stones, might you be headed that way?" she had asked merrily.

"It would be my pleasure to accompany you, Miss," he had replied eagerly.

"It's Emmalina. I'll be down now."

Minutes later she had appeared at the door in a crimson-dyed dress with an open neckline, ideally suited to a summer day; traces of repeated darning, in what he assumed was her hand. Her hair was plaited, drawing the sun to her face. It highlighted her freckles and her short, delicately upturned nose. As before, she was barefoot, something he later learned was her preference, keen to feel the earth under her feet, the mud between her toes.

They had walked side by side through the village, before taking a tight footpath winding behind the cottages and away from the village. As it stretched uphill and the cottages fell behind, they were replaced by rolling fields and clusters of trees in the full bloom of midsummer. Although conversation was easy, neither could avoid the deaths in the village, Emmalina sharing she had recently lost her father – something he was all too aware of. As Edwin, however, he had the opportunity to listen, give her time to talk. Her father had been popular throughout the village and surrounding area. A cooper by trade, the plague had dried up his work and left him at a loss. Emmalina felt this was a significant factor in him being taken by the plague, forced to spend more time with others, when ordinarily he would be tucked away with his barrels, in a modest lean-to behind the cottage. When she had become teary, Edwin had plucked a silk handkerchief from his pocket and offered it to her. Dabbing at her eyes, she had looked up at him and he had turned her gently into an embrace. As she sobbed onto his shoulder, he held her gently. They had stayed that way for a long time.

At the boundary stones, they had sat close on one of the larger rocks. Emmalina had clapped her hands together, seeing a buzzard circling, the sky the blue of painted fine china. Mr. Bliss had watched the buzzard and then without preamble – and somewhat unexpectedly for Emmalina – had asked her if she was betrothed. She had blushed and laughed, then blushed some more as his intention sank in. Her father, she had explained, had hoped she would wed a farmer, a local man she had met once or twice before the plague, at dances in the fields.

Emmalina loved her father dearly, but had made it clear that she had no interest in marrying that particular man. They had argued, her father registering disappointment at her decision – not to mention the vehemence with which she had voiced it. Had her family been aristocracy, she would have had even less say, property and land being the only considerations for a favourable marriage. Fortunately, her family though hard working, were not landowners, nor aristocracy and over time, she had persuaded her father to allow her agency in choosing a suitor.

The arrival of the Marriage Act of 1653, like much legislation of the time, reflected not only the increasing domination of the church, but also bit hard into the freedom of people to choose how they married. Rigorous parish records and an insistence of the issuing of church banns had been introduced, alongside an unrelenting push to standardise the vows exchanged – all of which had conspired to make marriage a more formal and stuffier affair. Then, as now, religious control masquerading as legislation, did little to prevent couples meeting, falling in love and having considerable sex with one another.

It was against this backdrop that little by little, a plan formed in both of their minds, albeit an unspoken one, based solely and passionately, around coming together in blissful harmony.

Following that first walk out, they had fallen into each other swiftly and completely. As the summer reclined long and lazy, whispers stole through the village almost as fast as the plague. People talked over fences, shouted across the street to one another about Emmalina and the strange, pompous man that went by the name of Edwin. Emmalina was well liked and little of the meaner conversation was directed at her. Edwin, however, the villagers tended to keep at a distance.

"Happen he *might* make her happy," Emmalina had heard the landlord's daughter saying as she entered the inn one afternoon, her voice trailing off as soon as she saw her.

"Or take her breath away," sneered Granny Sullivan, not seeing Emmalina, "forever, like," she'd added, folding her arms over the bar.

Despite the reservations, the conversations that would fade as she approached, neither Emmalina or Edwin had any intention of paying them heed, let alone changing their decision to spend as much time together as possible.

"Let them chatter and gossip. I care not!" Emmalina had laughed one evening as she linked her arm in his.

They had been passing the inn as night was falling, where a group of men, traders mostly, packing up and preparing to leave, had sniggered and jeered.

"Then I too, care not," Edwin had said with a broad smile, tilting his head back and walking taller as the men roared.

That was the night, some hours later, Emmalina had first accompanied Edwin to his room, sneaking up the back staircase having first made sure everyone was safely ensconced in the bar downstairs. Undressing her, Mr. Bliss had found his hands trembling. Even when her dress had slipped to the floor, he felt anxious when she took him by the hand and pulled him to the bed. He had learned that night – and eagerly – that allowing Emmalina to take the lead eased his nerves considerably.

And so, they found themselves wrapped in one another the following morning, as the new day nudged its rays through the wooden shutters. Waking slowly, each reaching to caress the other, Mr. Bliss had tried to ignore the squawking raven outside, grateful when the sounds of traders had drowned out its croaking. Without warning – or dressing – Emmalina had slid from the bed. With a stout swing of the shutters, she had sent the bird spinning into the air, before diving under the blankets, and wriggling into Edwin's arms as she chuckled to herself.

Three days later, having spent each night together at the inn, they had wrapped themselves in the blanket and shared a jug of ale – an action that led to them spending a lot longer in bed. Afterwards, as Emmalina had stood by the mirror arranging her hair, Mr. Bliss had watched her, entranced. In the small walnut cabinet beside the bed, scratched and candle-scorched by countless occupants, was a silver and diamond ring he had acquired in the nearby town of Buxton.

Each time she had stayed with him, he had drifted off to sleep planning to ask her the next morning, yet the drowsy combination of nakedness and morning ale always seemed to prompt a change of direction. One that more often than not, concluded with her sitting astride him, as he gradually surrendered the power of speech.

This time, however, he would not be distracted. Slipping on a pair of trousers, he gently slid open the drawer of the cabinet as Emmalina concentrated, tugging at an eyebrow with a pair of tweezers. Padding softly over, he bent on one knee behind her.

"Emmalina?"

She turned, gazing across the room unable to see him at first. Then, with a grin, she looked down at him.

"Edwin…"

"Emmalina," he asked holding up the ring, "would you do me the honour of becoming my wife?"

At the sight of the ring and the sound of his words, Emmalina's face had lit up and she had squealed. Slipping the ring onto her wedding finger, twisting it this way and that in the light, she reached down and took his face in her hands.

"Edwin, there's nothing I'd –

At this point, a look of confusion had crossed her face as she coughed. It was a heavy cough, lasting a while; the first note of a sombre tune.

"There's nothing I would love more," she replied after the coughing had passed, "of course I'll be your wife!"

Mr. Bliss leapt up and scooped her into his arms, lifting her off the ground. Setting her down, he was about to kiss her, when another cough rattled through her. "I'm…so…happy!" she told him between coughs.

When they separated later, she headed for home and he headed out for a day of collections, he knew there would come a time when he would have to tell her about his work, if only to explain his sudden and frequent absences. The coughing was forgotten, as each set out, heads aswim with wedding plans.

Sometimes, she didn't stay through the night, Mr. Bliss struggling to explain why he wasn't always available. It was one such morning two days later, that Mr. Bliss returned from London, sweating and smelling of smoke. He found an angry raven pacing the sill and tapping furiously at the shutters. Flinging them open, almost knocking the bird from the sill, the raven had rushed into the room and flung the parchment at Mr. Bliss, before flapping and squawking its way back out.

As he did each morning, he took bread and a jug of light ale in his room. He supped at it thoughtfully as he unrolled the parchment and took stock, making a plan for the day. Whilst Eyam remained a priority, he covered every nook, cranny and corner of the world, plague (and death of any kind) by no means unique to Derbyshire, appearing and disappearing as necessary until headway had been made.

That morning, chilly even for early September, whilst reading through the names and locations of his collections, one name had made him sit bolt upright, a sickening panic overtaking him. Three names from the end of the parchment, was written the following:

Emmalina Ashton, 19. Eyam village, Derbyshire, England.

Chapter 27 – Blood on Snow

Ulla pushed the door gently, not wanting to wake anyone. The day before had been a new moon, with her serene gaze looking the other way, the garden was dark and obscure. The paving was hard against her bare feet and she hurried across to the grass, to where it was damp and overgrown. Her feet were less used to grass, but she liked the way its delicate agility tickled her feet; not at all like the packed snow and ice she had grown up with.

Few people understood her need to be outdoors, not least the three she shared the house with. One of them Ulla had never seen. They rented the room above hers and all she knew of them, was a hefty footfall. She pictured them as male, short, and probably balding; feet booming when he stomped back and forth. More than once, he had had made her lightbulb flicker.

Ms. Olsson, she sometimes ate breakfast and the occasional evening meal with. It was never arranged, they just shared the old-fashioned Formica kitchen table, if they happened to be there at the same time, arguing good-naturedly over the best of the mismatched, unsteady chairs.

Ms. Olsson was a music teacher who ate a lot of tinned tuna, whether breakfast or her evening meal. She would smear it over thick slices of heavily buttered toast with tomato ketchup, or mix it with pasta, mayonnaise and a few aggressive twists of black pepper. Whichever way she had her tuna, whether followed with dessert or not, her evening meal was always washed down with three large bottles of German beer; cloudy and hoppy. More often than not, she would force out a damp belch into her hand, which did nothing to mitigate the beery, fishy odour that could easily swamp the modest kitchen. If she had dessert, which was rare, it always came from a paper bag in her cardigan pocket. She would lay out three chunks of coconut ice on a small china plate and eat meticulously, with a small knife and fork, one morsel at a time. After each piece she would dab her mouth with a napkin, fold it carefully and lay it on the table, before tackling the next chunk.

Ulla took her to be around fifty, but her preference for brown and beige, combined with sensibly bobbed mousey hair, made it hard to be certain. Beneath her faded appearance, she could have just as easily been thirty-five. They would exchange the most basic of pleasantries, both really preferring to eat in silence. Whilst each took comfort in the presence of the other, neither felt the need for anything approaching a friendship – anything relying on regularity or commitment – to develop.

Mimi, the other member of their household was from Australia, and talked at length about only passing through and moving on. Mimi had lived there longer than any of them. Mimi was twenty-one, blonde, bubbly and usually seen in the early hours, returning loudly from what they referred to as "one of their gatherings". What they did for work, who their friends were, what they did with their days, was a mystery to Ulla.

Where possible, apart from sharing a meal with Ms. Olsson, Ulla kept herself to herself. A rota for cleaning and using the washer had been devised by Ms. Olsson. On the first day of each month, it would be printed on stiff card and displayed in a plastic pocket stuck to the outside of the fridge. Ms. Olsson had colour-coded each person and the rota was never challenged. Ulla was green and the rota had recently revealed the name of the heavy-hoofed man living above her: Dag, who was red. Mimi was pink; Ms. Olsson, oatmeal. What the rota couldn't regulate, was those moments when people might pass in the hallway, or bump awkwardly for the same kitchen cupboard. Shadows on the landing catching a door closing; the sound of a key rattling a lock.

With Mimi rarely home at night, Dag usually pacing himself into oblivion by 10pm and Ms. Olsson tucked up in bed around the same time, night time was when the house and the garden belonged to Ulla.

With no one sharing the table late at night, Ulla would enjoy cheese and crackers with a spicy Piccalilli she had found in the cupboard and taken into her heart. Afterwards, licking her lips, her mouth still spicy, she would brew a black coffee and take it out into the garden.

For Ulla, the garden was by far the best part of the house. Cramped and overgrown, managed occasionally by the owner, someone that no one had ever seen; Ulla had heard a lawnmower once, early on a Saturday. It was a long, narrow, garden filled with shade that mirrored those either side. Much of the day, it lay within the silhouette of its neighbours, its share of the sun not coming around until late afternoon.

A pair of willows had claimed one side of the garden, always bent close, softly murmuring. At the far end, beyond a lifetime of grass, was an abundant hawthorn hedge. It was here that Ulla liked to spend her free time, settling each time on the ground, patiently waiting for an audience.

A breeze flapped her pyjama bottoms as she crossed the garden. She zipped up her hoodie and peering into the inky gloom, made for the hedge. Before she reached it, she froze: she could smell blood. Its metallic whiff filled her nose before she could see blood; work out where it came from. Her heart raced as she reassured herself. *This is a memory, no more.*

To her left came a sudden, frantic rustling in the bushes; the clamour of an animal unsure of its way. She scanned the garden, the dimmed house offering no illumination. It was only when a security light came on next door – the result of the animal and its nocturnal adventures – that she saw feathers spread across the ground in front of her.

Ulla knew birds, but what bird this had been was hard to identify. *Corvid?* Feathers darkened the grass like storm clouds; the inside of the bird now outside. In the short snap of light, innards steamed as a claret puddle seeped into the grass. Faced with the blood, the iron taste catching at the back of her throat, she was thrown back to that day as a child, more than twenty winters ago. The day hunters stalking reindeer, had killed her grandmother, Eija.

What the men had done that day, had put her beyond the reach of any help. At eighty-three, Eija had seen enough births and deaths, people and animals, to have lost count; memories enough to swell a runestone bag. She had been happy, hungry and lost. Laboured until her fingers bled. Lived on shoots and snow more times than she hadn't. When a bullet from a hunting rifle shattered her skull, she had sagged like a puppet.

Ulla had raced over to her the moment she saw her crumple. She found her grandmother lying on her side, dark blood oozing from her temple. Ulla had cradled her head, as her grandmother had many times when she was a child, blood congealing in her lap. There had been nothing she could do, besides hold her hand as she left for the light. Eija had died where she had been born, in the snow. Surrounded by the hot breath and low grunting of her circling herd, beneath a covering of hard stars.

Even after Ulla had scrubbed and cleaned the dress over and over, the blood had remained.

She had kept it for a long time, folded carefully inside a wooden box. The box had come with her to Sweden, when she had been put in the care of a distant auntie; distant in both her connection to Ulla and her care.

Eventually, Ulla had burned the dress. The ashes lived in a blue glass jar, hidden in a drawer, until the following spring. Her grandmother had liked spring the most and watching them gently float away on a wide river, Ulla had said goodbye.

The memory of blood on snow remained inside of her; a soundless trauma the colour of memories.

That had been many years ago and the last thing she had expected, was for that memory to rush her unbidden; hauled from her depths by the smell and sight of the bird on the lawn.

Chapter 28 – Amor Fati

As the coffee machine babbled away, Gabriel squeaked open the window, flooding the kitchen with birdsong. The melodic tweet of a blackbird piped up, mingling with the two-tone skank of a wren. As if prompted by the competition, the squeaky-wheel call of a black and white warbler joined in. Exploding suddenly, a riot of gulls drowned out the others. Circling in a wide arc, higher than all of them, was a Red Kite; its lone cry like a soul moving on.

Gabriel wandered outside with his coffee. He hoped Daisy had received his message; he had been thinking about her a lot. He felt sleepy and the unexpectedly sunny, dry day slowly felt cosy around him. Beyond the rusting swing, rocking back and forth in a low wind, was a patch of earth he had thought might take some vegetables. Red and white onions, garlic and perhaps parsnips – all resilient enough for him to forget to check in with regularly. This plan for a vegetable garden, was around the same age as Daisy.

Two-thirds of the way through clearing weeds, ivy and dead plants, having already filled countless garden sacks, he realised he had no onion sets. *Surely garlic was no more complicated than just planting a handful of cloves?* he thought, surveying the freshly turned earth and picturing an autumn bounty. It looked ready enough. Apart from larger stones here and there, a persistent root straining from one corner, his clumsy forking having left nicks revealing its white flesh. Like many a novice gardener, the first hurdle, that of planning ahead, waited not too far in the future, ready to trip him up spectacularly.

Satisfied enough, he was about to head indoors when he heard a crack from the wood beyond the garden, closely followed by a furious rustling. Shielding his eyes from the sun, he peered into the trees, hoping it was the Dik-dik.

He saw a figure struggling to free themselves from the branches. "Hello?" he called out.

Closer now, he saw it a red-haired woman with a rucksack, who stumbled from the woods, swearing as she brushed herself down.

"I'd know that cursing anywhere! Hello Daisy."

"Dad!"

Daisy rushed towards him, still picking leaves out of her hair. She had heard someone call out and it had sounded like her dad – and they were stood in his garden – but until she got closer, it didn't look like him, wrapped up in copious, snowy white hair.

"What the fuck…happened to your hair!" Daisy cried as she launched herself at him.

"Daisy, it's so good to see you again!"

"Please tell me, you're actually alive?" Daisy said squeezing his arm, "I've experienced some strange stuff, so I need to ask!"

Gabriel grinned as he took a step back. "Yes, I am alive. Very much so."

Daisy let out a deep sigh of relief. He looked alive, in fact he looked very well – it was only the long hair and full beard that confused her. "Umm…how come you've got so much hair, Dad?"

Gabriel shook his head slowly. "I'm not sure. I've been somewhere else, I guess time's different there? And what about yours, it's very red."

"Fancied a change," she said with a shrug. "How long you been back? And where exactly have you been? Have you heard any news on Suni?"

"I like it. I've been back a day or two I think…and I'll tell you all about where I've been. Sorry, no, nothing about Suni. What about you, are *you* okay?"

"I think so. No, yes, I am. How I ended up in there," Daisy said pointing behind her, "I've no idea."

"I think you and I have some serious catching up to do! Coffee?"

Daisy nodded eagerly as she linked her arm in his and they made their way indoors. "Definitely."

Later, the day still mild, they sat outside, Donovan's *A Gift from a Flower to a Garden* drifting from the open window. They had talked like two babbling brooks desperate to make a river. Tall grasses and overgrown shrubs bent in the wind, their conversation underscored now and then by the kite, its gliding silhouette shading in the vegetable patch as it passed.

"I heard you – when I was in the tunnel. I mean, sort of heard you?"

"That," replied Gabriel with a grin, "was down to Morfydd. She helped. I wasn't sure it had worked…"

"It worked. Being at Tor's Leap, probably helped too. There's so much more I've not told you, about magic…and about –

Daisy was about to tell him about Lysh but stopped. She wasn't exactly sure what to say; wasn't exactly sure what she was telling herself.

"It'll come out. All in good time."

"It will. Right now, do you mind if I try Suni?" she asked abruptly. Reaching into her pocket she brought out her phone, which was starting to pant, as messages and voicemails that hadn't come through when she was on the island flooded in.

"Dad...dad! He's awake, he's messaged!"

"That is brilliant news."

Daisy didn't reply, already calling Suni.

"Suni! It's so good to hear your voice!"

"Hello, Daisy."

Daisy pulled away from the phone screwing up her face. He sounded preoccupied, like she had interrupted him. "Is now a bad time?"

"Why weren't you here Daisy, when I woke up?"

"I came, a few times. It was really hard, seeing you like that. I thought you might die, or never wake up."

Daisy heard him sigh; his tone softer when he spoke again. "I hadn't considered that, sorry. Thank you for visiting. Where are you now?"

"At Dad's. He's back and safe. I wanted to visit more, but I got caught up with Gwen – you remember Gwen? I've been to this island...actually, if you're up for it, why don't I come see you?"

"I'm at the B&B, in Aberystwyth. My Mum's been staying too – not here, in the town. She wants to take me back to Manchester, fuss over me."

Daisy felt hurt. She had wanted to see him; fix things, if things needed fixing. "Makes sense, I guess. You going back right now?"

"Not right now. Soon, I think. My life is in Manchester."

"What about tonight? Can I come see you, pleeease?"

Suni smiled. It was hard to stay mad at Daisy for long – and he did want to see her. Really wanted to see her. "I'd like that, Daisy. Message me when you're on your way."

"I will and –

"By the way, Daisy...I've got a LOT to tell you!"

"Good! So have I!"

"You want the last bits?" Daisy asked, her fingers hovering over the remains of a giant plate of nachos.

"Yes! Fight you!"

Suni lunged forward and grabbed at a sticky clump of nachos and sour cream, just as Daisy tried to snake her hand around his. He stuffed them into his mouth, trying not to laugh. Any disappointment at her not being at the hospital when he came round, had evaporated the moment he had seen her outside the B&B, the red of her hair catching him off-guard. She'd been surprised to see him wearing his glasses (which she always thought made him look even more serious) and that he'd kept his dark stubble, what he repeatedly insisted was actually a beard.

They had both been hungry and ducked into the first pub they had passed, the Angel. It was busy, students and locals mixing amiably amidst brightly coloured cocktails and heavy rock music. They had squeezed into a corner, taking the only seats left.

Daisy had been telling him about falling off the battlements and the magic she had learned. She had just started telling him about getting drunk and joyriding in the boat, when the nachos had interrupted them.

"You stole a boat?" Suni asked between mouthfuls of food, spitting out crumbs in his excitement.

Daisy had nodded whilst trying to swallow. "Uh-huh."

"Only you Daisy, would get pissed and steal a boat! You could've died."

"Tell me about it!" she said rolling her eyes. "Twice. There was this moment in the water – and I was pretty much drowning – that felt like I was able to...communicate with it, with its energy?"

"Really?"

"Yeah. I can't explain it – like a lot of what happened on the island," she paused, holding off telling him about the drone. "Anyway, how about you? You're the one that's been in a coma or whatever?"

Suni grabbed at a serviette and wiped his mouth, reaching for his beer. He took a long drink, which was no more than an excuse to look at Daisy. To really look: the pale, washed out look he knew she preferred, her bright red hair, her green eyes always searching, her silver thumb ring flashing as she gestured wildly, snatching frequently at the nachos.

"Well..." he began, savouring the pause as he saw Daisy leaning in, eyebrows raised. "Come on!"

They said 'tell everyone', he thought to himself and Daisy was a good starting point.

"Whilst I was...out of it, I left my body. I saw myself in the hospital bed, saw you visit. I tried to let you know I was there, but I couldn't touch you, or get your attention. It was like being invisible."

"Shiiittt." Daisy replied, taking a swig of beer as she thought about her experience in the stone chamber. "You left your body? How did *that* feel?"

"It felt good. Weird, but good. I saw everything the nurses were doing, heard them talking. I thought I was literally going to be like that forever."

"I get that, I felt something similar. Yours sounds kinda amazing though, too? When I –

"There's more. I had...umm...other *visitors*. They just appeared, from this bright light. They were like people, made of light –

"Made of light? Did they look like we do, like, human?"

Suni giggled, pulling a face. "No one looks like you Daisy!"

"Funny. Get on with it...*did* they look like us?"

"Yes...and no. Similar shape, two eyes, mouth and so on. But they shone, like they were lit from inside. I think they healed me, Daisy; it felt like it."

"Then I'm very grateful to them. You should talk to my dad about this as well, at some point. It's so good to have you back!"

"Stop it, you'll make me blush!" Suni said beaming.

Daisy stuck her tongue out then moved closer, checking around before continuing in a lower voice, "I think it's something to do with the light on the cliff. It's changed us. Can you remember what happened?"

Suni nodded quickly, urging her to continue.

"Arwen told me we'd be changed. I do feel different, and all the things at Tor's Leap, definitely felt different."

"I feel different too and -

"Oh, and my dad...he's different – come back with long white hair and a massive white beard. He looks like the fish finger guy!"

Suni grinned at her excitement at being able to talk about her dad again. "So, you, me and your dad, we've all experienced out-there stuff? Maybe that's how I was able to see myself in hospital, see the visitors?"

"Maybe," agreed Daisy. "It's the Kindness, I think," she added. Then, "Did they feel dangerous, these light people?"

"Not at all. They had a power to them, but it was like...like they were made of love. This huge, loving energy. I felt so safe."

"Have you told anyone else, like your folks?"

Suni shook his head. "I wanted to tell you first – my dad's away, with work. I will be telling people though. They want me to."

"*They* want you to?"

"Yes. People need to know they are here, around us. *For* us. Once I'm home I'm doing a video, so I can tell as many people as I can."

"Do it. Maybe there'll be other people who've had experiences like that?" she said eagerly.

"I'm going to. It feels like, I'm meant to do it."

"Oh my god, you're gonna be like that Bridget girl...those videos you made me watch over and over!"

"I'm not even close, Daisy," Suni said in a serious tone. "She's an intuitive...and she's incredible."

"She's incredible," Daisy mimicked, hands over her heart. "You should DM her."

"Like, ask her advice?"

"It can't hurt. The things I saw on the island, like, I don't feel like I want to tell everyone, but you and I, we've both experienced magic, or something like it anyway."

Suni held up his pint glass and Daisy chinked hers against it.

"Here's to magic!"

"Here's to magic!" she replied, pulling her best spooky face.

Chapter 29 – Je Suis Lui et il Est Moi

The moment he had seen her name on the parchment, Mr. Bliss set out to do anything to avoid collecting Emmalina. Whilst there were delaying tactics he might rely upon, the last thing he wanted was to leave her waiting between places.

Ignoring it hadn't worked. Her name appeared each day and gradually moved up the list, until she was his only OVERDUE – something he was more than aware of, not needing the irascible raven alerting him to the fact each morning.

To say that he had been reluctant to use the eagle fetish, would be putting it mildly. Sleepless night followed sleepless night, buried beneath the heartbreak of knowing that Emmalina would have to move on. The eagle was one of his treasures, and he wasn't a man of vast treasure, although he did have a small collection of items acquired over the centuries. Locked in a metal cabinet in one of his quieter offices, a room at the back of a village hall in Derbyshire, the treasures remained.

It had been a rainy day, way back in Iron Age Cymru (Wales), when he had happened upon the carved eagle. He had been collecting souls felled by various diseases, accidents and inclement weather. One of those, an old, wise woman from a settlement deep in the wooded heart of the country.

Heledd had been ready for him. Fully aware of what came next, she had dangled the eagle charm in front of him as they talked. Seeing the glint in his eyes, she had stepped it up, talking of its power; of the magic contained within the smooth stone. How it might be used to travel between worlds, to connect with what she had called 'big magic'. As soon as she started telling him, easing out her tale and delighting as she reeled him in, he had coveted the carving – as was her intention. With him snared, all she had needed to do then was negotiate.

In the end, it had been simple. He had taken the carved eagle and in return, had walked away from collecting her. At her request, Heledd remained between places. She had chosen to remain and watch over her community. Appearing around the settlement, she was still seen and spoken to by the children; by the adults who believed and a handful of older, wiser women who knew the magic allowing them to communicate with Heledd.

With time running short, Mr. Bliss had found Emmalina at the boundary stones. As Edwin, he had done his best to answer her questions, not least her confusion as to how he could see her. She knew she was dead, but Mr. Bliss was keen to spend time with her as Edwin, rather than as Death; anything that might keep her from moving on.

By giving the carving to Emmalina, he had permitted her to remain longer. When she was wearing it, it helped him to know where she was. They had spent time at the stones, as they had when she had been alive. These were precious moments for them both, walking and talking, circling the meadows or sitting close by one another, whispering and giggling as lovers do.

After Emmalina had gone – in the end guided on by Tallulah when he refused, who had also taken the eagle carving from her, Mr. Bliss had split open.

He had turned his back on his outstanding collections and the following morning when the raven appeared, he had strangled it and thrown it into the fire, closely followed by the parchment. Heading downstairs, he had got drunk for the remainder of the day; then the remainder of the week, with no plans beyond continuing the trend.

People passing through the inn had given his table a wide berth. Some whispered about him, others sniggered and pointed without bothering to lower their voice. Marshall had sat nearby once or twice, but unable to get any sense out of him, had added to the local gossip of Edwin having gone mad with grief, frequent mutterings of how losing Emmalina had reduced him to a tangle of tears and fury.

He had been unable to escape his work indefinitely, Tallulah having made it clear that was not an option available to him. With a bitter and furious reluctance, he had eventually returned to work. Whilst the majority of his work was travelling to collect souls, there were those too, who through sudden death or abject confusion upon dying, found themselves lingering at one of his offices, or hovering around the situation or event that had led to their demise. Those who lingered through confusion, he dealt with swiftly: an aloof explanation and a gentle push, and they would be on their way to the light, for a restorative return to the Kindness, each participating in their life review and enjoying their own aftershow party.

One of the situations requiring a delicacy he did not find easy to connect with, were those who found it difficult to move on; those with no interest in moving on. These were the lovers, the poets, the lost, the damned and, in his opinion, the thoroughly stubborn and scared. Those of iron bonds and promises made whilst alive – all those 'I'll never leave you' and 'We're together forever' exclamations (not to mention threats) – that meant certain souls refused to leave. There were souls determined to stay with their family, with lovers, with their cat, their dog, their hamsters – and in more recent years, their SUV or sports car; even their mobile phone.

And so it was, there came a time, one hundred and nine years after losing Emmalina, that Mr. Bliss discovered a shocking secret.

It had been a regular day, one of travelling without having to travel, simply arriving wherever he needed to arrive. He had been in the south of France, one of those delightful villages filled with bees and sunshine; wine and cheese.

He was there to collect a girl of fifteen, Eléa, who had died falling from a mountain path. One minute, she had been crouching to sniff a bunch of bright citrine flowers, the next, she had tripped over her long dress getting up and lost her balance. When he arrived, she had been sat on a rock at the base of the mountain perplexed, a scattering of yellow petals all around.

He had greeted her in French, assuming that so soon after passing she would prefer her recent tongue. Their conversation had been sparse, Eléa asking questions impatiently. She had been furious that she had only made fifteen. This was mainly due to her having recently met a girl of seventeen, Ise, from the next village and their attraction had been immediate.

Pacing on the spot, glancing at Mr. Bliss and back up the mountainside, she was desperate to return to the path and pick the flowers. She had insisted he allow her to collect some, bind them with a vine and leave them outside Ise's home, even if she wasn't able to talk with her.

Mr. Bliss had been unbending. There was no time to be picking flowers; no time for love. Moments away from encouraging her into the light, which looked very much like a shimmering doorway in the mountainside, her countenance had altered drastically. Where before, he had been addressing a slim, dark-haired young woman, he now found himself faced with a stocky man of around sixty, bulky and square-shouldered, with a scowl of menace.

This had not happened before.

When he spoke to the man, he gave no reply. A firmer demand resulted in no change and Mr. Bliss realised that either the man could not hear him, or was unable to communicate. As he was waiting to see what would happen, without warning the man once more took on the appearance of Eléa. She had looked at Mr. Bliss, shaking her head in confusion and said, "Je suis lui et il est moi." – "I am he and he is me."

Before he could talk to her, the man appeared again. This time he had grinned as he jabbed his fingers toward his chest. Mr. Bliss had stared, convinced he was about to become the butt of a joke he had neither the time nor patience for. As the man vanished, he was replaced not by Eléa, but with a naked baby bawling loudly as it wriggled on the dusty earth. Mr. Bliss had stepped back immediately, having no idea what to do with a live baby. It had stared up at him, brown eyes gleaming with an inner light; depth enough to catch constellations.

He had shooed the child away with his hand, which hadn't done much. One last time, the child became Eléa, then the surly journeyman, before finally shimmering in front of him as Eléa. She had raised her eyebrows and opened her eyes wide. That was when the secret fell away, the moment the penny dropped – the eyes in each of the three...had been the same eyes!

Once he had guided Eléa into the warm, woozy light she had paused, giving him a grin before she had stepped into the vibrating light and disappeared. Left standing at the foot of the mountain, with a view that would cause an office of travel agents to implode with slavering dreams of commission, Mr. Bliss tried to process what had happened. He reasoned that what he had seen, had been some kind of reminiscence, of two of Eléa's previous manifestations. Lives lived before arriving here, before growing into the soft-spoken, freckled teenager that had fallen from the mountain path.

Although this had been the first time Mr. Bliss had seen this, and something that since had proved rare, it was not an isolated incident. Forty-seven years later, it had happened again – a soldier killed during the Battle of Dervenakia, during the Greek War of Independence. He too, had changed from the man stood over his corpse, to an elderly man, then a particularly obnoxious nine-year old child. None of them had spoken of it, in the way Eléa had, but it had felt very similar.

With this first experience and those that followed, the origins of a way back to Emmalina had crowded his head. A desperate need took hold: he had to track her down, discover who she had been after her life as Emmalina; to eventually find her in a new place and time.

Dragging his awareness back to his immediate predicament, he paced back and forth in the cave. His time out had become only about Emmalina – and he had to get out.

Outside the cave was a clear day with a cloudless sky, the waterfalls gleaming. A perky wind swayed the crowns of the trees, leaves like scalloped shells, as sunlight flickered and curled through the foliage. Looking down, the rocks fell away steep and sharp. There was no way he could climb down; no way to leave easily. There was one way that might work...

Rushing to the rear of the cave, he tensed and took a deep breath. With all his might he ran at the mouth of the cave, launching himself into the air. Seconds later, he plunged through the air, crashing into the branches of a stiff fir. Bouncing off a sturdy bough, he cartwheeled into a tumble. Faster and faster as the ground raced to meet him, small and sturdy branches alike doing little to slow his descent. As the ground came nearer and nearer, he closed his eyes...

He was back in the cave, as if the last few minutes had never happened. His body had no signs of injury; no signs of having just plunged a few hundred feet through a packed forest.

Disappointed but undeterred, he ran even faster and jumped again. As a fall, it was identical to the previous one. Once again, he found himself transported to the cave at the precise moment he should have hit the ground; as though someone, somewhere, was pressing a reset button.

Frustrated, and cursing under his breath, he took stock. Having tried five more times to escape the cave, only to plummet through the air and return, it was time to try something different. Inching along the ground he shifted around until he was able to lower himself out of the cave, legs dangling as he held on. He released his grip...and ricocheted down the prickly rocks, colliding with a jutting outcrop that sent him spinning into the air. This time the ground came even faster, the tree-cover thinner at the base of the mountain.

Fuming, he glowered at the mouth of the cave. Returning to the back, tucking his shirt into his trousers as he went, he rushed forward and executed a delightful series of cartwheels, the fourth of which took him further out than before, arcing through the air, before sinking like a stone into the bright green...

"Can I help you?" a woman asked. She looked to be around fifty, wearing a stylish navy business suit and polished black brogues, with a luxurious mane of expertly arranged grey hair. White Musk surrounded her – not to mention the entire building – like tear gas.

Mr. Bliss looked around. He had expected the cave, but this was an open-plan office, of smoked glass, chrome and beige wood. People were sat on tall stools – seating he felt was better suited to bars.

"I doubt it."

"Well, you can't just stand there. I'm Evelyn. I work here Wednesdays and Fridays. Customer Experience Manager, that's me."

"My name is Mr. Bliss. I am looking for my office."

"Nice to meet you, Mr. Bliss – loving that visor by the way, very purple – do you have a first a name?"

"Yes, I do," he responded coolly, removing the visor and stuffing into a nearby bin.

"Right. Erm…so you can set up anywhere. Just login, the details are on each desk, and you're off."

"Login?"

"Yes, the Wi-Fi code is on there."

"The what?"

"Wi-Fi. Makes the internet work."

"I just want my desk. My computer and my phone."

"That's no problem," Evelyn said with a practised smile, "any desk is your desk."

"What do you mean, 'any desk is your desk'? I want *my* desk. *My* things."

"Ahh, I see what's happening here…this is your first time, first time hot desking, yeah? It took me a while to get jiggy with it."

"This is not my office, I'm in the wrong place…and hot desking sounds horrific."

"Oh, it's great. Occasionally, I even get a window."

Mr. Bliss stalked off without comment, headed for what he took to be a door that would allow him to leave. It turned out, it led to a narrow, windowless room, garishly bright beanbags on the floor and two sets of lurid fuchsia shelves. On one set, a stack of tatty board games and on each shelf of the other, a repugnant plastic plant waiting to outlive time. A young man in a t-shirt and jogging bottoms, with a pointed beard and gigantic green headphones, turned and looked up from one of the beanbags, lifting the headphones to one side.

"Don't mind me dude, just chilling. You do you."

"No."

"Heyyy man, steady on, that's some heavy hostility there," the man bleated. "Here's where we chill. Drama-free zone, this."

Mr. Bliss pictured himself taking the man's breath from his body – and snapping his neck for good measure – but managed to restrain himself. Since the cave, since his plan to find Emmalina had reawakened, he was trying hard to follow the rules; to collect only those who had already died, without intervening or drawing attention to himself – despite having quickly decided this man was an imbecile.

He turned for the door, pausing with his hand on the handle. "Enjoy chilling, young man –

"That's more like it," the man interrupted nodding slowly, "see, we're all friends here."

"As I was saying, before you cut across me...enjoy chilling young man. I'll be back for you, very soon. See. You. Next. Tuesday."

Having navigated identical stairwells, side-stepping another couple who seemed hellbent on helping him waste his time at a random space beside other random spaces – none of which fell anywhere near the description of a desk – he finally made it out of the building.

He found himself on a busy city street, though which city he wasn't certain. Exhaust-fumes and noise swamped him – traffic, people, ringing phones, car alarms, non-specific clattering and banging – and he ducked into the first alleyway he saw. Closing his eyes and concentrating hard, he pictured his office in Wales...

When he opened his eyes, he was there. The dark, drab wood panelling had never looked so appealing.

Back in the office, collections filling up a cheap mobile phone that had appeared on the desk without him having asked for it, Mr. Bliss settled into his chair. In his absence, someone had adjusted it and it took him ages, fiddling and cursing, until he got it right again. He switched on his computer and as it started up sluggishly, he began working through the phone messages.

Little had changed: numerous collections to attend to, many of which were overdue. In amongst these, was a message from Tallulah:

Ivor, I hope your time away has been restful and productive. Please catch up as soon as possible, the agency staff have left a right fucking mess. I appreciate you. Thanks, Ivor.

Well, that was something, he concluded, to no one. It also read like she wasn't about to return him to the cave any time soon.

He was now overdue in Barking, Malmö, Tuscon and Stornoway – and that was just for starters. As he was preparing to leave, still wading through the messages, having at least reached the ones that were due soon rather than overdue, he was surprised to see one of his collections was an unusual one; by no means straightforward. One, that although it would take him back to somewhere increasingly familiar, was not without considerable risk.

Chapter 30 – The Kicker

As Gabriel wandered into the kitchen, the early morning creaks and sighs of the cottage could be heard. A dream had come with him, trailing like a lost ghost: he had been at the house in Manchester with Rebecca and Daisy. It had come like a memory, but in the dream, Daisy was older than when he had left. Smoking a cigarette waiting for his coffee, it lingered, taking effort to remind himself he lived in Wales; that this was not the kitchen in Manchester. Teasing reality from the dream was like trying to remember where he had put his keys.

Although she had been there for the last week, he still hadn't told Daisy everything. Physically, he felt the best he had in years, but his mind felt increasingly spongy and fragile, like it might shift on its axis any minute. In an attempt to hold on to something, he began to fixate on garlic – something tangible he could hold in his hand, push into the moist soil. New life to be nurtured. *Perhaps this is what dementia is,* he pondered staring out of the kitchen window, *a slippage between this world and the next, as our earthly time grows shorter?*

Had Daisy not wandered in at that point, he might easily have spent most of the day staring out of the window, tracking a faint white glow that seemed to pulsate and peep now and then, from deep in the woods.

"Happy Birthday my love!"

"Aww, thanks Dad. Nice to see you're wearing your jumper. You got coffee on?"

"What do you think," Gabriel answered happily as he handed her a steaming mug, which she drank from eagerly. "Right, come through to the lounge…"

"Can we sit out? It looks like a nice day."

"Why not. I'll be out in a minute…"

As Daisy wandered into the garden with her coffee, Gabriel ducked into the lounge to retrieve an envelope and a small parcel wrapped in tissue paper. As he was on his way outside, Daisy came stomping back in. "I literally got outside and it started pissing it down!"

"How lovely, a little bit of Manchester, just for your 24th."

Daisy grinned. "Twenty-four. Fuck, I feel old. You been working your magic, making it rain!"

"My magic, yes!" Gabriel replied, waving his hands around his head as he laughed. "And if you're old, I'm fucked."

As Daisy sat beside him on the settee, he handed her the envelope which she tore into, sliding out a card, birthday greetings in blocky, garish green neon.

"You been saving this?! Very retro."

"All the rage, according to the lady in the shop."

Reading the message inside, she felt her stomach turn over. His handwriting was worse than ever. It looked like he had stopped halfway through writing her name, correcting it with heavy scribbling. Either that, or he'd decided to call her Doosy from now on. She jumped up and jammed the card between the clutter on the mantlepiece.

"You'll love this," he said waving the parcel at her, "you've waited a long time…"

Daisy took it from him. It was heavier than it looked. "Aww Dad, is it the keys to the Jensen! Is it!"

"You'll be lucky!"

Squeezing it, sniffing it, her anticipation grew. Pulling the tissue paper away in clumps she revealed what was inside.

"Dad!" she shrieked delightedly as she tugged out the carved eagle.

"It feels like the right time...and actually, it's more yours than mine."

And you're gonna need it, he said to himself.

Daisy was about to put the necklace over her head, when Gabriel stopped her with a hand on her arm. "Don't put it on just yet. I want to tell you more about it, prepare you, I suppose."

Daisy nodded quickly and set it down on the arm of the settee, glancing at it frequently. "Whilst you're there," she said, getting comfier as she moved the cushions about, "tell me about Quscu – have I said it right? – I found all these journals when I was tidying my room..."

Hearing her refer to it as 'my room' made Gabriel smile. It was still hard to accept Daisy and he had found each other again, even more so that, she'd allowed him back into her life with what, to him at least, had felt like very little fuss. He still nursed a private doubt – that she might change her mind unexpectedly.

"Quscu?" he repeated with a confused look.

"Yeah, apparently you were there in the seventies. With some dude called DeSouza...?"

Gabriel stared at her for what felt like a long time. He was bewildered, trying hard to bring back something to mind that wouldn't come. "I was?"

"According to the journals. They go way back. Before I was born, before Tom and Charlotte, I think. The bits I could make out, read like you learnt magic from this DeSouza?"

"It rings a bell, like I should know? I can't make it come back, right now."

He looked panicked, unable to remember. Daisy sighed, trying to ease it out without him noticing. There was so much she wanted to know; wanted him to remember. Still, she reminded herself, she had the eagle – which definitely needed more questions.

"So, this eagle…" he continued as if their previous conversation hadn't happened, seeing her pick it up and turn it over in her hands. "I told you how it came into my possession, the night before you were born…"

"Many times," she said happily.

"I had it before then, I'm sure of it now. I lost it. It was never mine to keep, which is why I think I lost it. It does keep coming back though."

"Good! You know I've always had my eye on it."

"It helped me, when I was doing magic. It can aid passage, or in my case, escape. Between here and…well, other places."

"Like where you went when you died?"

"Not there. When I went into the light on the cliff, I think it was the carving let me to do that. That man, the one who attacked me…he's Death –

"Is he? He looked familiar. You saying he doesn't need anything to come and go, you mean?"

Gabriel nodded. "Yeah. He appeared as my friend Davey – and you've definitely met him when you were little. Once we'd gone through, into those woods, he and I were separated by his…I think boss is as good a word as any. I don't know where he went and I've not seen him since – is this making sense?"

Daisy nodded. Maybe it shouldn't, but it was.

"Maybe Death is, dead? When I got lost again, I think it was the carving helped me get out of the wood. That was when I started to remember," he said trailing off. "Before I forgot again," he added sadly.

As she listened, she noticed he was more serious than usual, less reliant on being funny. She lit up a cigarette and smoked as she played over what he was saying. "Can Death die? Like, is that a thing? Now you're back, how come you're giving it to me?"

"It's your birthday – and as for Death I've no idea – and you've always wanted it. Hearing about that stone door, the one on the island, and where it led, I think I'm meant to give it you now."

"I came back from the island without it though?"

"You did," he said nodding to himself. "It sounds similar to the light on the cliff. You said there was drumming too though?"

"I thought it was the sound of the sea, echoing along the tunnels, but the more I think about it, the more I realise it wasn't just drumming –

"More than the sound you mean?"

"I'm not sure. One minute I was in the chamber with the drumming getting louder and louder, then a light appeared and it got bigger...and suddenly I was here, in the woods out back. It was the sound that was the stronger sensation, if that makes sense? I felt it and heard it, *inside* of me."

"Like a vibration?"

"Exactly like that."

"I wonder if the carving can allow you to go back to the island the same way. A journey in reverse?"

Back to Lysh, Daisy thought. "Whatever it does, I'm taking good care of it," she said proudly, wrapping the cord around the carving and putting it carefully into her jeans pocket.

"I know you will. Besides, if you lose it, it does seem to have a habit of making its way back!"

~

"This is, amazing. Thanks everyone," Daisy said with a sheepish smile. After more coffee, she and Gabriel had not long made their way over to Morfydd's cottage.

Arwen and Pol were curled up on the settee. They had brought a card and Arwen had given her a dark green scarf she had knitted herself. Arwen also brought best wishes from Kara, who was still in Paris chasing down a missing Balzac manuscript – one that purported to contain what the author had believed to be secrets of immortality – Arwen and Pol expecting her back for Beltane, returned safe and well.

The cottage windows were open and Morfydd had obviously been out especially, fresh flowers in a vase on the table and another on the sill overlooking the sea. Daisy noticed the entrance to the world's smallest kitchen was now hidden behind a dark red curtain hanging from a wooden pole.

"That new?" Daisy asked pointing.

Morfydd opened and closed the curtain a few times, grinning. "Yes, Eleanor sent it. She made it. Lovely, isn't it?"

"It looks good. Adds an air of mystery!"

Morfydd gave her a wide grin before flitting around the room, topping up wine, vanishing behind the curtain and returning moments later with fresh bread, hummus and olives.

Not long after, satisfied everyone had enough to eat and drink, Morfydd had picked up a parcel from the table and handed it to Daisy. Unwrapping the brown paper, she found a heavy journal inside. "Your first grimoire," Morfydd said with an enigmatic smile, "Your book of spells."

The journal looked ancient. Around the size of a paperback book, its edges were dusty and Daisy wondered how long Morfydd had had it. Opening the stiff cover, which looked like animal hide, the blank pages seemed to shine with their own light; as though waiting.

Thinking about what she might write in it first, there was a fierce knock at the door that sounded like a police raid. As was her wont, Gwen had arrived by boat and huffed and puffed her way up the zig zag path from the beach. She was wearing a heavy cloak, one Daisy thought unnecessary for a mild March Day – but wasn't about to challenge her. She brought no gift, but Daisy had been surprised when she flung her arms around her, with a hug that could have fractured both their ribs.

"Glad to see you made it safely off the island..."

"You and me both," Daisy replied cheerily. "Have you –

She wanted to ask if after Lysh, but stopped. Gwen rarely spoke kindly of them and Daisy, having cut herself off, tried to push Lysh to the back of her mind. Gwen looked puzzled, staring expectantly as she waited for her to continue.

"Sorry," Daisy went on, "have you heard, Suni's doing really well."

"That's good news, it was quite a knock to the head."

"Where there's no sense..." Daisy giggled as Gwen headed over to Morfydd.

Looking around, at everyone there for her birthday, Daisy felt embarrassed, but secretly pleased they had made a fuss. She had just sat down beside Arwen and Pol, keen to catch up properly, when her phone vibrated. It was a message from Suni: On my way birthday girl...check this out in the meantime! x

Daisy settled back, reaching to tickle Maya's chin, who was perched on one arm keenly eyeing them for scraps. Suni had sent her a video and a few minutes later, she was lost for words. This was a side of Suni she had not seen before: so much more confident. It had been recorded on his phone, at the neat desk in his bedroom. He talked enthusiastically of his time in hospital, describing what it had felt like seeing himself outside of his body. It was hard not to be drawn in.

He summarised the visitors appearing, how they had healed his injuries and talked with him. It finished with Suni beaming at the camera and running a hand through his hair, imploring anyone watching the video to share it. To tell everyone.

Daisy watched it twice more, Arwen leaning in and watching with her, without comment. As soon as it had finished, however, she had leaned toward Pol, and Daisy watched them speaking animatedly, too low for her to hear.

Trawling through the video posts, there was a mixed response. There were vicious comments, ridiculing both Suni and the video; some out-and-out racist. There were kinder ones that praised the recording rather than the content. A few people had left bible quotes, but here and there, there were comments from people sharing similar experiences. He was clearly on to something and she was still thinking about the video, when he arrived.

"Hi, Suni. It's so good to see you up and about again," Morfydd said brightly.

"Trust me, it's good to be up and about again."

"OH…MY…GOD! It's you, isn't it? That famous guy from the video!" Daisy exclaimed, pretending to swoon, before breaking into fits of giggles.

"You should see how many views it's getting! I added my email and already I've had people telling me about their experiences. This could be huge."

"Hospital seems to have done you good, Suni! I swear, you're glowing!"

As the light outside the cottage dwindled, absorbed into the setting sun, Morfydd lit the fire and closed the curtains. After an extended round of hellos and a large glass of red wine, Suni handed Daisy a bulky carrier bag.

"I might have gone a little over the top, but Happy Birthday Daisy!"

She settled cross-legged on the floor with Suni opposite and upended the bag, a collection of neatly wrapped presents, each with a matching gift tag, spilling out. One by one she opened them, until she was surrounded by enough candles to illuminate West Wales, a bottle of Dior Poison, coffee beans from Kasbah, a new pair of black Hi-Top Vans and a keyring with a tiny cartoon witch dangling from it.

"Suni, I love them!" Daisy announced as she shuffled over and gave him a hug. "You've spoilt me!"

Before long, after they had all eaten enough cheese and crackers, fruit and nuts, bread – and polished off a small lake of red wine and coffee – they sat in clusters talking, each throwing a comment from one conversation to another now and then.

Suni had squeezed between Daisy and Arwen, Pol having moved to the floor to settle between Arwen's legs.

Conversation with Pol was difficult, like trying to start a fire with two stones. Despite his best efforts, she seemed happier to slouch into Arwen, letting her stroke her head as she ignored him.

Watching Daisy open her presents, it felt like the moment was moving closer. Since being in hospital, it needed to be said more than ever. What he expected after, was less clear. Seeing her parading up and down the room in her new green scarf and Vans, swinging her hips in an exaggerated parody of a catwalk model, the words had almost leapt out of him.

Oblivious to Suni's private panic, Daisy was enjoying her birthday. Buoyed by red wine, her thoughts had turned to Lysh and she wished they had swapped numbers. However unlikely it was, she really wanted them to show up, even though she wasn't sure if she had even mentioned her birthday. When she had asked Gwen if there had been anything else like the drone, she had hoped Gwen might mention Lysh.

Gwen had reassured her the island was safe, making it clear she had taken greater steps to protect it, even making a joke about boat repairs. She had not mentioned Lysh and Daisy realised how little she knew about them. Nothing of where they lived, came from? How they even came to be on the island?

When Suni stood up and announced he was leaving, Daisy was grateful for the interruption. His auntie had driven him and his mum over for the day, with plans to see more of Aberystwyth and take a walk around the stunning waterfalls at Devil's Bridge. As Suni said goodbye, Arwen took him gently by the arm and walked the two of them away from the others.

"I saw your video, Suni..."

"You did? What did you think?"

Arwen paused, tilting her head closer so she could speak softly. "It's very eloquent, Suni. I sense it's really affected you, the experience?"

"It blew me away," he began, lowering his voice. "They felt wise. Like they were made from a big loving energy that knows everything. That's the only way I can describe it really."

"It does feel like that, doesn't it."

"You've seen them too?" he exclaimed, trying to keep his voice down. He glanced over his shoulder, but no one had noticed.

"Oh yes, pet. Many times. I suspect you and I will talk about this again."

"You have?"

Arwen nodded and looked at him with twinkling eyes. Putting her arm around his shoulders she pulled him nearer and whispered. "Oh yes, they are my kin."

As Daisy came over, Arwen having returned to the settee, she found Suni staring into space looking stunned. She clicked her fingers in front of his face a few times. "Hey...hey, you okay?"

"Yeah...I'm...okay..."

"Thank fuck, I thought you'd gone again!" She tugged at his sleeve, "Do you really have to go?"

"I've got work tomorrow," he groaned. "Come outside, see me off."

The two of them slipped out of the cottage and wound their way along the path to the main road. Passing the sea, Daisy glanced at the water. A couple of days before, whilst her dad had been napping in his chair, she had gone to the beach. Since returning from Tor's Leap, each time she had been near water, she felt weirdly energised. She had gone to the beach the following day as well. Keeping close to the water, it had started to feel similar to when she had fallen from Gwen's boat; as though she and the water were connected, in a way she didn't understand. Seeing Suni up ahead, pacing back and forth in the layby beside the main road, she shrugged it off.

"Thank you so much Suni, coming all the way down here just for me."

Suni smiled. "Like I'd miss your birthday."

"And I'll be back for yours. Maybe by then, I'll have worked out what I'm doing with my life!"

"It gives you six months. Come back before then though, if you can. You know you're always welcome at mine, if you don't want to see your mum?"

They were interrupted by a sleek saloon skidding to a halt in the layby, having almost overshot it. Seeing Mrs. Panchal and her sister inside, Daisy gave them a wave.

"Yeah, not in a massive rush to see her. But you, I'll see soon. Promise."

"You know Daisy, with everything that's happened," he started carefully, "it's got me thinking, about a lot of stuff. There's something I want to tell you..." He paused taking a long, deep breath and letting it out slowly, "I love you, Daisy."

"And I love you!"

"You do?"

"'Course I do, silly!" she chuckled digging him in the shoulder. "You're just like the brother I never had!"

Suni felt sick to his toes. Darting for the car he dived into the back seat eyes brimming and slammed the door. His auntie wasn't one to linger and the car was away over the hill in no time, a small cloud of dust settling in its wake.

Daisy thought it odd Suni hadn't turned and waved. Ducking under a branch and heading back to the cottage, she couldn't understand why he hadn't even looked back.

Chapter 31 – When You Tell Everyone

"...what happened with the drone, *that* was a success?"

Hand raised, it looked like he was about to hit Donne, who flinched in his seat as Wordsworth circled the table, each stride rattling cups and saucers.

The seven men had all been summoned by a 6am message from Wordsworth. Now, they were crowded around a meeting table deep underground, sleepy and hungry. Some drank watery tea as others gazed blankly at tepid instant coffee. Wordsworth presided over his own cafetiere of exquisite coffee, enjoying each exaggerated sip.

"I just meant," Donne urged, "that the drone itself operated well. It reached the island *and* it did take photographs before –

Wordsworth bristled. "Before it was destroyed. A resounding success."

"We might take positives from the operation," Blake offered hopefully.

Blake, or No.4, was a quiet, reliable man who had been with the A-9 many years, longer in fact than Wordsworth. He still remembered the previous Deputy – and the sudden way they had disappeared. Blake's wife was proud of his regular attempts to bring lightness to his work, which he had long hoped might rub off on his colleagues. Most Mondays he brought flapjacks or a traybake to work, made by him and his wife over the weekend. When it was one of their birthdays, he would usually turn out a more-than-competent chocolate and buttercream cake.

"Some positives?" mocked Wordsworth, glaring at him.

"For sure," Blake went on, "we know exactly where the island is now and we know who was there that day; the images are reasonably clear. All three of them can be seen, which means ultimately, they can be identified."

"And have they been?" asked Mr. Panchal.

When the photographs had been displayed on the large screen at the head of the table, he had recognised Daisy immediately and said nothing. The older, white-haired woman and the shaven-headed figure he didn't know. Caught by the drone camera, all three were frozen with the same incredulous look.

"We're working on it. As a priority."

It was Marlowe, No.6, that responded. Small and round, with short greying hair he worked predominantly underground, giving him the narrowed eyes and shuffle of a mole. A man of ingenuity and dogged determination, he was known for his ability to take any image and ultimately turn it into an address, full social media history and up to date contact details. The secret to this, lived somewhere between intuition and illegality.

At this point, Coleridge, No.9, a tall man who appeared to be partially asleep most of the time, yawned and nodded at Marlow, intending to convey agreement. Recently, he had been giving a lot of thought to how he might leave the A-9; what life might look like if he were actually able to.

"It had better be," Wordsworth said with a snarl. "I want to know who these people are – and where we can find them, if not on the island."

"Find them?" echoed Mr. Panchal. It came out louder than he had intended and the group turned to look at him.

"Yes. This has gone on long enough. There are portals opening all over the place. It cannot be allowed to continue – and if

- 257 -

these witches have anything to do with it, I want them rounded up...and removed."

A hush fell over the table. Whilst there was little Wordsworth wouldn't do, the rest of the men had their limits. Byron and Shelley – No.7 and No.8 – who more often than not wore combat fatigues and masks, stretched in their seats. They had no limits, recruited for their muscle and intimidation, not to mention their unquestionable loyalty.

In recent weeks, Wordsworth's insistence on pushing on with the Witch Whistle carried with it a level of malice most of them found difficult to condone. Save for Byron and Shelley, the men were scientists; measured men who liked lives of logic and rationality. It was hard to justify what increasingly felt like Wordsworth's own agenda; his seething contempt for everyone, particularly women, something he had given up disguising some time ago.

"So, we continue to focus on the portals, the crossing places?" Mr. Panchal confirmed, keen to divert the subject as best as he could.

"We continue with that," Wordsworth replied sounding bored, "and with eradicating these women, this so-called Sisterkin. For all we know, they could be opening these portals. It is a threat to national security, which I refuse to tolerate."

The men at the table started to shuffle and murmur, gathering up their belongings; cautious overtures toward leaving as soon as possible. As Donne rose, followed by Mr. Panchal, Coleridge loudly pushing his chair backwards, Wordsworth slammed his hand on the tabletop.

"Sit down!" he barked, with a glacial look that had them back in the chairs. "We have another matter for consideration..."

"We do?" said Blake, visibly deflating as he let out a sigh.

Wordsworth leaned back in his chair and pressed a button on a remote control on the table. "Very much so. This, I'm taking very seriously."

At the end of the table the screen blinked to life as a video began to play. Clearly filmed on a mobile phone without the luxury of editing, it showed a young man with dark hair and stubble sat at a very tidy desk. He held up a piece of paper to the screen: Tell everyone.

As Wordsworth paused the video, Mr. Panchal froze.

"It's just some kid, surely? Not an actual threat?" he scoffed. He had hoped it had sounded innocent, but inside he felt great fear. Wordsworth would not stop until he had found out who the man in the video was. Sunil, by releasing the video, had put himself in mortal danger.

"Kid or not, we're monitoring him. Hear what he says next, about beings of light…" urged Wordsworth.

They all watched intently as the young man gave a short, factual introduction of how he had ended up in a hospital. After that, his demeanour changed, becoming more animated as he leaned forward, eyes wide. After describing being able to watch over his body in bed, he gave details of the three figures that had arrived beside his bed. Three figures made of light; what he referred to as a glorious, shimmering loving energy.

"And they told me," Suni continued, "and I think I knew already, that I need to tell everyone. They are here for all of us. We need them now more than ever."

In the last few moments, Suni could be seen to lean even closer, keen to emphasise his closing point. "They are here to help us become more connected to each other, to the universe. Please, tell everyone."

The video finished, a frozen image of Suni smiling from the screen.

"He talking about what I think he is?" asked Shelley.

"Interdimensionals?" said Blake.

"Err...we don't call them that anymore," Coleridge interjected drowsily, "it's considered offensive; there was an email..."

"He could just be nuts?" Mr. Panchal cautioned, turning to the group. "Come on guys, we really giving this our time?"

"Multidimensionals," corrected Wordsworth. "And yes, we are giving this our time. In case any of you are in any doubt, I think he is talking about what's been referred to as –

"The peace bringers?" Donne said as he twisted his coffee cup back and forth.

Wordsworth jerked round and eyed Blake with disgust. "They do not bring peace, No.3. You make it sound like they are in charge. We are."

Wordsworth stood up and reached to switch off the screen. "Gentlemen, there is much work to be done," he said from behind the chair, gripping the back, "deeply covert work. This man will be found and interrogated. The women on the island, will be removed. Meeting over."

The men hurried toward the door. As Donne bent toward the security scanner, the others bunched up behind him, eager to get out. Wordsworth called out, addressing them all.

"Please be under no misunderstanding, anyone not following orders, I will remove myself."

Chapter 32 – Three Stones

Ulla had never forgotten turning eleven. That was a cold year.

She had nestled into her grandmother and waited patiently. There would be a gift – there was always a gift – but she had no idea what. She had not long learned to ride and wondered if her present would be something related to that. Bringing out a small parcel, Eija's eyes sparkled as she patiently unfolded a piece of green velvet – remains of a scarf Ulla recognised immediately as one that had belonged to her mother. She remembered, even now, the reverence with which Eija had pressed each stone into her hand one by one.

From the first stone, they had been warmer than the hand that passed them to her. Two of the stones were around the size of a conker, but darker coloured; a dull brown that shone red when wet. The other, a glossy black stone, larger than the other two combined and around the size of a crab apple.

Even at eleven, the value of the stones was no secret to her. They held secrets and power; companions that had journeyed down through the women in her family. Never had they been separated, for their true strength lay in union.

Until her younger sister was born, the stones had belonged to her mother. Nina's birth had been too much for her; she had died minutes after clutching Nina to her chest. Ulla was nine and her brother Jaská, twelve, when their mother had passed. As she had taken her last, misty-eyed breath with her new-born, their father had been drinking with friends; passing around a bottle as they fished through a hole in the ice. At the death of his wife – news delivered later by Eija as she tried to console three wailing children – he had knocked back the dregs and jabbed the bottle menacingly in her direction. He mumbled threateningly, before tossing it aside and reaching for another bottle.

Jaská had been desperate to live with his father, bawling around his legs the following day. He had knocked him sharply to the floor and walked off. There had been no further explanation, Jaská left watching the sun travel across the sky as he waited for him to return. None of them ever saw him again and a sullen Jaská was looked after by Eija, along with his sisters.

All that ended two years later when Eija was killed; her family lacerated. Ulla never found out what happened to Jaská. The last time she saw him, he was following the group of men his father had been part of when the time came for them to move on with the herd. Nina was taken in by a couple in Helsinki desperate for a child, whilst Ulla was sent to a paternal aunt, a woman she never knew existed, who lived in Uppsala.

Ulla had arrived at the tall and narrow dark building, with her small life in a small suitcase. The building was poorly lit, cold and gigantic. Stairs reached for the sky and the grimy, damp hallways and landings refused to end. The larger rooms upstairs, had heavily plastered ceilings; like avalanches waiting to happen. She had been shown to a room on the first floor with an unmade single bed, a wash basin and a miniscule chest of drawers. What wallpaper hadn't peeled away, was striped brown and lime green. Ulla had dropped her suitcase onto the bed and sat down beside it.

She had waited until it was dark, clutching the suitcase to her when she heard footsteps outside the room. Opening it later, she found it filled with neatly folded clothes – packed by a social worker who had not troubled to share their name. This same woman, an imprecise scribble of thick, tangled hair and large glasses, she later discovered had enrolled her in a school without asking her, picked out a uniform without measuring her and before leaving that first day, waved a dirty blue Care Bear at her without explanation – which Ulla refused to take.

Watching the woman head briskly down the path from the house, Care Bear dangling from her hand, she left without closing the gate and Ulla knew she wouldn't see her again.

During the long journey to the house of her aunt, Ulla had concealed her stones, zipping them into an inside pocket. Wherever she went, she wanted to feel the safety of them close to her heart; needed to breathe them. And so, the stones had remained, hidden away, only to be taken out at night or when she was alone in her room.

That was, until, the insolence of Mr. Cotton.

Ulla emptied out the pocket of her dress and laid the three stones on the desk. Mr. Cotton must have been watching her for a while, noticed her not concentrating and singled her out. Perhaps it was her newness, her unusual ice-white hair, or the fact she had interrupted his class midway through the year – something he bitterly reminded her and the class of frequently.

Her stones had been more than happy within the warm, fluffy folds of her pocket and she frowned as she set them down. As Mr. Cotton reached for them, she flicked her fingers toward her and the stones followed, sliding across the desk together. She closed her fist around them and jammed it into her armpit, folding her arms.

"What on earth are those, Ulla?" Mr. Cotton demanded as he stood over her.

"They are my stones – and it's pronounced, ool-lah," she snapped squeezing her fist tighter. "They chose me. Not you."

A ripple of nervous giggling started, but faded quickly as the class fell silent as he returned to his desk. No one challenged Mr. Cotton; few dared answer-back. The only English teacher in the school, Mr. Cotton was stooped and ancient, old enough to have invented English itself, and clearly resented every single one of his pupils. The entire class watched, waiting to see what punishment awaited Ulla.

"They chose you?" mocked Mr. Cotton, his face hard.

Ulla nodded furiously. She felt the first sting of tears and held them back by sheer will. This stupid English man would not have the satisfaction of seeing her upset.

"Stones always choose their owner," she said in a tone that suggested only an idiot wouldn't know this. "These stones are my protection and my guide. You will not have them."

Although she hadn't been at the school long, she had seen enough to know that when one of the teachers confiscated something, it was never seen again. There would be talk of it being returned at the end of the day or the end of the week, but the items would always disappear into the staff room without being returned.

Ulla locked her arm tight. Unless he intended to physically overpower her, hold her down and prise her fingers loose, she would face permanent exclusion rather than give up her stones.

Mr. Cotton glowered at her as the class watched. Before he could reply, Ulla stuffed her fist into the pocket of her dress, eyeing him with a gaze harder than the stones themselves.

He had crossed the room slowly. Grabbing at her arm he had yanked her hand from her pocket and pulled her to standing. Gripping her forearm, he had jerked her to the front of the room. She had held her head high as she stared down the rows of eyes watching from behind their desks. Unsettled by the sight of an adult man terrorising a child, they were still able to appreciate the thrill of someone else being in trouble.

In front of the class, Mr. Cotton dug his giant hand into Ulla's dress, ripping the pocket and bruising her thigh. His fingers moved like rats in the dark, his long yellow nails pinching her skin. Closing his hand around the stones he brought it out and raised his fist high.

"Chose you, did they?" he announced to the class with a sneer as he turned his back on her. "Looks like they've chosen me now – and don't you move."

Before what came next – events that ended her time at the school – Ulla spoke once, in a hard, determined voice. "You will return my stones, or you will be sorry."

At this, his face turned crimson, a vein twitching in his neck. He rounded on her as though he was about to leap from his chair and beat her with his bare hands. Aware of this possibility, he stopped halfway out of his chair, sitting back down carefully. One by one, he placed the stones on the desk in front of him. He lay them in a line and sat back, folding his arms. He stared at her, then at the stones. Then at her. She saw the challenge in his eyes, the immediacy of her stones within his grasp.

She knew that she could dash forward and grab them with relative ease; she was perfectly able to move faster than he was. She knew too, that he would try and prevent her. In all likelihood, he would seek to humiliate her, in an attempt to regain some semblance of masculine authority. She also knew that she might not be able to grab all three of them before he intervened.

How events unfolded, was told afterwards in differing accounts. Many of the children were interrogated by the headmaster in the days that followed. The truth was coloured by panic, admiration and disbelief in equal measure. The only certainty, and on this everyone agreed, was that Mr. Cotton, after the incident with the stones, was never quite the same again.

"Well?" Mr. Cotton said sarcastically, "I don't see me returning these stones..."

Ulla looked at him and smiled warmly. With a growing look of disbelief, he watched as the stones arranged themselves into a triangle, the largest at the apex. As he grabbed for them, the triangle started to revolve anti-clockwise, faster and faster as the stones lifted off the desk.

Children strained in their seats. Mr. Cotton sat boggle-eyed, one hand still lingering over the stones. Still smiling, Ulla raised her eyebrows as the stones rose higher. Spinning in a tighter and tighter circle, they were a few feet above the desk, revolving so fast a whooshing sound filled the room.

Extending her hand Ulla made a slow, coaxing motion with her fingers. Almost immediately, the stones shifted from spinning horizontally, pivoting sharply into a vertical spin.

Moments after, following a flick of her hand, the triangle of stones slammed into Mr. Cotton's chest, lifting him out of the chair before hurling him against the chalkboard. With a jerk of her arm Ulla brought the stones closer to her, singing through the air until she cast them out once again, Mr. Cotton scrambling across the floor toward the door.

Revolving faster and faster, the stones charged across the front row of desks, sweeping books and pens onto the floor with a clatter. Children cowered, some diving under their desks as the stones smashed through the window of the class room, soaring high into the sky.

Ulla raised both hands high and brought the stones back again, shattering another pane of glass before they stopped abruptly in front of her, hovering in the air as they slowed. She held out her palm and the stones dropped one by one into her hand, before she returned them to the safety of her pocket.

She walked back to her desk quietly, still smiling. In the commotion her chair had been knocked over. Righting it, she sat down and stacked her books into a neat pile. Bending to retrieve her pencil from the floor, she blew dust from it and set it down beside her books. Turning to Tomas, the boy who usually sat beside her, she winked at him.

Inside her pocket, the stones were warm. Although it wasn't heard over the noise of children talking, over the gasping of Mr. Cotton spreadeagled on the floor, Ulla heard the stones singing their song; felt them chiming together in harmony.

Chapter 33 – This is the Space

A gentle draught wound over the ground, between the grasses. A day of blooms and balance, everything poised for the sun to heave itself up into the sky; a thrill in the air for the grand opening of spring.

Waking half-heartedly, Daisy turned over and dragged the covers over her head. Thumping at the pillows until the lumps relocated, she fell back to sleep easily, squeezing in another hour or so.

When Daisy had turned on the tap to fill the coffee machine, water had sprayed up the wall. Laying her hand on the tap again, she felt a faint tremor and wondered if it had something to do with the spray. Emptying the jug into the machine, she was amazed to find the water was warm.

She watched the garden through the window, gradually filling up with the brightness of the morning. Dew still clung to the grass and the birch catkins spun gently in the light. She was looking forward to helping her dad. It felt good, the two of them finally in the same place at the same time, hosting Morfydd and her friends.

Gabriel meanwhile, had flushed the toilet and was watching the water swirl away. Sickness woke him and he had hurried to the bathroom, where he had collided with his mannequin, Tanechka, who was staring blankly at the dark. In the end, it had been dry heaving, that left his stomach sore.

Peering into the mirror he tried to tidy his snowy mane. It was an odd look, but one he was quickly warming to it. Brushing his hair back, he thought of Morfydd's reluctance at him hosting, even when he had explained he wanted to return the favour. He had more room, inside and out, so when she had talked about celebrating Ostara, it seemed an obvious suggestion. She'd agreed in the end, but not without him having to cajole. Running his fingers and thumb over his beard, tugging at a loose hair, it was definitely a mustard jumper day.

"Morning Daisy," Gabriel said merrily.

Daisy reached for a mug and filled it with coffee. "Hey," she said handing him the mug.

"I could get used to this."

"Nice jumper. I'm gonna get you another, then you'll have two outfits. What's the plan then?"

"Well...Morfydd said she'd be early. We've got food, we've got drink. Seems like everything?"

"We got plenty of baccy?"

"I think so, yeah. I feel like the special tin might come out later."

"Nice. I'll help you put stuff out in a bit. Sooooo, today is the spring equinox, Ostara," Daisy began proudly, "a moment of pause, of balance. You feeling balanced?"

Gabriel grinned as he stood on one leg. "Reasonably."

Daisy sniggered. "That was such a, dad joke. You should be ashamed. As I was saying...today is about balancing the rational with the intuitive, light with dark. About looking inside, checking our balance. You getting this?"

"Rational and intuitive. Light and dark...inside, I'm getting it," he said good-naturedly. "I could probably do with more rational."

"Yeah, Suni's always good at that. I —

"You heard from him?"

Daisy shook her head, a pained look crossing her face before she forced a smile. "No, I haven't."

"He'll be in touch. You've been friends ages."

Yeah, maybe, Daisy thought, not quite believing it. At first, she'd paid it little attention, but having not heard from him at all, it was on her mind. She did love Suni, very much, but now it was uncomfortable. She realised now, that he had said it in a very particular way. It should feel good, feel comfortable, but she was left feeling irritated, unable to shake the idea he been expecting more from telling her.

Having tried unsuccessfully to call him, Daisy was glad when she heard a knock at the door. Morfydd breezed in, giving Daisy a quick half-hug as she called out for Gabriel. As she headed for the kitchen, Daisy was sure she smelled fresher than usual. Hugging Gabriel, she set down her basket and brought out two freshly baked loaves and two bottles of red wine.

As the three of them were talking in the kitchen, Arwen and Pol arrived, followed not long after, by Gwen and two of her friends, Viv and Bina – the three having met at Greenham Common and remained close ever since. Daisy kept herself busy, happy weaving between everyone, pouring wine or ferrying tea and coffee from the kitchen.

Viv was a woman who found little to trouble her, one of those wise souls able to go with the flow; find something wonderful every day. Petite, and similar in age to Morfydd, she had short greying hair, large silver hooped earrings and seemed very much at home in tatty black jeans and a red-and-black striped jumper. She settled in easily, chatting to everyone as though they were all old friends.

Bina, Daisy took to be nearer Gwen's age. Tall and curvy, with long blonde hair, she arrived in a magnificent indigo cloak and her presence was felt immediately. Quiet, but confident when she did speak, Bina had a strength that didn't need loudness, didn't need to be pushed to the forefront, but was unflinching when necessary. Daisy thought of the trees behind the cottage – solid and sure, difficult to imagine them not always being here.

Gwen and her friends had each brought a small drum and as they were getting them out, Daisy was taken back to the drumming at Yule and her time in the tunnels at Tor's Leap. If there was to be drumming, she hoped that with Morfydd and her Kin being here, she'd manage to at least stay in the same place this time.

Once everyone was introduced and had caught up with one another, Daisy settled on the edge of the settee beside Arwen, who had promised to tell her about scrying; show her if they had time. Gwen, Viv and Bina formed a pack on the floor and Daisy noticed how Gwen, in the company of her friends, was softer. More like the Gwen she had seen glimpses of on the island. Morfydd walked in, as they waited for her to get things started.

Inside the wood was cooler, the ground damp. Shadows wound around the trunks, wriggling free of the sunlight; holding it back. A flutter of wings, a crack of twigs sounded as the group approached.

As they had made their way through the garden – Morfydd insisting Gabriel join them, despite Pol's obvious displeasure – they had all stepped carefully between snowdrops as they entered the wood. Grey squirrels scattered, one scuttling up a trunk beside Arwen before leaping to another tree, then another, until it was out of sight. As they disappeared, their rustling sent birds skyward. Further in, where the evergreens wore darker shades, a piney scent hung in the air.

"This is the space," Morfydd announced, stopping suddenly a few minutes later. Everyone slowed and fanned out around Morfydd in a natural clearing within the trees.

Ambling around the clearing, eyes flitting up into the knitted branches she turned to the group. "I was thinking, it might be nice to spend time with the trees." Although there were pines, the majority were established oaks and silver birches, the odd beech squeezed between. Not far from the clearing, watching over proceedings, stood a trio of moody elders.

Daisy stood with hands on her hips. "What should we do?"

"Find a tree, one you're drawn to. Lean against, sit with it, see if you can clear your clutter."

"I can do that," Daisy answered merrily, looking around for a tree she liked the look of.

"Gwen and I will be drumming – is that okay with everyone?" Viv asked.

"Drumming's okay," Daisy answered hopefully, the others in agreement.

Arwen and Pol wandered hand in hand into the undergrowth and as Daisy made her own way deeper in to the wood, she saw that she was inadvertently following Bina, who seemed oblivious to the fact she was behind her. Gwen and Viv stood in the clearing, tolling a slow, steady beat with their drums. She saw her dad and Morfydd deep in conversation, looking like two people in no rush to go and find trees to hang out with instead.

As the drumming faded and she moved deeper into the wood, Daisy pushed the clutter from her mind, whispering away each thought as it popped into her mind, the woodland absorbing her words. In this part of the wood the trees were tighter together, Daisy having to grab onto trunks and branches as she ducked and weaved her way through. Further on, she tripped over a mossy bump on the ground, a stump left after a tree had split and fallen some time ago. Patting the moss with her hand it was dry enough, and she sat down and took a few slow, deep breaths.

Sat straight-backed, her hands on her knees, the clutter slowed. She could hear birdsong, wishing she was better able to identify each melody. Whatever they were saying it was lively, branches quivering as the birds landed suddenly, or pushed off in flight. As she allowed the woodland to envelop her, it felt more like the place beyond the stone door on the island – the same sensation of being held by the surrounding environment; seen by the aliveness. She settled into the feeling, trying to keep her mind free. Minutes later her eyelids felt heavy. Closing her eyes, she followed the birdsong as it carried her higher and higher...

~

Wordsworth flicked his cigarette onto the road, barely missing Mr. Panchal, where it hissed itself out. A plaintive drizzle had pushed in from the sea the last hour, doing little to improve his mood. Having demanded that the Witch Whistle be altered, made more powerful, now he was impatient to see what it could do; to finish this once and for all.

From the passenger seat he watched Byron and Shelley setting up a barrier to block the road south. The road north was already blocked, watched over by Blake and Coleridge in another Defender. He glanced down at a silenced revolver between his legs. A little more haste wouldn't hurt. Leaning over, all but knocking into Donne who had driven, he pressed heavily on the horn. As the men turned, he gestured for them to hurry things along.

With the barricade complete, they clambered into the back of the Defender, where Marlowe was hunched over a military-issue laptop oblivious to anything else. Only when Byron bumped against him, did he look up and give him a nod.

"Marlowe, what's happening?"

"They're close. Looking at the data, there's a few of them."

"Easy day," sniggered Shelley.

"Do not assume this will be easy," snapped Wordsworth from the front. "Byron, go join Blake and Coleridge," he said fixing him with a steely gaze. "Now."

Byron tried to squeeze out, but with limited room he was forced to clamber over Shelley, becoming temporarily wedged on his lap. "Fuck's sake," Shelley cursed, shoving Byron as he tried to swing round and let him pass. Both men jumped from the vehicle, Shelley vaulting straight back in. He was about to shut the door when Mr. Panchal climbed in.

"Marlowe...?"

"Marlowe!" Wordsworth called louder, the man eventually looking up from his laptop.

"Yes?"

"The photos, hand them out. Come on!"

Marlowe reached into a leather satchel at his feet. Sliding out a brown A4 envelope, he handed a series of photographs from the drone to each of them. "I've cleaned them up as best I can," he said matter-of-factly.

Wordsworth turned in his seat, so he could see Donne beside him and the three men in the back. Holding up the first photograph, he addressed them all.

"Daisy Lowry, 24."

He held up a second photo. "Gwen Butterfield. We're not sure of her age, late eighties at least – there's a long file on her. Her age, makes her no less of a threat."

Holding up a third photograph, he scowled. "This one, we know less about. Goes by the name Lysh. Mid-thirties approximately."

"Now," Wordsworth said as each man cycled through the pictures, "we think there's more than these three. Butterfield has a lot of known associates, some of which we suspect will be here: Arwen Lewis, Pol Sarson and Morfydd Evans. I have an image of Lewis and Sarson," he said, pausing to show them a grainy photograph of two much younger women. "Take any of them."

"Take them?" questioned Donne.

"Yes, take them," Wordsworth replied impatiently. "By any means necessary. We can interrogate them, work out who's who later. Then there's the testing, before removal."

Donne, Marlowe and Mr. Panchal let out a collective sigh. Wordsworth glared at each in turn, waiting for whoever had the courage to challenge him. No one spoke, the increasing patter of rain on the roof suddenly louder; a faint squeak as Donne shifted in his seat. Unfastening his seatbelt, he opened the door and stepped out. Glancing momentarily at the sea, he took a deep breath and turned to face Wordsworth.

"Some of these women are older. You sure you want us to take them, by *any* means?"

"My instructions were clear," bit Wordsworth, fingering the revolver. Waiting for Donne to respond, he reached down and checked that the silencer was fastened tight.

Donne stared at Wordsworth teeth bared, neither disguising their contempt for the other. "We're scientists," he began wearily, "our work is about safeguarding these energy gates, the portals and —

"Your work," Wordsworth hissed, "is whatever I say it is."

Donne leaned through the open door and jabbed his finger at Wordsworth's face, looking like he had a lot more to say. "Not this time. You can —

Wordsworth brought the revolver from his lap and pulled the trigger. Donne went down with the first shot, which hit the centre of his forehead, a mist of blood spraying across the inside of the door before he crumpled to the ground.

"Shelley, Tennyson. Sort that, we need to move. It'll be dark soon."

Chapter 34 – My Soul Is My Sat Nav

Ulla stepped from the train lugging her suitcase. Although she hadn't long in Copenhagen before her evening flight, she was looking forward to spending time with Nina, even if it was on her home concrete.

Having ridden the escalator from the lower level she bumped her case over the step, its tiny wheels clattering over the impressive red-and-black tiling. Slowing, she scanned the crowd of people coming and going under the vaulted wooden roof and grand chandeliers of Central Station.

Regardless of how long it had been since they had seen each other in person, Ulla could always find Nina in a crowd. Momentarily distracted by Danish flags on long poles either side of the hall, unable to work out what was making them flutter indoors, she stood on tiptoes searching for Nina's wide, pale forehead and bright blue eyes – the brightest light in any station concourse.

Catching sight of her sister, Nina waved frantically as she hurried over, Ulla twisting her sister into a tight hug. She held on to her, unable to remember the last time she had felt another body against her own. There had been so much time apart. Nina had been so young when she was sent to Helsinki; like yanking out a seedling before its roots were strong enough.

Nina stepped back with a grin. She always enjoyed Ulla's entirely random visits and even now, still found herself admiring Ulla's wilful refusal to fit in, with anything; the way she always looked like a woman from another time and place.

"You're wearing shoes!" Nina joked as she bumped shoulders with Ulla, ducking to sneak in a vape, exhaling across the concourse.

Ulla smiled as she gave her sister a distinct shrug. "Not allowed on the train without – and that's not allowed in here," she added, nodding toward Nina's vape.

With a frown that could cut glass, at odds with her easy personality, Ulla's short, stocky frame was wrapped in a dark-dyed reindeer skin tunic that stopped at the knee, beneath which was a heavy linen skirt berry-dyed red and hefty, animal-skin boots. The only thing missing was a dusting of snow. Whenever Nina thought of her sister, it was always with snow melting into her ice-blonde hair – currently in two long, tight plaits down her back – or dripping from her clothes. It was her pale hair, gunmetal grey eyes and milk-white skin, that gave her a delicate look more suited to fireside fairy tales. A look that in the past, had led people to assume she was frail, or easy to coerce, though neither could be further from the truth.

Weaving between people flooding the entrance, Nina vaped and babbled away as they left the station behind and headed along Bernstorffsgade. It was chilly, barely above freezing; made colder by a vicious wind that sliced across the broad street. The sun did its best, shining furiously as it reflected off the damp pavements and glinted over passing bicycles.

Had she longer, Ulla would have liked to explore. Taken in the old port of Nyhavn, walking beside the canal whilst encouraging Nina to show her the best of the bars and cafés. The bright painted buildings, the boats straining at their ropes, added to an air of anticipation that filled the streets like perfume. For Ulla, these were sights rarely experienced, preferring the solitude and safety of her snow and forest.

Passing the extravagant Neo-Baroque Central Post Building, designed by Heinrich Wenck who had designed the adjacent Central Station, Nina had taken Ulla by the arm and pulled her into a soft-lit coffee shop, guiding them to a corner booth out of the way.

Sipping at their coffees they jumped from subject to subject, their conversation following its own beat. It was curious, Ulla considered when Nina had gone to the toilet, that they could talk easily on a vast range of topics, rarely disagreeing, but the one subject neither ever brought up, even now, was their brother Jaská.

Watching her cross the room, Nina looked thinner than she remembered. She looked like she wasn't eating enough, her short, savagely bobbed blonde hair adding to her slight appearance. Nina was taller than her, what some call willowy, which Ulla acknowledged might be skewing her outlook. She was glad she would never be tall.

"I like this coffee," Ulla announced as Nina sat down, chinking her mug against Nina's.

"It is good here. Shame we can't do Tivoli, but it's not open for a few weeks. That would have been lovely."

"I am not here long. How is your life?"

Nina had moved to Copenhagen just over a year ago, and as though having waited for Ulla to ask, now updated her on *everything*: her new flat (including its confusing and intermittent hot water system and her odd neighbours), her job in a jazz bar she was holding on to until she found something more permanent – "more adult" she insisted with a groan – and the wild nights she regularly had with her workmates. She talked softly and quickly, her hands filling in the details. Ulla said little, but Nina had no doubt that she was listening, warm acknowledgement in her nods and frequent chuckles.

Ulla had always been the quieter of the two, people mistaking her as rude or shy, but Nina understood that whilst she could be rude, shy she definitely wasn't; Ulla heard everything and missed nothing. When she did speak, it had always felt to Nina like someone had told Ulla a long time ago, she was only allowed a finite number of words and phrases in her life and that she must choose them carefully; not waste any.

Moving on to telling her about a recent relationship, Nina wasn't sure Ulla would be interested, being someone with no relationships to speak of. Nina explained, how four months in, it had limped to an unspectacular end brought on by spilled red wine and a stubbed toe. Ulla had rolled her eyes repeatedly, before downing her coffee and ordering beer for them both.

Ulla sniffed dismissively as Nina wrapped up her relationship story. "That sounds unsatisfying."

"It was definitely that," Nina said flatly. "I can do without a man who cries when he…finishes."

"I wouldn't know."

"You still not dating, Ulla?"

Ulla shook her head vehemently. "Where I live?"

"There are people aren't there, sometimes?" Nina pushed.

"I will date when someone impresses me. Most people are wary of me."

"Would you like to change that?" Nina suggested gently.

"No, I wouldn't."

"But you're not scary, Ulla," Nina said with a thin laugh. "You can love – you do love. Deeply."

Ulla didn't reply. She took a drink of beer, long enough for her sister to drift off and reach for the menu instead. "You hungry?" she asked sliding a menu across the table.

"Yes. I have a long journey. Do they have a chicken sandwich?"

"I'm sure they will – and this is on me. You want anything else?"

Ulla drained her drink in one go and set the glass down carefully. "Chips we can share – with cheese and hot sauce – and another beer, please."

By the time they had eaten, there was hardly any time before Ulla's train to the airport. Between nibbling hungrily at her food and drinking her beer, Ulla had told Nina of her plan to fly to Manchester, the next stage in an already lengthy journey taking her through England and mid-Wales, the longest section around eight hours on the National Express #409[9].

"It sounds expensive!"

"I have many reindeer. I sell as needed."

"You make it sound like there's a rush? Why don't you stay with me a few days?" Nina asked hopefully. "I'd love that."

"I must be there tomorrow, for the equinox. I will stay on my way back."

"This is those stones again, yeah?" Nina asked cautiously.

Whenever they talked about Eija or the stones, Ulla never let them out of her sight and there was always a slight chance it would end in a conversational stalemate. Nina had never quite understood how Ulla allowed herself to be led wherever the stones took her.

Nodding, Ulla automatically reached into her pocket, keen to check she could still feel the warmth of the stones at the bottom.

"Do you think you'll ever settle down Ulla, find your place?"

Ulla arched her eyebrows. "Give up, you mean?" she replied cooly.

---

[9] A journey not for the impatient, where time can stop completely, or feel as though it is going backwards at times.

This was not a new conversation. Ulla knew Nina worried about her, struggled to comprehend the way she lived her life. She wished she didn't; there was no need. Nina, with all her enthusiasm for her life in Copenhagen, still needed structure; the comfort of routine. Whilst Nina was happy to allow herself some freedom, Ulla knew she needed rigid edges, to prevent her life from becoming too unpredictable.

Nina winced. "Does it have to be giving up?"

"To me, it is the same."

"It'd be so nice to see you more often," Nina continued, changing tack.

"I would like that. Maybe when my task is complete."

"Your task? That make it sound very grand..."

"I have to do it."

"How do you know that, Ulla?"

Ulla smiled, humouring her. "Because, my soul is my Sat Nav."

"Your soul is your Sat Nav?"

"Yes. It guides me, like the stones."

"And they guided you here, to Copenhagen?"

"No," Ulla answered with a broad grin, "the train did."

Nina rolled her eyes. "I always forget just how hilarious you are Ulla!"

"Aren't I."

"Would you like me to come with you, to the airport?"

"I know the way."

"I just thought it'd be good, more time together?"

"I love you dearly, Nina. More time is good."

"Right," Nina said getting up from the table, brushing crumbs from her jeans. "we'd better get going then."

"Just remember," Ulla said firmly as she followed her sister across the café, "you won't change my mind."

Chapter 35 – Twryf[10]

"There you are! Where've you been?" Morfydd demanded.

Coming inside, Daisy had got the sense she'd interrupted Morfydd and her dad. The kitchen was heavy with cigarette smoke and smelled of coffee. Behind their conversation and those in the lounge, she heard Neil Young playing at a low volume.

"With the trees," Daisy replied, pointing vaguely at the door. "I think...I nodded off."

"You're wet." Gabriel said handing her a tea towel.

Hearing Daisy in the kitchen, Arwen got up slowly and stepping between Gwen, Viv and Bina made her way over.

"Daisy, are you alright?"

Drying her hair, she turned and peeped out from under the towel, as though not recognising her for a moment, "Yeah...I feel a bit, spaced, though."

Arwen put an arm around her shoulders and guided her under the staircase into the darkness of the dining room. She fumbled a hand along the wall until she found the light switch, which didn't bring a great deal of light to the room.

"Let's sit down for a bit."

They sat side by side on the window seat overlooking the drive, the meagre glow of the solitary bulb doing little to upset the darkness beyond.

---

[10] Twryf (turrif) – a loud noise, or tumult that often precedes a strange event or an unexpected arrival of people.

"We can talk here, it's quieter. Would you like to know more about scrying?"

"Scrying?" Daisy repeated softly. She had a patchy recollection of Arwen having talked about this before, but since returning from the wood, her thoughts felt boggy.

"I thought water scrying might be a good start…"

Daisy shifted position and back again. "Something doesn't feel right, Arwen. I can't concentrate on what you're saying. I feel fearful, but I don't know why?" She searched Arwen's face for reassurance; for something she could hold on to as an answer.

"Fearful of scrying?"

"No. When I was in the woods, I wanted the trees to communicate with me. I tried, really tried, to let go of all my clutter. I think I fell asleep. Before I did, I heard the birds then…then there was this uneasy feeling?"

"Some woods can feel like that, darker? I wonder if –

"I think something bad is going to happen," Daisy persisted. "Do you feel it?"

Arwen shook her head softly. "I don't, no. But I trust that you do. Let me get Pol," she said getting up, the two of them returning moments later.

Crouching in front of Daisy and Arwen, Pol was still nearly as tall as them. She laid her hand on Arwen's. "What is it, sweetheart?"

"Daisy has a bad feeling. Would you mind taking a look outside, check everything's okay?"

"Of course, I will."

Pol stood up and was about to turn for the hallway when she stopped. Leaning in she planted a kiss on the top of Arwen's head. "Love you." With a nod to Daisy she was gone, the sound of the front door closing echoing down the hallway.

Pol checked the back of the cottage first, prowling through the garden which was dripping wet and squelched underfoot. She skirted the woods, shining the torch on her phone into the trees, moving it back and forth slowly as she looked. As the beam struggled to penetrate the darkness, she heard movement, but it sounded too light to be people. Close by, an owl hooted. Satisfied, she rounded the corner of the cottage and squeezed down the narrow passage to the drive. At the front door, she stopped and listened. She heard the hum of conversation and laughter from the cottage behind her, the sound of the sea out beyond the road.

Arwen had been worried – more than she had let on in front of Daisy, Pol thought. They had been together long enough for Pol not to doubt her intuition. Her ability to know exactly how Pol was feeling, to have a sense of future events, had been something Pol had found disconcerting when they first met; so unlike any of her other relationships. It had left her feeling like she had nowhere to hide.

Her thoughts were interrupted by the soft thud of what sounded like a car door closing; carefully, as though someone were trying to limit the noise. Cocking her head, she waited to see if it happened again. When it didn't, she edged down the driveway, keeping to the shadows beside the gorse hedge. Whatever she heard, it had come from the road and before going inside, it couldn't hurt to check.

Crouching, Pol poked her head past the end of the hedge. With no street lighting and no visible moon, it was difficult to make much out. Still crouching, she shuffled forward, convinced she had heard talking. It had been whispered and even as she scanned the area, she was ready to dismiss it as the sound of waves rolling over the shingle.

Standing up, she shook herself and smiled – a grown woman spooked by the sound of the sea! Had she walked further out, she would have seen one of the blockades, intended to prevent anyone making an escape. She would also have caught sight of masked figures in black combats advancing on the cottage. Had she done that, instead of turning her back on the road, it might have prevented her being struck on the back of the head with a revolver; stopped her crumpling into a heap on the driveway.

"Go now!" Wordsworth hissed as he padded quickly up the drive. "Blake, keep an eye on this one," he hissed over his shoulder.

As Byron and Shelley sprinted for the cottage, Byron darted down the side passage to mark the back door, Shelley taking his place beside the front door. Coleridge followed close behind Wordsworth, Mr. Panchal bringing up the rear.

Despite the increased power of the Witch Whistle, Wordsworth had insisted they conceal their faces behind masks; blend into the night. Byron and Shelley were heavily armed, something neither were strangers to. Marlowe remained in the Defender as a potential driver, but also as the one responsible for keeping track of everyone and ensuring there were no issues with the Witch Whistle.

As Wordsworth, Coleridge and Mr. Panchal spread out across the driveway, there was a moment of pause: Byron stood by the rear door semi-automatic in hand, Shelley similarly positioned at the front. Coleridge stood with his arms at his sides, as though unsure what to do next.

Wordsworth stole closer to the front of the cottage and peered through the window, shrinking back into the shadows at the sight of two figures bent in conversation, barely illuminated by the light within. He motioned furiously for Coleridge to get out of the way, away from the middle of the driveway where anyone might see him. Yawning, he skulked out of sight and ducked behind the Jensen parked outside the cottage.

Hunched behind Wordsworth, who was rummaging in his trouser pockets for the remote, Mr. Panchal silently hoped something would interrupt proceedings – and fast.

Unseen by any of the men, beyond the northern blockade, a car slowed to a stop.

"Here," Ulla commanded, leaning between the front seats of the taxi. Glancing at the road closure further ahead, caught in the headlights, she added, "turn off the lights."

The driver turned the taxi into a layby, stopping beside a black Fiesta and turned off the lights. When he'd picked her outside the pier in Aberystwyth, she had said little and avoided all attempts at small talk during the journey.

"We weren't going any further," he grunted, tipping his head toward the ROAD CLOSED sign.

She felt the heat of the stones through the fabric of her pocket; it was increasing, as they started their harmonious ringing. As soon as she paid, she was away into the darkness.

Still with the lights off, about to start the engine and turn the car around, the driver leaned toward the rear-view mirror. Sweeping his greasy hair back, Mr. Bliss started the engine and having turned the car around, parked further down the road out of sight. He sat back, drumming a finger on the steering wheel. He was close enough.

As soon as Ulla had ducked into the driveway, she saw movement ahead. Using the sound of the taxi firing up the engine as cover she slipped quickly into the gloom. Hidden behind the gorse, she peered through the twisted branches and tried to read her surroundings.

Turning to Mr. Panchal, Wordsworth looked him up and down with a smirk. It was time to give Tennyson a push, see which way he jumped. "This is for you," he said holding out the remote control. "Take it."

Mr. Panchal's mind raced as he weighed up his options: he could take it, try and find a way to hold off using it, maybe even pretend it wasn't working, buy himself and everyone inside more time. Maybe he could just break it and damn the consequences? He could make a run for it, try and get inside the cottage and warn everyone. Even as the scenarios flashed through his mind, he knew Shelley would not hesitate; nor Wordsworth.

Taking the remote he looked at it in his hand. "And now what? I don't know how to use this?"

"You only have to press the button, hold it down."

He could just leave all of this behind, keep running and never stop...but Daisy was inside. If anything happened to her, he would never live with himself – and Suni would never live with it either.

"Are we close enough, out here I mean?" Mr. Panchal queried innocently, mentally lining up as many questions as he could.

"We are close enough. Get on with it."

"I just press it, then hold it down? For how long?"

There was a rapid movement as Wordsworth slipped a hand inside his jacket and Mr. Panchal caught a glint of something metallic.

"Do not test my patience, Tennyson," Wordsworth said as he levelled the revolver at his face.

"I think that's, a little unnecessary," Mr. Panchal said backing away. "I –

"Need I remind you what happened to Donne?" Wordsworth interrupted, pointing the revolver toward the device in Mr. Panchal's hand. "Do it, or I'll put you down like a dog."

Mr. Panchal stepped in front of him and was about to press the button, when Wordsworth spoke again. "Oh, and No.5..."

Mr. Panchal turned. "You're a very competent scientist, undoubtedly an asset to us. Now we've all seen that video, I expect you to bring him in – Sunil that is – within the next 48 hours. Regardless of what happens here. Trust me, it'll be much..." Wordsworth took a moment, "kinder, than if I do it."

Sorry Daisy, Mr. Panchal mouthed as he brought his thumb down on one of the buttons and held it there, legs shaking...

Inside the cottage, Gabriel and Morfydd were still in the kitchen, talking about Daisy as they made more coffee.

Arwen and Daisy remained in the front room on the window seat. Time around Arwen had helped the anxious feeling settle and Daisy was feeling more like her old self, not to mention hungry.

"Arwen, I'm starving. Do you mind if I grab some food? You want anything?"

"I'll have some cake, if there's any?" Arwen replied, settling back into the seat as she drew her legs up, knees under her chin. "And see if you can find where Pol got to."

"Cake it is!" replied Daisy, "And I will."

Gwen, Viv and Bina had spent much of the evening in their own bubble, reminiscing over times of protest, times of pain – celebrating the enduring strength of their friendship.

As Daisy walked into the kitchen, Gabriel noticed her face screw up in agony and hurried toward her. At the same time, Morfydd yelped as she brought her hands up to her head...in the lounge, the instant Gwen heard the noise she knew exactly what it was, desperately trying to protect the three of them, Viv's mouth hanging open, as Bina keeled over backwards. Crawling over the floor toward the kitchen, Gwen felt the searing pain inside her head. The room passed in and out of focus as she tried to summon the energy to keep going, catching sight of Morfydd slumped on the floor beside the kitchen counter, Daisy howling on her knees opposite as Gabriel stood over her...

Catching Gwen's eye, Morfydd pushed out a low sound from her belly, hoping she would be able to do the same. "Daisy," she cried weakly, "Daisy, if you can, connect!"

Daisy knew Morfydd was saying something, but was distracted by a commotion as the front door, kicked in from the outside, slammed into the wall...

Pol came round to find a man stood over her. The second he saw her move he was on her, attempting to pin her down with a knee in the small of her back. Twisting loose, she rolled over and discovered her wrists were cable-tied. Struggling to her knees she wobbled from side to side as she tried to stand, thinking only of Arwen. As the man squared up to her, convinced her bound wrists would make her easier to subdue, Pol launched herself forward and headbutted him, knocking him to the ground. She wasn't about to wait and see if he got back up and charged up the drive head down...

In the dimly lit room, Arwen had been thinking of cake when suddenly it felt as though she had been hit her over the head. A screeching filled her skull, blinding her momentarily. Feeling for the edge of the seat, she put her feet on the ground and tried to visualise her surroundings. She called softly into the blackness. "Daisy...Pol?"

She sensed movement in the hallway, heard what sounded like Morfydd. The last thing she heard was Pol bellowing her name from outside, followed by a series of gunshots. She collapsed and slipped from the seat, her head hitting the flagstones with a dull crack. Blood began to pour from her nose, before a thick, dark stream pushed between her lips...

Ulla heard shouting and screaming. At the sound of gunfire she froze, unable to work out exactly where it had come from. Finding the courage to leap from her hiding place, she ran toward a cottage up ahead.

Stopping halfway along the drive, she dug into her pocket and brought out her stones. They were hot, their sound now heard all around; chiming in unison. With the road behind her, the cottage in front, she stood in silhouette, no one having noticed her. The door to the cottage hung open and she saw two men in black flitting around the entrance, two more off to her right. Closing her hand around the stones, she brought her fist up to her mouth and kissed it, before tossing the stones high into the air...

Wordsworth and Mr. Panchal heard a strange ringing sound and turned abruptly...Coleridge flinched, separating from Shelley and dashing down the passage to the rear of the cottage.

Above them all, the stones sailed higher, tight together in a spinning triangle, their whirring chiming filling the air as they spun faster and faster. Ulla crouched, ready. Stretching her right arm above her, she closed her fist and pulled her arm down sharply...the spinning stones shot downwards and smashed into the ground just in front of the cottage.

Bolting over to where they had embedded themselves, an electric blue radiance could be seen expanding in all directions. She brought her palms down over the stones and tipping her head toward the sky, released the most beautiful sound; a long, pure note like the call of a Siren.

As Ulla lifted her hand from the stones, the intense, dazzling blue light spread out, higher and wider than the cottage; a pulsating energy of love drawn from the heart of the earth. One that continued to grow and grow, until it enveloped the entire cottage and everyone inside and out...

~

Coming autumn 2024, book 3 in the Keepers of the Song series, (provisionally titled) The Gathering.

Acknowledgments:

Much love and gratitude to everyone who bought, borrowed, stole and read The Kindness, especially those who left reviews online and spread the word far and wide.

Thanks to all my friends new and old, to my family, especially my unique and wonderful siblings and to Mum, without whose guidance, encouragement, love and deep wisdom, I'd not have got this far. Gratitude to Pops, for his enduring support and encouragement with these books. Thank you to abctales.com, for supporting writers of every kind, with their wonderful website and encouragement, please check it out.

Huge thanks again to Emily Southwell, the artist who created the magnificent cover artwork. As before, her guidance, inspiration and patience along the way is deeply appreciated.

Special thanks to my good friend Sarah L. Dixon, poet extraordinaire, for proof-reading this book. Sarah is a warm and wonderful poet, who I encourage you to go and see on one of her many poetry tours: www.thequietcompere.co.uk

Warm wishes and thanks to Wirksworth Heritage Centre, for inviting me to have a book signing at their book weekend. I would also like to thank Ian Skye and Radio Derby, for having me in for an interview and making me feel so welcome – thanks to myself, for managing not to swear once during a live broadcast.

Love and gratitude to my spirit guides and spirit companions, who continue to keep me safe and well. Heartfelt acknowledgment and gratitude to the Kindness; the magical Source of all.

This book was written to the music of Radical Dance Faction, Incredible String Band, Windy & Carl, Dub the Earth, Jaya the Cat, Quintessence, Chapterhouse, Steve Hillage, System 7 and Mirror System, Here & Now, Llyn y Cwn, Gene Clark, Alpha & Omega, Hawkwind, BT and Neil Young. Much of the editing was done to the sounds of early 90s house, including mixes from Sasha & Digweed (together and separately), Dave Seaman, John Kelly, Carl Craig and Bill Hamel. Thank you all, for keeping me singing and dancing away as I write.

During the writing of The Sisterkin, the work of Glennie Kindred remained a source of inspiration and wonder:
www.glenniekindred.co.uk

As did the wonderful work of Rae Beth:
www.knibbworld.com/rae/

In addition, *Witchcraze*, by Anne Llewellyn Barstow offered a fascinating insight into witch trials and the persecution of women and witches throughout history.

SJ Howarth lives in Derbyshire and when not writing, works as a counsellor, past-life regression therapist and trainer. He can also be found growing herbs, making daal and drinking coffee. More often than not, he smells of patchouli and has never knowingly turned away anything made of liquorice.

For news on the next book in the series and other books available or coming soon-ish, to say hello, or invite me for an interview please visit:

www.haveyougotthekindness.com

<u>Emily Eliza – cover artwork</u>

London based artist, Emily Eliza, paints colourful pieces to brighten people's homes. Painting from a young age, she continues to use a range of mediums including gouache, watercolour and acrylic. Her work has previously been displayed in the Lakeside Gallery and Djanogly Art Gallery in Nottingham, and she has interned for Sir Frank Bowling OBE.

Inspired by nature and folklore, Emily's prints contain flowers, plants and mystical themes. Her prints aim to bring the outside inside and add a touch of magic to people's homes.

Etsy shop - Emily Eliza Art Studio

Instagram - @emilyeliza_art